FORGOTTEN

GEORGE C. KYROS

Order this book online at www.trafford.com
or email orders@trafford.com

Most Trafford titles are also available at major online book retailers.

Print information available on the last page.

ISBN: 978-1-4907-9847-9 (sc)
ISBN: 978-1-4907-9849-3 (hc)
ISBN: 978-1-4907-9848-6 (e)

Library of Congress Control Number: 2019919561

Trafford rev. 11/26/2019

 www.trafford.com
North America & international
toll-free: 1 888 232 4444 (USA & Canada)
fax: 812 355 4082

To my four Grandchildren
Jack, Cassiopeia, Logan, and Benjamin

CONTENTS

PROLOGUE

I t is hard to imagine that wrongdoings of men against other men go unnoticed or are plain forgotten as time marches on. Of course, we still remember the tragic events of the persecution of the Jewish people in Europe during the 1940s and are reminded that whole tribes of Native Americans were annihilated here in our own country. But how many of us are aware that millions of Armenians perished at the hands of the Ottomans during the Russo-Turkish struggle for control of the lands around the Black Sea in the Bosporus? How many of us are aware that the people of Constantinople were herded out of their city like cattle by the conquering army of Mahmud the First in 1453 to be sold as slaves? "Give me the city, the people are yours," Mahmud declared to his faithful followers, before they scaled the wall of the city to put an end to the glory of the Byzantine empire. Last, we will be hard-pressed to find more than a handful of people who know that thousands of children were taken away from their homes in northern Greece in the 1940s and sent to neighboring communist nations. Only a few of them returned home. These innocent angels were rounded up by the communist faction of the combating revolutionary armies and expatriated to other countries, never to see their parents or their homeland again. They either perished from hunger, illness, and other hardships of living away from their families, or were assimilated into their new communities and became members of their new society. The International Red Cross and other independent researchers have documented that camps in Bulgaria, Rumania, Hungary, Czechoslovakia, Poland, and Yugoslavia housed thousands of these Greek boys and girls during the 1940s.

Just after the forces of the German army left Greece in 1942, resistant groups of patriotic Greeks took advantage of the lawlessness and each one of them attempted to form a government. They polarized into two camps and the civil war erupted. The nation became divided into two camps. One camp supported the governing system with its king, while the other was against it. The opponents wanted to depose the king, re-write the constitution, and establish communism in the country. Those who were loyal to the king were supported by England and the United States, while the others were aided by countries of the communist bloc of nations behind the Iron Curtain. Finally, in 1948, the army that was protecting kingship, won several decisive victories over its opponents and the civil war came to its conclusion.

Controversy still shrouds the truth about this most unfortunate expatriation of children. The perpetrators claimed that the children were at risk in northern Greece, for they expected the war to be escalated with the help of their communist neighbors. Children had to be tucked away from harm's way until the civil war was over. They claimed that the children were safer in a concentration camp, away from impending fierce battles. The opponents saw a sinister plot in the so-called *Paidomazoma* (rounding-up of children). They claimed that the children were sent behind the Iron Curtain to be indoctrinated into the principles and philosophy of communism and return home as fully fledged communists. Once back home as adults, they were to enter the society and spread the principles of communism throughout the nation. Eventually, the movement was intended to get enough followers to topple the old governing regime and make Greece a satellite of Russia.

The author of *Forgotten* feels that taking a stand on the controversy will serve no purpose. To the contrary, it may rekindle the flames of hate and promote social hostilities among still polarized groups of Greeks. He only wishes to tell the story of the tragic event of Paidomazoma during the Greek civil war. He wants to say something important to his reader. He experienced the brutality of the war and wants to bring to our attention a part of it, not because he wants to just say something. He wishes to tell us a true story. As a child, he witnessed the calamities of that war and wishes to bring to our attention the fact that thousands of children were deprived of the pleasures of growing up as Greeks in their own villages and towns. Most of these boys and girls were lost in new lands, among people who couldn't understand either their language or their way of life. Those children's destiny was to reach adulthood, become members of another society, lose their identity as Greeks and disappear in the masses of another social environment. These are the *Forgotten*.

CHAPTER ONE

E arly on a Sunday morning, a rebel's voice blared through a loudspeaker from the hills above the village of Vivitsi to awaken nature from its peaceful slumber. Dogs barked and people were heard calling their neighbors. The loud voice, coming from the mouth of some rebel woman, announced that all children between the ages of eight and fifteen had to be on the grounds of the church by six o'clock that morning. The revolutionary authority had convinced the parents and guardians of children, during previous meetings, that it was safer to remove underage children from pending battlefields. Parents and guardians of orphan children had accepted, or were forced to accept, the idea that small children must be sent away for their safety and protection. Many parents were the victims of the war, for one reason or another, and grandparents, close relatives, and neighbors had shouldered the burden of raising these orphans. The authorities had decided that children less than eight years old were unfit to travel and to put up with the hardships of camp life away from home. They had to stay home and face the pending dangers of fighting armies. Those over

1

fifteen were deemed that they were old enough to carry a rifle and participate in the revolutionary struggle.

Fotis and Georgia were fifteen-year-old twins. They were born to Mr. and Mrs. Liakos two years after the couple became husband and wife and before the civil war erupted. Their father, George Liakos, was born in a remote village of the Peloponnese, up in the mountains of Mani, an area located in the southwest part of the island. He attended grammar school there and received his high school education in the same village. At the age of eighteen, he graduated from high school with high marks. Two years later, that bright young lad was drafted in the Greek army and served his country for two years. His education and his patriotic leadership were soon recognized by his superior officers and that outstanding young soldier was promoted to the rank of an officer in the military intelligence branch of the king's army.

After his military service, he returned to his birthplace and took the entrance exam in an academy that trained young men and women to teach in grammar schools. His name appeared at the top of the list of selected candidates and he entered the academy with high hopes for his future. Three years later, he received his teacher's certificate and the department of education offered him a position to teach grammar school in Vivitsi, an isolated village close to the Serbian border with Greece. The young ex-officer and new teacher met Fotula by chance. He was taking an early evening walk to get acquainted with the village of Vivitsi when he laid his eyes on a young lady standing at the threshold of a fur store. She stood there, graceful and magnificent, like a dream fairy. At that moment, she was thanking a lady customer for the patronage she extended to her parents' fur store. Her black eyes, her luscious lips, the pitch-black hair that framed her dark, oval face with a slightly elongated nose and a perpetual smile, captured the attention of the young teacher. Tall for a woman, at about five feet eight inches, with a well-proportioned chest and noticeably curved hips, she forced George to stop and introduce himself. He bowed slightly in front of her and told her that he was a stranger in town, the new teacher in Vivitsi. Fotula Bizeli became the lawful wife of George Liakos a year after that afternoon.

Fotula was the only child of a couple from some unknown town of Pontus. Following the tragic Armenian genocide of 1914-1918, her parents abandoned everything they had at their birthplace, sailed southwest through the straits of the Dardanelles, and ended up in northwest Greece. They were Greek Christians, a potential target of constant harassment by the Muslim majority in their birthplace. Permanently separated from their motherland and the rest of their families, they settled in Vivitsi and started their new life there. Fotula was born in Vivitsi and earned her grammar and high school education in town, but she chose not to go on for higher education. Contrary to her father's insistence that she continue her education at a university in Salonika, she insisted on staying home. She lived with her parents and worked at their store until she met and married George Liakos and became the mother of twins. Mr. & Mrs. Bizeli did not have the good fortune of seeing their grandchildren past the age of four. The couple died from a deadly pneumonia epidemic that swept through their town. Fotis and Georgia were just four years old at the time and they barely remembered their grandparents.

Fotula loved being a wife, a mother, and a storekeeper. As the charming mother of two lovely children and the wife of one of the teachers in town, she was proud of herself and her family. After George and Fotula became husband and wife, they built a three-bedroom home with a roomy garden in front. They landscaped the place with fruit-bearing trees, seasonal flowers, and other perennial plants. Their garden was a showcase for the lady of the house. She grew vegetables and spices. Fotula became active in social activities at school and, when time permitted, she helped her store clerk to manage the only fur store in town.

The young couple were indescribably happy now. They were the example of what parents should be and they relished the love and the friendship they received from their neighbors and friends. The future looked rosy for them, especially when God blessed them with their twin babies.

"Choose the name for the girl, for I already decided to call the boy 'Fotis,'" she said to her husband, moments after she was told by the midwife that she brought a boy and girl into the world.

"Okay, then," George said, and meditated for a few moments. "You gave the boy the masculine version of your name. I will do the same for the girl. Let's give the girl the feminine version of my name. Let's call her Georgia," he said, and that's how the twins were named Georgia and Fotis.

The bell on the steeple rang at seven o'clock and the children, escorted by adults, trickled into the grounds in front of the church. All had walking shoes on, were dressed warmly, and without exception had a small bundle of clothes strapped on their backs. The girls had a warm scarf covering their heads and most of the boys wore home-made caps that covered their heads all the way to just above their ears. Some of the adults brought a donkey with a load saddle fastened on its back. Four baskets, woven with long splinters of reed, were secured with ropes on the load saddle, two on each side. Small or ill children were to be placed inside these baskets for their trip. Several young women dressed in military attire, with red berets over their short-cut hair and World War II rifles strapped on their shoulders, were buzzing around among the arriving children. They were taking a count of the children in the gathering and were registering their names and ages. The Greek letters Epsilon, Lambda, Alpha, and Sigma were woven, in capitals, on a piece of cloth stitched on the front of their berets. The four letters abbreviated the words Hellenic Public Liberating Army, which was the accepted description of the fighting revolutionaries. George and Fotula had been executed several years earlier and their widow neighbor, who was taking care of the children for seven years after the demise of their parents, arrived with them a bit late.

The leader of the women's fighters ascended to a temporary podium in front of the church and spoke briefly to the frightened adults.

"Civil war is a terrible thing to live through. As you already know, our leadership finds it necessary to relocate our children in order to keep them away from danger. Sacrifices and blood-spilling are inevitable. We must save our children! We must get rid of the king, who is not even a Greek," she shrieked.

"Let it be, if we kill some of our fellow Greeks who follow the king," she barked, and repositioned her beret on her head. She wiped her foaming mouth with the palm of her hand and, turning her attention to the terrified children, added in a moderate tone of voice: "Girls and boys! You are the future of Hellas. Today, you take your first step toward bettering yourself and the land you call 'your country.' You are going beyond our borders and you will learn many new things in the company of new friends. Be brave and don't cry! Your ancestors watch over your heads. Don't desecrate their memory. Someday, you will return to the motherland to change things that are wrong for a long time. The tomorrow rests in your hands. Let us start our historic mission today!"

Her comrades assisted each smaller child to a comfortable position inside a reed basket on the back of the animals. When the tumult for the marching calmed down, armed guerrillas, children, and donkeys formed a marching line for the voyage. Finally, everything was ready. At this moment, a cacophony of children's cries and a muffled sobbing from the parents erupted. Nothing else disturbed the morning silence.

The air was crisp that morning. The rays of the early sun painted the treeless parts of the undulating hills a bright crimson. The trees appeared to have a lighter green hue and the grass was still wet with its morning dew. Partridges began to chuckle their love-coded messages to other partridges across the valley, but larks were still sleeping. It was early April and nature celebrated the arrival of Persephone. Except for a honking from a donkey, a whining of a horse somewhere in a corral, the crowing of a rooster, and the barking of some lonely dog, the village was quiet and peaceful at this hour.

The travelers took their marching position according to the instructions of the leading fighter. She and another of her comrades, carrying automatic weapons on their shoulders, led the way. The burdened animals, with their precious load of four children in baskets, followed behind the leading rebels. The rest of the children, dispersed between the rest of the fighters, labored single-file behind the donkeys. Two of the fighters occupied the tail of the marching line. In that traveling arrangement, the group marched on for three hours until they came to the foot of a treeless hill. It was still early morning and the commander ordered a brief rest. Everyone, including the donkeys, lined up in front of a spring to get a drink. Water was gushing out from a fissure at the base of a huge tree and rolled down the flat face of a rock below. Shepherds had chiseled a bowl-size cavity on the rock where fresh water was always replenished from above. Some of the children put their lips at the bowl and drank some of the water and others just splashed it on their faces. After their brief intermission, they resumed their marching, uphill this time, until they reached the summit of the hill. There, the group made another brief stop, and the leader walked ahead to get a clear view of the valley ahead of them. She climbed a protruding rock, took a pair of binoculars out of her pocket, and surveyed the grounds in front of her. In the meantime, the children had a brief rest and received a modest snack. Each of them received a piece of bread and a wedge of cheese from the hands of one of the freedom fighters. Thirty minutes later, the group resumed its marching and moments later disappeared on the other side of the hill. At a moment when the twins found themselves alone, Georgia confessed to her brother that she was afraid and worn out. The guard traveling with them stepped off the walking formation to relieve herself. In view of everyone, she took the rifle off her shoulders, laid it on the ground, pulled her slacks down below her knees and squatted next to a low bush. In view of everyone, she shamelessly urinated and defecated, just as their donkeys did, as they were laboring up the steep hill with their human loads on their backs. Before she returned to take her marching position, Georgia added with despair that she was sick to her stomach and that her legs refused to obey her brain. She was disheartened to the point that she would rather be with her parents in heaven. Fotis scolded her for her negative attitude and pointed out that they were still young and that their future was ahead of them. He started to remind her of things that their late father said, but he cut short his sentence. The freedom fighter was returning, and he did not want her to hear Georgia's disheartening talk.

"Keep walking as if nothing is wrong with you. Hear me? It will get dark soon, and we will eventually reach some place to eat, sleep, and rest for the night. Don't despair and get us in trouble! Shush," Fotis whispered and fixed his stare straight ahead as if nothing had happened. The freedom fighter took her walking position between the two siblings and the downhill walk was resumed.

The group kept moving down the slope in dead silence until they reached the valley in front of them. A long, cultivated field extended in front of them and at the far end a tall mountain blocked the view beyond it. Houses were visible in the farthest part of the valley and that sight rejuvenated the travelers' spirits. They assumed that one of the edifices would be their resting place for the night and that food and shelter would be waiting for them.

The mountain ahead appeared to be steeper and much taller than the hill they had traversed during the early morning. Snow topped its summit and a rugged canyon split its peak in two parts. An hour later, the group reached the far end of the valley where the houses were. Everyone was extremely tired from walking all day. Besides, they were hungry and thirsty. The commander announced that they would spend the evening there and tomorrow they would scale the mountain ahead of them. She also emphasized that they must get a good rest, for tomorrow they would need all the energy they could get to climb the mountain that loomed in front of them.

"Ahead are some of the most treacherous grounds of our trip," she announced and paced the ground several times. During her back-and-forth pacing, she specifically said that a path along a deep ravine on their way was narrow and quite dangerous. She tried to lift their sagging spirits by telling them that the land on the other side was flat like a pancake and that they would board a train to travel in safety and comfort the day after tomorrow. Last, she pointed out that the twin peaks in front of them marked the borderline between Greece and one of the friendly countries to the north.

The caravan finally arrived in front of a one-story building with GRAMMAR SCHOOL painted directly on the wall above its entrance. When the travelers arrived, the doors opened and several local women greeted the frightened and bewildered children with motherly love and compassion. The women tied the animals to posts and gave them a bucket of barley. They helped the small children off their baskets and escorted everyone inside the school. An oversized wood-burning stove was blazing hot in the center of the room. Bread, cheese, a big bowl of yogurt, and several wooden pitchers with water were resting on a long table. Blankets were piled against another wall. The children formed a line and one by one helped themselves to the food. Georgia and another ill girl withdrew by the pile of blankets, sat on the bare floor, and refused to eat. After the rest of them had their fill, each child picked up a blanket from the pile, made a bed on the bare floor, crawled under it, and went to sleep. Georgia and the sick girl wrapped themselves in separate blankets, lay down, and, like chastised kittens, became silent and went to sleep. Fotis ate his food in haste, picked up his blanket, and searched the area for his ill sister. He found her curled under her cover, close to the wood-burning stove. He spread his blanket next to her, sat on it, took his shoes off his sore feet, and massaged them for a few seconds to improve the circulation. In the silence of the darkness, he reached over to his sister, gently poked her in the back, and whispered just loud enough for only her to hear him. He crept closer and asked her if she was sleeping. To his delight, he heard that she was still up and feeling much better. Furthermore, she asked him not to worry about her and her well-being. Fotis was elated by hearing that his sister was feeling much better and that her cynical attitude had improved. He handed her a hunk of bread he had in his pocket, wrapped himself in his blanket and before he could count to ten, he fell asleep next to her.

*

Eight years after George and Fotula were blessed with the arrival of their twins, the scourge of the revolutionary war was still in its infancy throughout Greece. The army of the nation was in shambles. They returned home defeated by the unstoppable, German might in 1940. The rebels, aided by their neighboring

Bolsheviks, gradually prevailed over the national army and the National Police, who kept order in the land and were driven away from their stations in the villages. Wealthy citizens and business owners were either arrested by the rebels, charged as capitalists and executed, or escaped to metropolitan cities still under the control of the king's authority. Schools were closed for shortage of money to pay the teachers and the territorial banks were ransacked and closed. The revolutionary commander of Vivitsi assured George and Fotula that no harm was on its way for them or their children. That bearded communist commander of the territory advised George to attend the weekly meetings in town and cooperate with the political leaders of their village. He hinted that he expected to see George personally involved in the cause of the revolution, since the school closed until the war was over.

"I advise you to make every effort to join the active struggle as an officer. We need your knowledge as a military man. The revolution needs people like you!" the commander emphasized. "Be an active participant of the people's struggle to make our country a better place to live."

After dinner and in the privacy of their bedroom, George told Fotula that, in his assessment, the revolution would be successful and the king would be thrown out of Greece. He was deeply concerned that many heads would roll if the rebels prevailed. To avoid facing the noose or the firing squad, he started to think that he had to do as the captain suggested and asked his wife's advice.

"Are you thinking of strapping a gun on your belt, joining the rebels, and killing other Greeks, possibly some of your relative soldiers in the king's army?" Fotula asked with disgust. "I hope you do not entertain thoughts of that nature!" She moved several feet away from him to read the impact her comment had on her husband. George was surprised at receiving such a stern answer from his wife and rushed to calm her down and to assure her that he was only bringing up the subject for discussion. He stressed his concern about their safety. As a devoted husband, he wanted to hear his wife's response to the predicament. He laid on the table the considerations of either getting involved in the struggle or trying to stay impartial. He was deeply concerned that walking through the minefield between establishment and revolution could blow up in their faces. He was further taking under consideration their two beautiful twins. Fotula stood there, thunderstruck.

"Let's give some serious thought to both options," George responded in bewilderment. "Our future will depend on how we handle this problem."

"What if we take our children and move to the place of your birth?" she asked.

George took his time to present to Fotula every bit of information about returning to his birthplace. He told Fotula that, according to what he had read in the papers for the previous six months, conditions in the Peloponnese were no different. He told her that only a few big towns were still in the hands of the king's army and the local police forces. The rural areas, like the territory where he was born, were under the control of rebel forces. Running the fingers of his left hand through his uncombed hair, he made it clear that their problem was not where in Greece they should make their home. Rather, they must choose between joining the rebels and taking the risk of staying with the establishment.

"If you can predict the future, I can make the right decision," George declared to his wife, and the subject never came up for discussion.

Their life, from this point on, was turbulent to say the least. His teaching job was terminated, for the school was closed, and the fur business tumbled downhill. They were forced to cultivate some nearby patches of land to produce grain to make bread. They grew wheat and corn and kept two goats for milk. George erected a chicken coop where they raised chickens for their eggs. Poverty was bearable, but the harassment they received from the communist leaders in town was beyond acceptance. This hostile environment infuriated George and made him appear antagonistic to the revolution. On occasions, he did not feel like attending the very important Indoctrination meetings held in town every Sunday night. Furthermore, he neglected to register as an active member of the Epsilon Alpha Mu (Hellenic Freedom Front) organization in the territory. In the end, his apathy and failure to become an active participant in the revolutionary front became the Achille's heel of their existence. Accusations of being a fascist couple piled up against them and a summons, issued by the People's Court, was delivered to their doorstep. The summons specified that both must appear in court to answer accusations filled against them by the revolutionary comrades of Vivitsi.

Their court date came and Fotula and George appeared in front of the people's court, thinking that nothing serious had been filed against them. The judge, dressed just like Lenin in the portrait that was hanging on the wall behind him, sat in the main chair behind the bench. Two other men, wearing military attire and with dense beards and thick mustaches covering their rugged faces, sat one to his left and one to his right.

"Comrades George and Fotula Liakos, approach the bench," the judge said and repositioned himself on his worn-out chair.

When the defendants came close enough to clearly hear his voice, they stopped in front of "his honor's" bench.

"You are accused by the leadership of the revolution that you do not cooperate with us," he declared. Lifting a manila folder from the bench in front of him, he took out a single page and slowly read the charges:

Comrades George and Fotula Liakos failed to attend the weekly meetings several times during the last year. Furthermore, Mr. Liakos is not registered as an active member of EAM.

"How do you answer the charges against you? Are you guilty or not?"

George attempted to ask his honor to clarify the charges leveled against them, but the judge interrupted him with a vitriolic voice and a hostile look on his face.

"I did not ask you to question the sincerity of our elected officials," he boomed. "Do you consider yourself and your wife guilty or not guilty?" he repeated with a voice resembling that of a mad man.

"Not guilty, comrade judge," George responded, standing like a wooden statue. "I'm faithful to the cause ..." he began, but one of the two men seated next to the judge cut him off with a loud voice and a frightening look.

"Enough of these excuses, comrade judge," he said. Looking at the frightened couple, he added, "If you are not part of the solution, you are part of the problem." He sneered and, bending close to the judge, he whispered something in his ear.

"Recess for fifteen minutes," the judge announced and, dismounting his squeaking chair, led the two military officers out of the courtroom. Once outside, they walked several paces away from where the court proceedings were taking place. They moved under the shade of an ancient oak tree that stood there for ages. It had survived fires and lightning and was there to comfort men and animals in its cool shade for as long as the people of Vivitsi could remember. Folklore had it that freedom fighters of another era had held their meetings under this tree. The threesome walked in the shade, made a close circle facing each other, and reviewed the evidence against George and Fotula. Without any more deliberations, they reached their verdict. There were no defense lawyers to rebuff the court and no jurors to hear the case. Only two rebel leaders and a judge, who probably had to go along with the wishes of the revolutionary authority, were there to decide the faith of two devoted parents. George and Fotula wanted to stay impartial from the bloody fighting wishing to raise their children to become productive members of their society. Seemingly in a deep thought and with a heavy heart, the threesome judges returned to the courtroom. They took their places on their chairs and the senior judge called "order to the court."

"Defendants approach the bench," he said and cleared his throat to announce the decision of the court.

"The people's court carefully reviewed all the charges brought against you and finds you guilty of working against the cause of the revolution," he declared and fixed his eyes at the defendants. Desperately, George attempted to say something, but the booming voice of the judge shut him off.

"Take them away," he ordered without any further deliberations. Several armed men and women, who stood by the door, grabbed George and Fotula by their arms and forcefully led them away, not to be seen alive again.

At dawn of the following morning, rifle shots interrupted the tranquility. That afternoon, shepherds found the bodies of George and Fotula on the slope of a remote hill close to Vivitsi. They had been shot to death, execution style, and left there bathed in their own blood. The news of the gore findings spread around town and the next day, their compassionate neighbor, a poor and childless widow, went to the scene with a hoe and a shovel, dug a shallow grave at the spot where the bodies were found, and unceremoniously threw in the lifeless corpses of George and Fotula. Finally, she filled the hole with stones and dirt. She couldn't stomach knowing that the remains of her dear neighbors were about to be consumed by carnivorous birds and animals. Two days later, that caring soul moved into the house of her deceased neighbors and began to attend to the needs of the twins. She kept her nanny goat in her old dwelling, next door, for she needed its milk to feed the children. This arrangement solved two problems: the children had a loving guardian and the old lady had a comfortable bed in the house of George and Fotula. Often and when the weather permitted it after Sunday Mass at the church, the gracious lady brought Fotis and Georgia to the place where their parents were interred. There, in solemn isolation away from the rest of the world, the children deposited fresh flowers on the ground that covered their parents, lit a candle, and said a prayer in the memory of mom and dad. They kissed the wooden cross the good neighbor had nailed together and hammered in the ground at the head of the grave that marked the burial spot. The dedicated, trusted neighbor became the children's mother until they were taken away during the Paidomazoma.

*

A sharp, shrill whistle woke up the children the next morning. The freedom fighters came in the room and announced that it was time for them to wake up and resume their journey. The leader walked around the room, poked the sleeping angels with her walking stick and ordered them to get ready for their perilous walk toward the top of the mountain. Several of the smaller children started to cry. They were panicked by the shrieking sound of the whistle and the sudden poking they received in their tiny bodies. During the pandemonium of the crying and the confusion, some of the smaller children found it difficult to fasten their shoelaces, especially in the darkness of their room. Older boys and girls dressed faster and found time to help others do likewise. At last, everybody was ready for their second day of marching. They congregated at the grounds outside their sleeping quarters and meandered aimlessly. They were frightened to death, half-asleep, and thoroughly confused. Some of them were still rubbing their eyes to wake up and others blew their noses on the ground to clear their nostrils. Several of them stood motionless, just like the fence posts around the school grounds. Minutes later, they lined up one behind another and received their scanty breakfast: a cup of cold milk and a slice of stale village bread. While they were chewing their bread, girls and small children of both sexes were permitted to use the outhouse. Older boys found out-of-sight spots to relieve themselves. Finally, the whistle blew once again, and everyone formed their traveling formation to move forward.

At the beginning, the walking path was passable, but when they reached its halfway point up the slope, the path became uneven and treacherous. To their left, the summit was several feet above their heads; to their right, a rivulet meandered downhill, more than a hundred feet directly below them. At places, the path was just wide enough to allow one donkey at a time to squeeze through clearings. Several children joined hands to balance on their feet and to encourage one another to move forward. Only a few of them had set foot in terrain like this one. They were children of families who owned goat herds in Vivitsi. A few of them found it easier to advance on all fours, like toddlers.

Suddenly, a crashing noise forced everyone to freeze in their path. A donkey, with its precious cargo of four children on its back, lost its footing and went tumbling down the rocky slope. The four children in the baskets and the beast itself tumbled downward uncontrollably. The drama ended when four crashes and a deafening thud came from the bottom of the gorge. As soon as the deadly event was over, cries filled the air, but the high-pitched whistle ordered the group to resume marching.

It was early afternoon when the worn-out convoy reached the foot of the mountain on the other side. The commander called another stop, and everyone halted on a flat piece of land close to a stone bridge. This overpass stretched over the rivulet that had claimed the lives of their four friends and one of their donkeys.

Their resting ground was a sad site to behold. Little children walked around as if they were lost in a universal vacuum of nothingness. They wore pale faces with bewildered expressions. Their lips were trembling from fear, thirst, and hunger. They meandered without talking to one another and they dragged their little feet on the ground as they paced aimlessly in all directions. Some of them were silently weeping, others were crying uncontrollably, and still others were just wiping their tears away from their tender faces with the heels of their little hands. All of them were dead-tired and terribly frightened. The deadly accident that took place earlier made them feel that they were both vulnerable and worthless. They felt that no one cared for them anymore. There was no mother or grandmother to sooth the pain that started in their stomachs and climbed up to their hearts. Georgia and Fotis tucked themselves inside a small cavern under a huge boulder and cried bitterly until the commander's whistle called everyone to order.

The female commander told her assembly that the accident was predestined and she urged everyone to pray to God to place their friends in the legions of His angels. She made the symbol of the cross several times and repeated that the accident shouldn't make them lose faith for the tomorrow. She also told them that the future was bright for the rest of them. Lastly, she encouraged everyone to put himself or herself back together and think positively about their future.

"We still have a few more miles to travel before we stop for the evening. Soon, very soon, we will complete our mission and you will return home to reclaim our country from the hands of the capitalists who deny equality for all of us."

The freedom fighters, with four fewer children and one less donkey, formed the familiar line of marching and began to move forward in dead silence. The dreaded mountains were behind them and the sky above their heads was bright blue. The caravan had crossed into another country, somewhere northwest from their village.

To their right was an endless marshland dotted with immense birch trees. The land to their left was a vast field of violet flowers. It extended as far as their eyes could reach in all directions and resembled an immense purple blanket. The aroma from the flowers was pleasant and the chirping of countless nightingales, perched in the branches of the birch trees in the marshland, soothed their hearts. It was early spring and the birds were sending love messages to one another. The tranquility of the setting rejuvenated the children's hope for the future and the picture of the macabre accident began to fade away from their memory.

At some point in their marching, the commander called another halt. The children congregated in a circle around her and the animals were secured by their reins to sprouting trees. She made a cursory inspection, then stood in the center of the gathering and told them that the leadership entrusted their future to foreign comrade friends who lived beyond the end of the valley ahead of them. She cautioned them that these people didn't speak Greek but said that would be just a temporary problem for them.

"Children! Shortly after we get to the end of the valley, you will board a train for the last leg of your trip. My comrades and I will return to Greece to continue our struggle for freedom and equality for all Greeks. Meanwhile, eat the bread and the cheese you will get, and drink water from the creek," the commander concluded and walked away to inspect the grounds ahead of them.

Each child received a hunk of bread and a wedge of salty feta cheese from the unsanitary hands of two of the freedom fighters. They hastily consumed their allotment of food and, one after another, they kneeled over the gurgling creek and, like the donkeys, drank water to flush down the salty taste of the cheese. Several minutes elapsed and that dreadful whistle of their commander called everyone to congregate next to a bare spot where the donkeys were kept. Once again, small children were helped inside the baskets on the back of the animals and the group marched forward. The group moved onward in complete silence, just like zombies, except when one of them asked permission to urinate or defecate behind some overgrown clump of wild vegetation.

After two hours of walking along the creek, between the marshland and the cultivated fields, they saw a freight train standing on its track in front of a station. It was a very long freight train. All cars, except one of them, were open at the top and loaded with coal. The empty car was different. Gray canvas was stretched over metal beams that formed the sides and the roof. Two side doors stood open. They were designed to slide apart from each other along one broad side. When the children arrived at the station, they found the doors drawn apart. Padlocks on heavy, rusty chains were hanging from each door. Hay, some loose on the floor and some still in bundles, was the only visible content. The scene resembled a car prepared to receive a herd of sheep from New Zealand destined for some slaughterhouse.

As soon as the caravan arrived in front of the standing train, the children were ordered to assemble in a clearing. One of their escorts stood in front of the terrified listeners and told them to be brave Greeks and to learn all they could during the time they were to spend in the land they were going to. She wished them good luck with a fake smile in her face and turning around, she herded the donkeys and the rest of her comrades back to the mountain from where they had come.

Two of the train men walked around the congregated boys and girls and counted them twice. One of them made notes on a worn-out notepad with a stub pencil he pulled out of one of his pockets. The foreigners did not seem friendly, but again, the children couldn't understand what they said to each other to form a better opinion of them and their intentions.

"Up, up," two of the foreigners ordered in Greek. Pointing at the open door of the standing car in front of them, they encouraged the helpless children to climb the short ladder that led inside. Once everyone was inside the standing car, the sliding doors slammed closed and the heavy chains with the padlocks secured the doors. Most of the children freaked out hearing the screaking sound of the sliding doors and the rattling of the chains against the metal bars of the car. Several of them began to cry, a few of them uncontrollably. Georgia drew a frightened deep breath and hugged her brother for comfort. Fotis was less, shaken by the awful sound. His lower lip began to tremble, but he kept his cool. As soon as the pandemonium of crying and sobbing subsided, he rose to the occasion and said in a clear, crisp voice.

"Friends, hear what I'm about to say. Crying will do nothing for any of us. Let's wipe our faces clean, put our heads together, and figure out what we must do to face our predicament. Our lives are not in danger; only our comfort is. Yes, our food is not of the quality we ate at home, but honestly, all of us were hungry at one point or another during our village living. Let it be, if our parents are not here with us to help. Ask me and my sister about growing up without parents and we will tell you all about it. Let's act like Spartans and be brave like them."

A fourteen-year-old girl dragged herself up from her sitting position, wiped her pretty eyes with the end of her shirt, and attempted unsuccessfully to clear her throat. She took several deep breaths to fill her lungs with fresh air, and in her teen-age, high-pitched voice supported the statement made by the previous speaker. She stressed the need to help one another, especially the little ones, and volunteered to take the place of the older sister for two little blond girls who were cuddled in one of the corners. Fotis was surprised by his own courage and brave initiative to say something encouraging. He kept walking among the rest of the children and made positive suggestions and spirit-lifting comments to everyone around him.

Their train sat there for the rest of the afternoon and most of the early evening hours. At some point during the night, it started to jerk forward, then it accelerated at a higher speed. Finally, it gained more speed, leaving behind a black and gray raccoon-tail of smoke that eventually was swallowed up by the glittering night sky above. The laboring train kept advancing, while the abducted children went to sleep. At the suggestions of some of the older children, the group lay on the floor in a circular configuration. The smaller boys and girls occupied the center of the circle and the older ones occupied the outside periphery. Plenty of hay was spread under them and a generous portion of it covered their tender feet and backs. Several bales of hay were arranged in a circle in one of the corners of the floor. This confinement was their toilet. It offered privacy for the occupant. When the straw on the floor was saturated with human waste, two of the older children pushed the soiled mess out through the space between the bars that formed the walls of the car.

The train sped along, non-stop. Two railroad men visited the children in the late morning and again in the early evening. They brought several jugs of water, one basket with bread, one aluminum tray with several slices of cheese, a half dozen smoked herring cut in pieces, and a small caldron filled halfway with a soup made from boiled potatoes, black-eyed beans, hog fat, and sauerkraut. The children sat cross-legged on the floor with an aluminum bowl and a spoon in their hands. Three fifteen-year-old girls went around and delivered the food equally to everyone. Everyone drank water directly from the jugs, for cups were not available. During their morning visit, one of the guards handed an apple to each child.

All the children slept during the dark hours and most of the day. Generally, their riding went without serious complications. Many of them were engaged in conversations regarding their past and cried frequently; others isolated themselves in corners, covered their faces with their hands and prayed to God for help. But most of them socialized with one another, with an occasional burst of laughter or a carefree giggling.

Fotis and Georgia talked a lot. Sometimes they sat with their worrisome faces wedged between the metal bars that formed the walls and gazed at the landscape the train was traversing. At times, the scene was interesting to watch, but at other times it became monotonous and boring for them. One could only see endless wheat fields as far as the eyes could reach, with an occasional farmhouse perched on some elevated ground. In other instances, the train meandered between rocky cliffs, along gurgling rivulets, just like a gargantuan millipede crawling along between boulders in a grassland. When they became bored looking at the landscape, the twins would sit side-by-side and recollect pleasant events of their past life. More than once, they reminisced about the wonderful times they had at home, especially when Grandma and Grandpa came for Christmas evening with loads of toys for them.

Out of nowhere Georgia asked her brother if he still had the charm Grandpa gave him at Christmas before he passed away. She proudly declared that she still had hers and, reaching under the opening of her blouse, retrieved a round object attached to a chain. The thing was the size of a half-dollar. Fotis fumbled under his shirt and came up with his charm. Georgia remembered that, according to what Grandpa had said, this thing was blessed by the patriarch of Constantinople and, supposedly, would keep the wearer from harm's way. As they kept turning the artifacts in their hands, Georgia placed her charm next to her brother's and noticed that the charms were identical. The image of some unknown saint was engraved on one side and the words *Do not lose it or do not give it away* were engraved on the opposite face. The children pondered the meaning of the writing and the name of the saint, but they could not come up with a tangible answer. Minutes later, they tucked away, next to their hearts, their precious possessions and the subject was forgotten for now.

During one of their discussions about their future, the twins talked of things that were waiting for them. Georgia expressed fear that "bad people" were waiting for them at the other end. She sank her face between her brother's extended arms and tried to get rid of the shivering thought that mistreatment was inevitable at the end of their trip. Fotis told her to be his brave sister. Pulling her face close to his heart, he promised that he would keep her safe for as long as he will be above grass. In order to emphasize his devotion to her safety, he told her that he was prepared to "walk over a pit of burning coals" to keep her safe and unharmed.

"We don't know what the future holds for us, but think about it this way," he added and continued his ambitious talking. "We will be educated in a country different than ours and we will learn the language they speak there. Eventually, we will return home more enlightened to reclaim our house and start a new life in Vivitsi. Tell me, dear sister," he asked, "what our future would be at home, under the supervision of a poor woman, with no education and no money to help us go on with our life?"

Georgia shrank in his arms, regained her courage to go on living, put her emotions under control, and thought that her brother's ego was a bit overinflated. In her whimpering voice, she reminded him that most brave men end up having a short life. Fotis responded that he would rather be a brave man with a shorter life, than live a long life in poverty, disgraced and ignorant. Finally, releasing her from his grasp, he pushed his bushy hair away from his face with his left hand and paced the length of the straw-covered floor several times.

Conversations like this one were conducted often between Georgia and Fotis in the camp. He was always optimistic for the future, but Georgia had second thoughts about her brother's ambitious outlook. She envisioned difficulties ahead, with many unpleasant consequences. She assumed mistreatment, predicted rampant sicknesses, and feared deaths at their "educational training." "Virgin Mary, protect us from all bad things and evil people," she silently prayed every night before she surrendered herself to the good fairy of the night. As time marched on, she convinced herself that there are big differences between a boy and a girl, and she caught herself gravitating toward boys for her companions. Unconsciously and without explanation, that propensity disturbed her a lot. She had no mother to discuss her teen-age problems and give answers to her perplexing questions. She dared not talk to her brother about her emotional uprising, for she was afraid that he would interpret things the wrong way. She kept her problems to herself, secret and without answers. Her brother was just a brother, and nothing more. He was just busy walking around among the rest of the children repeating his ambitious convictions about their future in the country they were going to.

After most of the day's riding on the train, their prison's-like conditions came to an end. The train reduced its speed, blew its loud whistle several times, and came to a gradual stop. The heavy doors slid wide open and the children saw a strange world in front of them. Anxious to get out of their confinement, they congregated in front of the open door ready to disembark and walk on solid ground once again. It was late in the afternoon and the sun was hidden behind heavy clouds. Wide streets extended in every direction and tall buildings stood on both sides as far as the children could see. An uproar of human voices, mixed with the rumbles of cars, trucks, and motorcycles, filled the air. Two young women approached the standing children and welcomed them in Greek. The older woman cautioned them with motherly love to watch their steps coming down from their confinement. The other woman spoke less and did more to make them feel at home. She offered her hand to those who needed support to descend and literally lifted some of the smaller children to safely plant their shaking feet on the ground. As soon as all the children were on the sidewalk, the two women took a careful headcount of the arrivals, made notes in their notebooks, and guided them to a canvas-covered truck that stood in the parking lot with its engine running. Like lost sheep in a meadow, the children followed one of their receptionists, while the other followed a few paces behind. The entire group mounted the standing vehicle and the noisy truck began to move forward. Moments later, they arrived at their destination, hungry, thirsty, and exhausted from bouncing around in an uncomfortable railroad car. They were led inside a public housing building and were congregated in an immense room lined with picnic tables and benches.

Bread and a pot of steaming goulash stood side by side on one of the benches. Wooden pitchers with water and clean, aluminum cups were lined up at the far end. The two guiding young women took their places on one side of the bench and readied themselves to serve the food to the hungry children. The children formed a line on the other side of the bench and one by one, each received an aluminum bowl filled with goulash. They picked up a fork and a slice of bread and sat down for their early dinner. While they were eating their supper, the two overseers visited each one of them. They registered the first and last name, the age and sex of each child, and then withdrew to another room. After diner, the two women returned and attached a nametag on the lapel of each boy and girl. Lastly, the children could roam freely around the room and use the toilet at their discretion, without asking permission from anyone to do so. Toward the end of the evening, the nineteen girls were separated from the twenty-six boys. Each group was led to separate buildings where they were to sleep at night.

There was a moderate-size room for the girls and a larger one for the boys. Canvas cots were set on the floor, one next to the other, and two home-woven blankets were neatly folded and placed on top of each cot.

One of the chaperons led the girls to their sleeping room and informed the group that, for safety reasons, they would sleep in a separate room from the boys. She told them with a sneer that it was risky to have boys sleep in the same room with the girls.

"You are not old enough to have any relation with boys and as you grow older, you will learn the nature of these beasts," she mumbled with obvious bitterness and distrust for men.

The room for the boys was furnished the same way as the girls' room. The other chaperone led the boys to their room, showed them where the toilet was, simply said good night, and went away.

It was nine o'clock in the evening. The girls set their beds at their selected spots in their room, took off their shoes and, like soldiers on training, laid down to rest. Georgia assisted two of the smaller girls to set their beds and, acting like their older sister, she escorted them to the toilet. She offered them water before bedtime, removed their footwear from their tiny feet, kissed them good night, and tucked them under their blankets. She dressed her cot with two blankets, placed it between the two girls, took off her shoes, recited her prayer, and crawled between her two blankets.

Most of the boys stayed up until 9:30. Fotis and another boy sat at the edge of their cots until ten o'clock and recalled events of their lives back home. Fotis bitterly lamented the unjustifiable execution of his parents and took an oath that he would never forget them for as long as God allowed him to walk on the surface of the earth. The other boy did not express any emotions at being separated from his parents. He just stared at Fotis with wide-open eyes and with a frightened expression. He only said that he was terrified to death and that he wished to see this experience come to a happy ending. When their conversation came to an end, they crawled between their blankets, like the rest of them, and went to sleep. Fotis tossed in his bed a few minutes longer than his friend did. He was trying to block out of his hearing the snoring of another boy, who was sleeping on his cot next to him. Eventually though, things became quiet in the pitch-dark room and he, too, went to sleep.

A loud rap at the door woke everybody up at seven o'clock the following morning. Some of the older girls assisted the younger ones to comb their hair and put their shoes on. Likewise, older boys helped the younger boys to put themselves together. At eight o'clock, all the boys and girls, forty-five of them, stood in line outside their sleeping rooms in the open air. They had to perform their morning exercises before breakfast. Their physical fitness instructor, a young, slender, blond woman with a piercing voice and a whistle in one of her hands, took the kids through several strenuous, body-stretching exercises for thirty minutes. Finally, boys and girls returned to the assembly room and like inmates in a county jail, lined up for breakfast, in single file. They received a freshly baked hunk of corn bread with plenty of black raisins inside it and a cup of cold milk. While eating their scanty breakfast, their two chaperones walked around the gathering and superficially examined their hair for lice infestation. At the same time, their physical fitness instructor checked their dirty hands and feet for any infected lacerations. Further, she examined their ears and eyes and, in some instances, asked the child to open his or her mouth wide open for her to inspect the inside condition of the child's mouth and teeth. That routine consumed most of the morning hours. At eleven o'clock, they returned to their sleeping quarters for the biggest surprise of their life. On each bed, regardless of sex, there was a shirt and a cap. Additionally, a pair of slacks was placed on each bed for the boys, while a skirt with a thigh-high pair of shorts was spread atop each girl's bed. All items were made with local cotton fabric, colored greenish brown. Several women holding manually operated hair clippers in their hands stood there to clip the hair of the boys to a fraction of an inch long and to trim hair shorter for some of the girls. One of the chaperones announced that every person in this country wore the same clothing. She pointed out that this was the land where there were no laborers or white-collar workers and that everyone worked at communal factories and farms that belonged to the government. She made it abundantly clear that the government would feed, dress, and take care of all its people the same way. She concluded that the new arrivals would wear the same clothes, eat the same food, and sleep in public buildings. She reasoned, with an air of authority, that since the children became a part of this community, they would wear the same clothes and eat the same food as the rest of them. Finally, she motioned to the hair-cutters to begin cutting hair. Most of the boys and girls had no objections to seeing their hair on the floor, but two fifteen-year-old girls with long, thick hair began to cry when they sat on the barber's stool. Needless to say, their objections were ignored. As an afterthought, the senior chaperon mentioned that all possible human efforts were made to guess the size of the garment and cap for each child, but if anyone didn't fit into the new clothes, he or she should try to find someone in the group with the opposite problem and make an exchange. If one of them reached an impasse in trying to fit into a new garment, he/she should see one of the chaperones. Lastly, she instructed everyone to pile everything they had on their backs on a designated spot on the floor.

Chaos ensued during the afternoon hours. Each child tried to find clothes and hats that reasonably fit over their tiny bodies. When they congregated for dinner in that evening, the group appeared different from the group that was there early that morning. Most of them giggled at each other's appearance, but deep inside, they were in shock from fear of their safety. Their cherubic faces appeared cold and lifeless like the face of Europa, the frozen satellite around Jupiter. Their dinner was a mixture of pork, diced potatoes, cabbage, a generous amount of barley, and haphazardly chopped celery that appeared to be an afterthought addition. The preparation was a thick mush. The vegetables were overcooked, but the pork was boiled to tenderness.

The evening hour was uneventful. Fotis and his sister sat at their bench until they were told that it was bedtime. They laughed at their appearances with their new haircuts, but primarily they talked about their life in Vivitsi. They silently cried in each other's arms, remembering their parents, grandparents, and their good old neighbor with her nanny goat. They relived sadly the happy moments they all had together during Christmas and Easter holidays and they laughed remembering some of the punishments their father handed down to them during their mischievous, preschool years.

"I missed Mom and Dad more than our grandparents," Fotis said to Georgia with a sigh that started in his stomach and exploded forcefully through his mouth. "I wish, so I wish, I can sit next to them and tell them that nothing on earth is more precious than them." He broke into uncontrollable, sobbing that made his chest rise and fall like the bellows of a blacksmith. Georgia attempted to soothe his bitterness, but her encouragement did not have the intended effect. She joined him in a symphony of intermittent sobbing until one of the chaperones interrupted their emotional communication.

"Okay, children," she said in a motherly tone as she interrupted the mental union between a brother and a sister. "The past is gone. Think of tomorrow, for only tomorrow counts." At bedtime the twins said goodnight to each other and withdrew into their sleeping quarters. Georgia cried in bed until the good fairy sealed shut her mind and her eyes and sent her to dreamland. Fotis tossed in his bed for a while trying to find justification for the things that were happening to them. "Dear God, help us get through the present trial, and lead us back to our motherland where we belong," were his last words before sleep prevailed. In the middle of the night, he swore to God, he had visitors. He felt his father's ouzo-smelling breath on one of his checks and the delicately perfumed breath of his mother on the other. He never forgot that preschool experience, when his parents kissed him good night before he fell asleep.

After breakfast the next morning, the children met one of their indoctrination teachers, a woman in her late fifties. She had short gray hair, was about five feet, seven inches tall, with broad shoulders and a narrow waist like an Olympic athlete. She had a rather pleasant smile, with an authoritative air of expressing herself. The children rose to their feet upon her entrance to the classroom, but she politely motioned them with her hand to sit down.

"Good morning, class," she said, and told them that her name was Antonia and that she was born in one of the Greek islands of the Ionian Sea. "I'll be one of your instructors for a while. Please call me 'comrade' from here on. For me to be able to associate your faces with your names, I will call your name and you must respond with a 'yes' and a raising of your hand, any hand," she said cheerfully.

Taking attendance took a few minutes and then she became serious with her teaching job. She briefly mentioned the names Lenin and Stalin and spent the rest of the morning pointing out the advantages of living under a communistic government compared to a democracy. Specifically, she pointed out that people in Greece paid a lot of money to go to school, to visit a doctor at the office, to feed themselves, and to have a bed and a warm house. She emphasized that in a communist country, all these things were free.

"Tell me what the king and his vultures do in Athens. They suck the blood of the poor, that's what they do!" she concluded. She vilified the Greek social structure that allowed only a few super-rich Greeks to have roomy villas, limousines, and servants. She went on to point out that these same super-wealthy families are hoarding the wealth of the country in Swiss banks while forcing the rest of the citizenry to dwell below the poverty level of a civilized society.

"Children, the time is here and now. Let's change all that for the betterment of our people and the country itself! You represent the beginning of this movement, remember that," Antonia bellowed.

Day after day, she kept going over these statements until the children began to react positively to hearing her preaching about social injustice in their motherland. At the end of each session and for several months that followed their first indoctrination into communism, the children were conditioned to salute the names of Lenin and Stalin. "Hurrah, hurrah to father Lenin and 'Uncle' Stalin," the children yelled before they were dismissed from their tutoring. For the rest of the year, Comrade Antonia was their teacher and their principal instructor, repeating the same thing with new emphasis on equality and obedience to "Uncle Joseph."

"Young comrades," a middle-aged man, dressed like the boys, greeted the classroom a year later. He told his listeners that he will be their new instructor, for Comrade Antonia was assigned to a new camp. The man was tall with chestnut-colored hair, with a smartly trimmed goatee that connected to his thin moustache around his mouth, a soft voice, and a pair of piercing, green eyes. For the year and a half that followed his first appearance, he lectured about the fathers of communism and their contributions to the rest of the world. He narrated specific circumstances that thrust Lenin, Stalin, Mao, and Tito to power and to world fame. At times, he organized field trips aimed to show the best part of the city and break the monotony of controlled living.

One bright fall day, the new teacher decided to make the session rather entertaining. He took the children for a tour in town. He led the children down a street lined with bakeries, dry food stores, and butcher shops, one next to the other for several blocks. At the end of that street there was a public area that was paved with cobblestones from one end to the other. An immense statue of Lenin dominated the center of the place. A message, carved at the base of the statue, was written in some foreign language that the children could not read. At the periphery of this quadrangular public area, several multilevel buildings stood tall. Some of them appeared to touch the clouds above them. Farther down the boulevard, the children saw a long bridge that extended over a wide river. In the expanses beyond the river, the children saw tall, chimneys that stood tall like gigantic telephone posts. Black smoke spilled into the clear sky above them. In this wonderland of big and new things, thunder was heard, and a light rain started to come down. The group was led inside an uninhabited, barn-size building to get out of the rain that had begun to change to a frightening hailstorm. This area was a historic place that served as a reminder that resisting the spread of communism was not tolerated in this country.

"The soil under your feet is saturated with the blood and the brains of two hundred traitors who dared to oppose communism in this town," the teacher said to his innocent listeners. "It stands as a stark reminder that no man can stand in front of progress," he continued. Turning around, he pointed at the markings on the brick walls. "These wells at the brick walls are made by the deadly bullets the execution squads fired at the chests and the heads of their victims," he added, and placed his index finger in one of the marks. Some of the children shivered at the thought that they were walking on dry, human blood. The majority of them paid no attention to the history of this ghastly place. They were accustomed hearing from their teacher stories of death and human suffering. Soon after the weather became clear and the sun appeared in the sky above their heads, the children were permitted to roam through some of the stores, but eventually, they regrouped at the square and walked back to their sleeping quarters. The teacher dismissed them an hour earlier, but their day was not over by any means. Their chaperones led them back to the lecture room and informed them that cleaning the toilets was their job.

"Your mothers are not working here to clean after your mess," the most arrogant of the two chaperones said sarcastically. "All of you, from ages eleven to fifteen, will take turns cleaning the toilets," she said, and called the names of the children who were qualified for the task. She, in turn, grouped the 11- to 15-year-old boys and girls in several cleaning gangs. From this point on, every morning just after breakfast, one of the girls' gangs were assigned to clean the toilets in their dormitory. Likewise, one of the boys' gangs was responsible to clean the toilets adjacent to their own sleeping room.

From this point on, and for the next two years, the children's lives moved like clockwork. They woke up at seven in the morning, did their exercises for half an hour, ate breakfast at eight, cleaned the mess they made overnight, and from 9 a.m. until 6 p.m. attended intensive brainwashing sessions. Finally, they ate their dinner at six o'clock and socialized before they went to sleep at nine o'clock. As time went on, their personalities changed considerably and their postures took the shape of adults. The older boys began to grow a healthy fuzz on their faces and the older girls had difficulties concealing their femininity under their cotton underwear.

There were no Christmas gift exchanges, New Year's Eve celebrations, family get-togethers, or birthday parties. These celebrations were invented by the capitalist merchants to "drain your pocket," the children were told by their teachers. Repeatedly, they were told that God was a myth and that He was invented by men to justify fear of the unknown. Occasionally, the children were taken to local factories where they saw women and men performing the same job, standing in line one next to another. Occasionally, they visited communal farms, where grain, fruits, and vegetables were cultivated and processed. Day after day, the children did the same task, just like automated machines.

Two and a half years went by, and five children died at their camp. Two boys and two girls perished from an epidemic of pneumonia. A girl suffered from a tetanus infection that settled in her foot due to unsanitary living. Amputating her leg, above her knee, made her condition worse. She developed a serious infection, which spread throughout her body, and the poor little girl died in agony.

Most of the children found themselves believing that the things infused in their minds were God's truth, indeed. They sang the marching jingles with gusto, always in the local language, and most of them were able to rudely communicate with the local people. Fotis thought that things were not as bad as he was expecting them to be and voiced his opinion to his sister. He told her that they were ready to go back to Greece and spread the ideas of communism to enlighten the rest of the Greeks. He unequivocally voiced that the king had no place among the Greeks.

"Be careful with your loose tongue, Fotis," Georgia responded in a hushed voice. "Even the walls have ears and hear what you say. Reconsider what comes out of your big mouth. Remember who killed our parents. The executioners of Mother and Dad weren't king's people, were they?"

Fotis shrank with shame, hearing his sister's bitter comments. He walked away from her and for several weeks after that he stewed in his own anger. He couldn't believe that the comment he made triggered such a negative reaction in his sister. Day after day, he sat away from her and ate his supper alone. He was angry with himself for admitting that things were not that bad in the camp. Weeks later, Georgia decided to bridge the gap between herself and her brother. She couldn't stand seeing her brother, the only brother she had, in such mental anguish. She took her dinner dish in her hands, sat next to him, and tried to soothe his pain with kind words. Away from the rest of the children, Georgia told her brother that he was the only person in her life. She said that she depended on him, and that he should depend on her likewise. She asked him to forget what she had said the other day and reasoned that whatever bothered his mind should not be that important to either of them. Silly things that came out of their mouths shouldn't split their familial love, she told him and hugged him tight. Seconds later, she heard him sobbing uncontrollably and felt warm tears spot the sleeves of her drab uniform. Fotis said nothing to her. He was engulfed in his own thoughts and emotional rebellion with himself. As a young man with principles, he couldn't justify betraying the memory of his parents. He couldn't excuse himself for saying to his sister that things weren't that bad. What was he thinking when he said such an awful thing that offended his sister and betrayed the memory of his parents? He should know better, for he was almost eighteen-years old and should have been wiser! Anyway, the young lad's pride was devastated.

As the days wore on, Fotis had frequent conversations with himself. Invariably, his other self won the argument and forced him back into his depressing mood. During one of his self-deliberations on the subject, he convinced his other self that what he said was not out of line, after all.

Who can convince me that staying home was better? he thought. *Maybe a stray bullet or a loony fanatic could have put an end to us, like they did to my parents. I never said that I embrace communism. I only said that things are not as bad as I thought they would be, and as far as the king is concerned, I still believe that the guy must be dethroned.* This argument satisfied both him and his other self and brought the young man in peace with his own conscience.

CHAPTER TWO

A month after young Fotis settled the debate with his other self, a commander of the revolutionary army came to the camp and asked to see Fotis Liakos.

"Fotis!" one of the chaperones called in a loud voice. "Someone here wants to talk to you."

Fotis got off his bench, rearranged his collar and his pants, wiped his lips with the part of his shirt that was hanging over his belt, and walked over to where the impressive stranger was standing.

"Are you Fotis Liakos?" the man asked and walked around the young lad several times.

"Yes, I am," Fotis said and paused to hear what the strange visitor wanted from him.

"Come with me, comrade," the other man said and started walking away from the rest of the children. Fotis followed, wondering where he was to be taken. Nothing was said while the two walked down the street. Minutes later, the twosome entered one of the big buildings. Fotis followed the stranger down one of its poorly lit corridors until the stranger stopped in front of one of the doors that lined the left side of the hallway. The man dug a key out of his pocket, opened one of the doors, and motioned Fotis to enter. The room was an office with simple, worn-out furniture. An old desk with a plush chair on one of its sides dominated the center of the room. Two rusty metal chairs without seat cushions lined the other side.

The enigmatic man motioned Fotis with his index figure to take his place in an empty chair. He, in turn, walked behind his desk and threw himself on his plush chair. He took a deep breath, took a fat folder out from one of the drawers, opened it, and took a page out of it. He looked at it for a second or two, rolled it into a tube, and, pointing it at Fotis, spoke in a serious tone of voice.

"Young Liakos, I have orders to go around the camps and find young men who are ready to participate in the revolution. I see you are a smart and ambitious young man. They also tell me that you are a fast learner."

Fotis thanked the stranger for his compliment and told him that he always believed that perseverance was the only way to overcome adversities in life. He made himself more comfortable and relaxed, and got ready to receive the big news.

"Our liberation struggle needs young fighters like you. The leaders of the KKE decided to increase the number of attacks against the softies of the king and to do that, we need more men to shoot rifles at them. You and several other young men from the camps in the area are chosen to leave the monotony of the concentration camps and receive training for active duty. Hang around here until the truck, with the rest of the selected fighters, shows up. It will not be long!"

"May I run back to camp to say goodbye to my sister?" Fotis asked.

"No time for sentimental adieus. The truck will be here momentarily," he said, and walking by his window, he glanced outside to see if the anticipated vehicle was coming down the street.

Fotis was frozen in his chair, as if a high-voltage electric current ran through his body. He envisioned himself firing a powerful rifle against the enemy, and that thought alone increased the flow of adrenaline in his bloodstream. The same thought turned his original reaction to dust, when he realized that the enemies would be fellow Greeks, some of them the same boys he had played marbles with on their grammar school grounds. They were young Greeks hoping to see the war ending soon so they could return home, hug their parents, kiss their sweethearts, dance their traditional dances, and share local wine in their neighborhood taverna. Worse yet, these very same men would not be firing marshmallows at others in actual battle. They would shoot real, deadly bullets. In the middle of this controversial thinking which flooded young Fotis' mind, the rumbling and screeching truck rolled down the cobblestone street and stopped in front of the door.

"Let's go," the other man said to Fotis. "The truck with several young men, just like you from other camps, is here. You have an hour's ride to get where you supposed to go, and it will get dark soon. The place you are going to is up in the mountains and the riding is treacherous, especially at night."

Fotis obeyed the command without objections. He knew well that any protest would fall on deaf ears. Thoughts of running away entered his mind, but upon careful consideration he found the idea ludicrous and suicidal. He did not even know where he was, or in which direction to run to get back to his country. *It's a good thing that he cannot hear what I am thinking,* Fotis said to himself with his mute voice, and he followed the other man out of the office. Like a well-trained dog, he increased his steps to keep up with the man in front of him and seconds later, they stood in front of the standing truck with its engine still running. Several young men of his age were sitting on wooden benches inside the vehicle. The driver, apparently a Slav, sat behind the wheel eating a sandwich and smoking a cigarette that smelled like it was made with the threads from old mooring rope. Fotis climbed into the vehicle and sat next to another man he had never met before. As soon as the driver finished his sandwich, he stuck his stinky cigarette between his lips and engaged the engine. The vehicle sent a cloud of black diesel smoke into the evening air and started to move forward.

The aged truck lingered on dirt roads for a while without a problem. It climbed a steep, uphill mountain road and handled with ease the sharp turns around narrow passages. Finally, it reached the top of an isolated mountain and stopped. The crowd of the young adults got off and stretched their limbs; some of them took a pee in the darkness. Moments later, every one of them took their seats onboard and the truck rolled downhill until it reached its destination and came to a complete stop. The men dismounted the vehicle and saw a huge tent a few yards in front of them. Four armed young men in their late twenties stood there to welcome the nineteen newcomers. Two of them looked Greek, but the other two appeared to be local men. They were tall fellows, with light complexions, blond hair, and bright, blue eyes. One of the Greek-speaking men ordered the newcomers to form a double line and to follow him. The other three members of the welcome party followed behind in military formation. The sky above their heads was dotted with an untold number of shining dots and the crescent moon was halfway up from the eastern horizon. Other than the symphony of howling wolves coming from the surrounding pine forest, nature was eerie and quiet. Once inside the tent, the door closed, and the four receptionists lit several kerosene lamps. One of them told the new arrivals that there was a good reason for no electricity in the place.

"The covert nature of our operation demands absolute secrecy," he said. "We must stay away from public view. The closest point of civilization is several miles from here." Another guy took the podium and told the young arrivals that this place was a top-secret camp for intensive training and that they were at this place to become familiar with some of the techniques of guerrilla warfare. Finally, one of the Slav-looking fellows informed the boys that they would stay at this place for the next six weeks to learn things that they would need to know when they joined the fighting men and women on the mountains back in their motherland. For now, they should sit around and relax. Finally, he introduced the four members of the welcoming party as Kostas Likos, Nikos Gekas, Bruno Sinkevich, and Alexander Sinofsky.

"You don't have to remember our last names. They are assigned names. Call us Kostas, Nikos, Bruno, and Alex."

Kostas, pacing the floor as if he were General George Patton, told his listeners that they would learn the basics of guerrilla fighting. They would learn to use a rifle, an automatic machine gun, a handgun, a knife, and a bazooka. Furthermore, they were there to learn things about explosives, booby traps, hand grenade launchers, etc. At the end of his introductory welcome, he walked around and shook hands with everyone. The arrivals mingled with the rest of the trainers, chatted with them at random, and asked questions about this place. Fotis was very interested to know why only these nineteen young men were chosen for this mission. To his dismay, he received remarks that did not answer his question.

"That is classified information. You are a smart and hardworking young man. Aren't you?" one of them told him. "Besides, why you are interested to know about this place?"

*

Back at the camp, Georgia was devastated upon hearing that her brother had been snatched away from her without explanation or warning. She kept asking her chaperones for answers, but she received unsatisfactory responses. "It's time for him to become an active member in our struggle for equality," one of them told her. When she was in private, she cried her eyes out to no avail. She was frightened and insecure without her dear brother, the only person she trusted with her secrets and her personal problems. Day after day, she woke up with puffy eyelids and was seen wandering around the camp aimlessly as if lost. There she was, an eighteen-year-old girl, without parents, siblings, or any other relative to ask for advice and guidance. One of her girlfriends, another eighteen-year-old girl in the camp, tried to console her and encouraged her to go on living without her brother. She reasoned with her that, sooner or later, she had to break away from her brother's shadow and live her own life.

"You learned to go on living without your parents, didn't you? It seems that the moment for you to be independent and get away from your brother is here! Quit bellyaching, sis," she told Georgia. "Fotis will go on living according to God's will and you should do likewise," she told her, and patted her on the back with sisterly affection.

"But I love my brother," Georgia responded with a muffled sniffle that interrupted the rhythm of her voice. "He is the only blood relative I have!"

"We all love our siblings," her friend added. "That does not mean we must chain ourselves to them for the rest of our life. There is that moment for all of us to be detached from our family and build our own nest. Mind you, dear, we still love our own folks."

Her friend's counseling had a positive effect on Georgia's thinking. She adopted a positive outlook for the future and her hope for a better tomorrow soared upward. Still, deep down in the unreachable depths of her heart, she was yearning to spend time with her brother and hear his optimistic comments about their future.

Dear God, grant me one wish. Please keep Fotis safe, she repeated every night, before she went to sleep. So Georgia went on living from day to day without a purpose or a tangible plan for her future. She went to sleep living the past and woke up hoping that each day would be better than the day before.

*

Things were different for Fotis, up in the mountains somewhere north of his birthplace. He was going through intensive training in active military life. Part of their daily routine demanded the physical fitness of an athlete and the courage and dedication of a devoted soldier. Daily, they ran a treacherous path under live fire for an hour. A cold shower followed, then a Spartan breakfast, and at eight o'clock, they lined up for inspection. During the rest of the day for the next three weeks, they were taught some of the techniques of guerrilla warfare. Discipline and obedience to the principles of communism were emphasized throughout the day. They ate dinner at 6 p.m. and from seven to nine o'clock they heard lectures about the importance of equality between men and women. Most of all, they heard the poverty, back home, was the doing of the rich.

One day, it was raining hard when they entered the dangerous path. Part of their exercise was to advance forward, creeping under a net of barbed wire. As always, two automatic submachine guns from two opposite hills were spitting real bullets that flew just inches over the heads of the crawling young men. When they reached the end of the gantlet, they took a count and discovered that one of their friends was missing. Everyone thought that he had decided to run away. The trainers called for cease fire and three of the boys crawled backward in the path looking for their missing friend. They found him lying face down in the mud, with a hole from one temple through the other. They brought him to the other end and realized that he was dead. No religious ceremony was conducted for his interment and no priest read prayers for the salvation of his soul. His remains were lowered into a hole they dug in the ground, wrapped in a worn-out blanket. He was buried in the middle of nowhere, somewhere on a mountain in a country that the boys could not even name. He was one of the *forgotten*.

Life in the mountain camp went on as usual until the first part of their training was over. After three weeks, the remaining eighteen young men moved to a more remote area that was void of any other human life. Here they were introduced to the art of dirty war. Day after day, they were taught how to effectively use a dagger and became well-versed in the destructive power of several types of explosive materials. They learned to make booby traps with explosives and were taught ways to infiltrate enemy territory. Fotis' instructors saw in him a young man with outstanding abilities to neutralize his opponent, effectively function behind enemy territory, and hit small targets with a World War II German bazooka.

The eighteen young adults had grown to manhood and appeared to have forgotten their teens and their dedication to Greece. They behaved as full-fledged communists, ready to return home and pick up their original mission. Two and a half years of indoctrination followed by a few months of training in hand-to-hand combat had been a complete success. Only two of them were sixteen; the rest were seventeen or eighteen-and-a half. Regardless of age, all of them were experts with conventional firearms and all of them had a good knowledge of explosive materials. Above all, they had acquired the skill to stand in front of a crowd and deliver short, persuasive speeches. In the eyes of their trainers, these eighteen teen-agers were a sample of the fanatic communists needed to infiltrate Greece. Alexander Sinofsky stood among the members of the graduating class and told them that they would soon go back home. Like the twelve apostles of Jesus Christ, they should teach the rest of the Greeks that Stalin was their friend. He pointed out for the millionth time that the governing system in Athens was corrupted and must be changed. Bruno Sinkevich told them the night before they departed for Greece that it was time for them to make Greece great again and gave a bear hug to each one of them. That evening, each of the graduates was introduced to his local guide. For the first time, the group broke up. That same evening, each one of them was led in top secrecy by their guides to a different hiding place.

All the next day, Fotis and his guide hiked over hills and through thick forests. The following morning, dead-tired and ravenously hungry, they reached a village where they found a safe house to rest for the day. Tiptoeing in single file, the two men entered a house before the sun was up. The guide told Fotis to sit down and help himself to the food and wine that was spread on a table. He also told Fotis not to venture outside the house until his next guide showed up.

"Your next contact will be here after dark. He is a local man and he is 100 percent trustworthy. The territory is infested with anti-communist, armed fanatics, who will not hesitate to slash the throat of a person who is suspected as a Bolshevik! We must be careful, comrade," he said, and announced that his assignment was over. His mission was to bring him to this point and turn him over to another guide. On his way out, he wished Fotis a safe trip and good luck. Finally, he reached over, hugged him with brotherly love, and advised him to be extra cautious. Before he opened the back door to go away, he gulped down a glass of wine, pushed a piece of fried ham in his mouth, stuffed a hunk of bread in his knapsack, and disappeared in the darkness, like a burglar.

Fotis sat by the table with the food in front of him and ate all he could push down in his stomach. He was hungry like a dog and his feet, not his legs, were aching. He took his boots off his feet, rubbed the heels and toes for a while, extinguished the kerosene lamp that illuminated his dark room, and spread himself on the floor to get some rest. His mind traveled back to the training camps, for nothing else mattered to a dedicated revolutionary soldier. He did not think about his parents, his grandparents or the good woman with the goat that took care of him for seven years. When he rubbed his overburdened stomach, he touched the chain of his charm, and that sensation triggered a mental contact with his sister, Georgia. He opened his eyes and he thought he saw her standing in front of him wearing her perpetual smile on her face. That mirage broke his heart. His experience for two and a half years with people he never met before did not cross his mind. He only kept asking himself: *Am I doing the right thing going back to Greece with the sole purpose of killing other Greeks to depose the king and changing the political system of the nation? Am I a hero, or a puppet of the Bolsheviks?* After a while, nature overtook his fantasies and when day extended over the land, the power that made him fatigued prevailed. He spread himself on the floor and went to sleep.

A rap at the door and a gruff voice woke him up just about the time the evening star showed its face from behind a puff of clouds on the western horizon. He opened his eyes and, before answering the door, inspected the grounds outside his window. Countless glittering lights were covering the expanse over his head and the crescent moon was barely noticed.

"Get up comrade. Time to go," an elderly man said as he walked into the room with a young man wearing a fisherman's cap. "I am the owner of this house and this is Petros, your new guide." He went on to tell the half-sleeping Fotis that Petros would guide him to the seashore where he was to board a fishing boat for the last leg of his mission. "I don't know exactly where you are going, but I know that from here on, you will travel in Greek territory. Only the captain of the boat knows where to pick you up and at what nook he will drop you off."

Fotis stuffed his shirt in his pants, put his boots on, straightened up, and introduced himself to his guide. The guide introduced himself only as "Petros." With a firm handshake and a friendly expression on his face, he said, "Time to hit the road, comrade. It's best to reach the forest after dark. I like traveling unnoticed. In the open, people see you and ask questions about your whereabouts. You never know who will cross your path. I would rather be safe than sorry."

Fotis looked directly at the aging host, took his hand in his, shook it firmly, and expressed his gratitude for the luscious dinner and the restful time he spent in his house. To accentuate his obligation, he told the gracious man that he would like to return, after the revolution was over, and renew their friendship.

"It's all for the struggle to throw that leech, the king, to the sharks in the sea and establish equality for all Greeks," his host responded and repositioned his cap over his shining bald head. "Son, I'll roast two lambs from my herd and we will have an unforgettable celebration in town, and if you are still single, I'll have the most beautiful girl for your wife," he added. Winking his left eye at Fotis, he reached at his moustache and twisted it with his bruised fingers. "Go with my blessing to where you go, son," he repeated and hugged Fotis one more time. Fotis walked out of the house with questions for which he had no answers. The host's last statement was foreign to an eighteen-year-old, but it stuck in his mind for a long time.

Fotis and his guide sneaked out of the house under the light of the stars, meandered through narrow streets for a couple of minutes, then entered an oak forest. Petros, a local lad in his middle thirties and with the body of a rock climber, led the way through the narrow and uneven paths, all night long. Fotis trailed behind him in complete silence. At some point during their stumbling through the forest, Petros broke the ghostly stillness and informed Fotis that he had traveled this path several times and he knew where each obstacle was in front of them. He also noticed that his companion had a problem choosing his steps and quoted a folklore statement.

"People around here say that 'a blind person is like a stranger walking in the dark,'" and handed his walking stick to his companion. "You will find it helpful locating flat spots to plant your foot," he said to Fotis with a concealed titter.

Their progress was tedious and slow in the darkness. There were roots to stumble over and sharp stones to stub one's foot. At places, tree branches were hanging low in front of them and blocked their advance. A strange howling sound, like the crying of a cat fighting a dog, came from somewhere in the forest. Fotis' hair stood up and the eerie sound forced him to freeze in his tracks. Petros looked toward the place from where the howling came and told his companion that wolves get crazy and make strange calls during their mating season. Fotis relaxed a little upon hearing that the alarming sound was part of being in a forest at this time of the year. He controlled his fear and continued walking behind his guide until the sun came up and lit their path. At this point, Petros casually called for a brief stop. He removed his knapsack from his back, took out his water canteen, uncorked it, and, pointing with it at his companion, asked Fotis if he cared to have a sip of water.

"Do you want some?" Before Fotis responded, Petros bent down and placed his sack against a young tree. Fotis reached over, took the canteen from his companion's hand, opened it, placed its opening against his lips, and swallowed several mouthfuls of its contents.

"Thanks," he responded, and handed it back to its owner.

"We are almost there," Petros said. "You stay hidden in the cover, while I climb the tree to check the shoreline ahead of us. We must be sure that the coast is clear before we get out in the open." Like a cat, he disappeared into a cluster of branches on a tall oak tree. Fotis sat on a flat rock and admired the other man's swiftness as he climbed to the top of the tree. Minutes later, he came down from his observation post and announced that he did not spot anything suspicious from there to the waterfront, but he advised waiting a few more minutes until the sun peeped clear from behind the trees. He wanted to be doubly sure that no stranger saw them. At long last, he selected a flat clearing next to his companion and sat down cross-legged.

"Where are you going?" he asked Fotis with his eyes fixed on the ground. "Mind you comrade, that's none of my business! I'm just curious ..."

"To be candid with you, friend, I know as much as you do," Fotis answered. "They only told me that the person who holds the secret of my final destination is the captain of the boat that will pick me up."

He must be a very important person to get all this attention, Petros thought, and dropped the subject. Instead, he remarked, "The man who offered you his hospitality yesterday is one of the most powerful and the richest man in the territory. He has the most beautiful daughter, about your age. He means what he told you before we left his home. If you ever come back, you will be his choice for his 'doll.'" Fotis blushed at his companion's comment and turned his face away to hide his emotion. He looked toward the eastern horizon and pointing at the sun said, "Petros – don't you think it is time for us to move on?"

Petros understood what his new acquaintance was attempting to say and responded with a friendly smile and a tap on Fotis' shoulder.

"You are right, buddy! Let's get going. 'Your business is your business,' we say around here. It's time for you to march on." They got up and Petros informed Fotis that they would walk to a clearing from where he would show him the cave where he would hide until the boat came. He cautioned him to be patient and stay put at his hiding spot until the fishing boat arrived sometime in the next twenty-four hours. He made it perfectly clear that whatever Fotis does, he should not attract the attention of passers-by. He reaffirmed that the people in the smuggling network knew where he will be, and they will get him as soon as it is safe for them to cross Albanian waters.

"Oh, remember the code!" Petros exclaimed. "They will ask you, 'Are you Odysseus?' and you must say, 'No, I am a hermit crab.' Can you remember that?" Petros said to Fotis and asked him to repeat the code several times. Finally, Fotis and Petros left the cover and walked side by side toward a rocky seashore.

The sea was calm like a huge puddle of olive oil. No wind disturbed its stillness and no dolphins were around to make ripples. The gulls and the pelicans were still tucked in their nests. The forest behind them was alive already. Partridges were chuckling on the highlands and nightingales in the lowlands were sending their thanks to their creator. Under their feet, the grass was the domain of a countless variety of insects and reptiles. It offered its protection against the night chill of the early springtime.

"Do you see that promontory that protrudes over the water?" Petros asked, and pointed with his finger at a rock formation that was sticking like a giant shovel several feet above the water. "You will find a cozy cave under that rock. You get in it and wait. Just be patient," and asked his companion to repeat the identification code for the last time. Fotis handed the walking stick to its owner, hugged him with brotherly love, and thanked him for taking risks to get him safely to this point.

"I'll be waiting to see you back to claim that beautiful girl after the war is over," Petros said and vanished back in the forest. Fotis, alone for the first time in his life, stepped up his pace toward the rock Petros pointed out. He tiptoed under the extending rock and found the entrance to the small cave. He crept inside it, like a reptile, and was prepared for a long wait.

It was early in the morning. The sun was only a little way above the horizon, and the sky was cloudless and blue like the sea below. Fotis positioned himself face down on a flat spot, pushed his feet toward the back of the cave, rested his chin on his folded arms under his face, and fixed his eyes on the endless sea in front of him. Not a soul anywhere to be seen, and that isolation frightened the young man. Gaping at the emptiness in front of him, his mind brought to life the picture of his late parents and his dear sister. He was alone on a seashore that he didn't even know if it was part of Greece or part of another country. His mind traveled back to Vivitsi and visited the grounds where his parents were buried. The simple wooden cross that the neighbor had hammered on his parents' burial ground stood in place just the way he left it three and a half years before. The wildflowers that he and Georgia placed next to it the day before they left the village had turned to straw, but they were still there. He wondered if the good neighbor still had that playful goat that she brought over to their house, and that thought made him smile. The picture of Georgia stayed with him longer, much longer. He wondered how she was doing without him, and that thought triggered a cascade of frightening scenarios in his mind. Was she okay or some bully was taking advantage of the eighteen-year-old Georgia!

My God, he thought to himself. *What will happen to her without my protection and guidance? I hope she is strong enough to endure.* At that instant, he felt warm tears wetting his sleeves and noticed that his nose was dripping. He elevated his head above ground level, lifted his face with his hands and took another look ahead, but saw no boat moving toward him. He only saw little puffs of waves littering the blue water in the far distance. He was not uncomfortable lying on his belly and was not tired either. He was just bothered by ominous thoughts about his future and the safety of his sister.

A new thought persisted in bothering him: he questioned the wisdom of becoming an active fighter in the revolutionary army. He could not find the reason and the audacity to fire a deadly bullet against one of his own countrymen. He couldn't accept the idea of lining up with the very same men who gunned down his parents in cold blood. Deep down in his heart, he felt that the king, who could barely speak Greek, had no place in government, but the rest of the governing system was okay. Most of all, he was not convinced that equality among all Greeks was a workable and just idea. The young adult thought that his father was entitled to have a nicer home than his neighbors. He invested time and money to go to school and become a teacher. He worked harder and got more for his labor than some guy next door who was idle all his life. The same thing was true with his mother, Fotula. His grandparents worked hard to open and keep a fur shop. It was not given to them. It was the product of their dedication and hard work. Only Grandma and Grandpa were entitled to enjoy the fruit of their labor. The store was theirs and only they should decide to whom they should pass it on, not to share it with some of the lazy dwellers of the village.

It was after midnight when Fotis realized that he was mentally exhausted. He stood up from his hiding position, peed into the water bellow, stretched his arms and his legs to get rid of the numbness from being immobile for several hours, and reconnoitered his surroundings for any signs of danger or for his rescuers. He saw nothing. He only heard the flip-flapping sound from the gentle waves, breaking against the rock formation several feet below the floor of his hiding cave. He repositioned himself back on the ground, curled in a fetal position, and asked his brain to let him go to sleep. An annoying yawning kept visiting him and he felt that the sea breeze blew sand in his eyes. Moments later, the young man surrendered to nature and fell asleep.

*

Georgia had a different set of problems back in the camp. Besides being alone and worrying about her brother, she had a young man following her like her shadow. Any place she went, this insistent and often arrogant young man followed her. While she was attempting to do tasks that she was assigned to do, he was next to her, and when he had the opportunity, his hands were all over her. He managed to sit next to her during mealtime and followed her even to the door of the girls' bathroom. The thing that bothered her the most was the apathy of her trainers and supervisors. They appeared to have problems of their own, lately. They did not care about the well-being of the children anymore. Something bad for the camp was on its way.

Most of the children were young adults now. Several of her friends had established serious relations with boys and two of them were not shy to admit it. Georgia was not yet ready to step over the line that separated childhood from adulthood. Granted, she was a grown-up, but still, she was hoping that her brother would return. She was confident that he would appear someday and take her back to Vivitsi. At night, before she went to sleep, she prayed to her favorite saint to bring Fotis back. She asked the trainers and chaperones about her brother's whereabouts, but to no avail. Her saint was mute, and the trainers and chaperones refused to be specific. So, poor Georgia was living one day after another while putting up with the bothersome acts of her admirer.

The fear, that she was *forgotten,* became more intense daily. Trainers and chaperones started to disappear, and despair became routine in the camp. The only thing that fortified Georgia's hopes for a better tomorrow was her belief that the charm around her neck had magic powers, just as Grandpa had said. Before she closed her eyes to go to sleep at night, she kissed it with devotion and asked it to bring her brother back. She felt desperate, for her future did not look promising at all.

On the international scene, things were changing drastically. Winston Churchill made a deal with Joseph Stalin to stay out of Greece's affairs and, in return, Great Britain and the United States would "look the other way" from Stalin's efforts to expand communism in other parts of the world. It was vital for Great Britain and the United States to have a free pass to the Middle East through the Mediterranean Sea. The present agreement among the three superpowers after World War II changed the Soviet Union's plan to provide all-out military and economic support to the rebellious Greeks. Consequently, the funds, that were allocated to finance the camps, stopped coming. Chaos prevailed when the trainers and the chaperones suddenly walked away from the camp. Children found themselves in a strange and hostile country, without food, shelter, or supervision. They walked the streets begging for food and shelter. A few of the good-hearted local people provided food and shelter for some of them. Eventually, the majority of the children fell victims to hunger, illness, the harsh weather. A good number of them fell victims to the exploitation by unscrupulous local residents.

Georgia stayed one more week in the girls' sleeping quarters after almost everyone was gone. She did not have the stomach to leave another younger girl alone, for she was ill. The other girl could not keep food or water in her stomach and at the same time was running a high fever. Georgia begged for a few stems of mountain tea from a neighbor, brewed a cup of tea with it, and tried to convince the sick girl to drink it.

"It's good for you," she said to the sick girl. "Every time I had an upset stomach, my late mother forced me to down a cup of that stuff." The other girl gagged at the first sip she sent down her belly and refused to go any further with Georgia's potion. She was just melting away, with fever under her blanket. When the local authorities came to claim the empty beds and to evict the tenants, they found the two girls huddled together in an isolated corner of their sleeping room. They threw Georgia and her belongings into the street and took the sick girl to some local clinic. Georgia retrieved a worn-out blanket from the pile of the discarded items, wrapped it around her shoulders, and took the street toward the center of the town.

A chilling rain was coming down and Georgia decided to get shelter in a nearby public outhouse. The lady responsible for cleaning the place allowed her to spend the night there. Georgia locked herself in one of the cubicles, wrapped her blanket round her shivering body, and stayed there all night long. The next morning, she took the road toward the center of the town and kept walking, away from the evacuated camp toward the center of the town.

On her way there, an old dilapidated house, at the far end of a dead end alley, caught her attention. It was a well-constructed edifice, but it looked to be deserted. Weeds grew at the threshold, its door was partially open, and two of its windowpanes were missing. Georgia thought that she could move into this place and make it her temporary sleeping place until the charm around her neck performed its first miracle for her. She turned into the alley and, with her heart in her throat, approached the seemingly abandoned house and entered through its partially open door. It was dark inside, but she could see cobwebs stretching over one of its open windows. A heavy dust deposit covered the warped wooden floor, yet fresh footprints were visible in the dust. Georgia became terrified, thinking that people were still living in this place. She thought that a gunshot would ring in the dark and a bullet would put an end to her life. Obviously, she was trespassing over a person's private property.

She stood at the entrance of the place, like a ghost, hoping that some miracle would take place. She had her old blanket wrapped around her shoulders and under that, she had her blessed charm to warm her heart and fortify her hope for a better tomorrow. She was scared to go inside, for she was sure that the footprints on the dusty floor were made by human feet. She did not dare to backtrack her steps, for she had no other place to spend the night. So, she stood there looking at the footprints in front of her. The more she stared at them, the more she convinced herself that they were made by a child or an old person. The distance between steps was short, a characteristic of some child's steps, not those of a healthy, adult male. *God help me decide to either go in or get out of here,* she said in her soundless voice and concentrated her entire attention to hear the voice of God. As her eyes became adjusted to the poor lighting, she also noticed little dot marks next to the footprints, an indication that whoever made the footprints was using a walking stick of some kind. It must be either an elderly or a handicapped person, she thought. In this state of mind, she stood there pondering what to do. While she was trying to sort things out in her mind, she thought that she heard a squeaking sound of a door opening and her nose detected wood smoke.

"Hello! Is anybody here?" Georgia called. "Are you okay? I smell smoke!"

The squeaking sound of the door came back to her ears again, and a woman's whining voice disturbed the silence.

"Go away … I'm an old woman and have no money … I cannot help you!"

"I am not here to ask you for anything," Georgia responded. "I only hope that you are kind enough to let me sleep under your roof for tonight. I'll be on my way tomorrow morning," Georgia pleaded, and stood fast by the door. The squeaking sound repeated itself and a few seconds later, a shadow appeared in the dark, coming slowly toward her.

"I mean no harm to anyone," Georgia repeated. "Please help me!"

The shadow was an old woman. She waddled slowly, balancing her weight on a cane she held in her right hand. A noticeable hump was on her back, and strings of thin white hair hung, uncombed, over her wrinkly forehead.

"Are you one of the girls from the camp?" the old lady screeched. When she lifted her face to look at her visitor, Georgia noticed that she had no teeth and only one eye was staring at her. The socket, where the other eye was supposed to be, was empty.

"Yes. I am one of them," Georgia responded with modesty and unconsciously let her blanket fall off her shoulders. She was shaking like a leaf from fear that the old woman would react unfavorably to her answer and ask her to leave.

"Oh, my dear little lady! Come in and become as comfortable as my poor house can offer," the woman exclaimed and taking the girl by her hand, she guided her toward the inner part of the house. Georgia started to believe that the charm around her neck had powers, indeed. *Thank you, dear lord,* she said in her inaudible voice that only her heart and God could hear. The old woman's aged hand felt good in Georgia's hold and her presence dissolved all the fears she had about her future. She felt her heart rejuvenate and her spirit soar high, just like a red eagle. The old lady and the young girl, holding hands, finally entered a room in the center of the house. There, the old woman closed the door behind them and declared modestly, "This is my palace, dear." She asked Georgia to make herself comfortable by the fireplace to warm her shivering body. "I don't have much of anything to offer nowadays, but I'll rummage around and find something for you to eat! Please, sit close to the fireplace. Poor thing, your hands are shaking. I'll join you shortly," she declared and wobbled away supporting herself on her walking staff.

Georgia couldn't believe her good luck. She sat on a low stool next to the fireplace and deep in her mind thanked Holy Providence for bringing her to the doorstep of this compassionate lady.

The room was spacy and comfortable, but not well-ventilated. A musty odor prevailed in the air. Items from some distant past were on display. The furniture and the other objects appeared to hold memories of some old glory. Medals of military accomplishments, antique swords, helmets from World War I and framed pictures of men from antiquity hung on the walls. Several certificates of military distinction, encased in massive, ornate frames, were on display on a long ledge over the fireplace. A small mahogany table with four red velvet-cushioned chairs stood in the center of the room, but the stone fireplace appeared to be the dominant attraction. Two small beds, one on each side of the fireplace, were covered with warm, homemade quilts. Only one of them appeared to be in use. The quilt on the other bed had accumulated a considerable layers of dust. An additional pillow, decorated with three calligraphic letters crocheted on its fabric, was resting against the solid mahogany headboard.

The old lady meddled around in one of her chests for a few minutes, then disappeared through a door into another room. Georgia sat, dumbfounded, on her low stool trying to make sense of the things she saw and experienced. The things on display made her conclude that the old lady was descended from some distinguished family of the remote past. Her conduct toward her was proof that she was a gracious, polite, and caring woman.

"Are you comfortable, my dear?" Georgia heard the voice of the old woman coming from behind her. Taking things out of her hands, she placed them on the table. The moment her trembling hands were free, she walked over to Georgia, took her hands in hers, held them for a moment, and announced with remorse that her scanty offering would have to be enough for now. She gently led her to the table, offered her a chair to sit down, and uncovered the antique crystal tray she placed there moments earlier. Bread, slices of preserved ham, cheese, an apple, and a glass of water were artistically arranged in a circle inside the crystal dinner plate.

"Don't be shy, my little lady and after you eat, tell me something about yourself." Georgia took her place on the chair in front of the food and the old lady sat on the chair directly opposite to her.

"My name is Anna," the hostess said. "Anna is a very common name for women here in Macedonia. What is your name, my young lady?"

"My name is Georgia," the bewildered girl responded and went on to tell the gracious lady that she was born in northern Greece, the twin sister of her only brother. She shuffled in her chair once, reached over to the food in front of her, took a bite from the bread and cheese and began to chew.

"Okay. Are you planning to be in town for a while, Georgia?" Anna asked her. "You are welcome to sleep tonight on the floor by the main entrance but eat your food first. You can close the door to be safe and to keep the northerly wind out. I'll be back in a minute." She walked out of the room. Georgia ate some of the bread and cheese, consumed the crunchy apple, and drank the water. In the meantime, she was so overwhelmed with emotions that she could not find words to thank the old woman for everything when she reappeared.

"Thank you for allowing me in your house and for the delicious food. You saved a life, my precious lady. God will remember that," she added and wiped her wet eyes with the palm of her left hand. The chatting between the two women continued a little longer. Anna asked more questions about Georgia's place of birth, her parents, and the circumstances of her being at the camp with the rest of the children. Georgia did not ask Anna any questions about her past. She was busy answering questions that Anna kept firing at her. It was almost nine in the evening and Anna suggested that they should retire for the evening. Georgia thanked Anna for her hospitality, once again, moved back to the entrance foyer of the house, retrieved her blanket from the dusty floor, closed the entrance door, wrapped herself with her blanket, and withdrew to the furthest corner away from the main entrance of the house. There, she curled in the corner, wrapped the old blanket around her shivering body and in the darkness of the old confines, she cried her eyes out. She cursed the day she was born, and the thought of climbing up a tall building and jumping out at the street below crossed her mind several times.

"Lord, either take me to your kingdom, or guide me out of my quandary," she whispered in the darkness. Before she closed her eyes to go to sleep, she retrieved the little charm that was hanging around her neck. She pulled it out from the cleavage between her full-grown breasts, kissed it tenderly, and – before she returned it back to its hiding place – asked it to perform its next miracle.

Her sleep was not peaceful. She felt cold and when she finally managed to fall asleep, she was tormented by bizarre dreams all night long. She saw her parents and her brother going by her without even looking at her. They were shadows in her fantasy. She attempted to draw their attention by calling their names, but no one responded to her cries. She relived the accident that claimed the life of the four children and her heart ached. Mean dogs and venomous snakes followed her everywhere she went. Finally, the sun came up, the darkness of her surroundings gave way to the light of the day, and she was relieved from her tormenting dreams. She sat up. She felt cold and uncomfortable, having had only the worn-out blanket to keep her warm, but she was up and still alive. She stood up, pushed her thick hair away from her face, and cracked the door halfway open to take a better look at the new day God awarded to His creation.

"Are you up, already? I heard the old door squeaking," Anna called from somewhere inside the kitchen. "Come in!" she repeated and announced that she had brewed fresh mountain tea. "Have you ever had mountain tea?" Anna asked, and disappeared back in her kitchen. Georgia followed her and sat on one of the chairs by the table. The old lady fetched two ornate teacups, filled them with steaming tea, placed one in front of Georgia and the other in front of her chair on the table, and said, "You look to be a trustworthy young lady. You can stay here for a while," she declared and fixed her one eye directly at Georgia to read the impact of her offer.

"It's very gracious of you, Madam Anna …" Georgia began, but she was interrupted in the middle of her statement.

"Hush, girl! Call me Anna, or Aunty Anna, if you prefer," and a smile blossomed in her aged face.

"Thank you very much, Aunty Anna, for allowing me to stay here." Georgia volunteered to do all the chores around the house while she was under Anna's roof, for labor was the only thing she had to offer. The emotional impact of Anna's offer was uncontrollable, and she was at a loss for words. She picked up her cup of tea, drew a sip of its contents, and put forth extra efforts to suppress a torrent of powerful reactions that formed lumps in her throat.

"My mother insisted for me and my brother to drink mountain tea, every time we had a cold or a digestion discomfort. She swore on its curing power."

"I don't believe that this weed has any medicinal properties. I only like to have a cup of it when I don't have coffee," Anna responded in a whimsical tone. The two newly acquainted women sat around the place for the rest of the morning talking about the things that crossed their minds. Georgia expressed her yearning to find her brother and to return home, but Anna had no desire for anything else in life. She only mentioned that she was not happy with the political system Comrade Tito had established over greater Serbia.

"We, the Macedonians are not Slavs," she said. "We are the true descendants of Alexander the Great."

Georgia chose not to comment on Anna's conviction about the Macedonian people. She did not want to debate the issue with the old woman, for she valued her friendship. She needed a place to sleep and be safe. She deduced from Anna's comments that she was in the Slavic part of Macedonia, not far from home. Months before, one of the trainers in the camp had told her that Macedonia was an area of Serbia bordering northern Greece. Putting together these two bits of information, Georgia concluded that she was close to her motherland. A yearning to return home was kindled anew. The prospect of seeing her old home became real and a faint smile blossomed on the face of the hopeless girl. If she only knew which direction Greece was, she would hike toward the border.

The days of living with Anna rolled uneventfully, one after another, for Georgia. She kept busy cleaning the inside of the house, boarded up two of the broken windows, and weeded the entire area outside. Her hope that she would find her way back home kept her mind going while she was working around Anna's neglected house.

There was an additional room next to the room where Anna had her two beds, but it was under lock and key. Two other rooms were empty, and their doors were always open. Anna never allowed Georgia to step inside the locked-up room and never said a word about what she kept in there. Likewise, Georgia honored the old lady's restriction and never asked questions about the contents of this room. A veranda on the other end of the house had an unobstructed view of a mountain range in the far distance. One could enter the house through this open veranda. A small door on the back of the house led into the veranda from a narrow street that separated it from the neighboring house. This door had a deadbolt lock, and Anna always kept the key to the lock in her pocket. She preferred to use this door, instead of the bulky front door, to enter the house. Georgia liked to spend time on the veranda, especially when Anna was not home. The mountains, with their peaks still covered with snow, were mesmerizing and reminded her of her home back in Greece.

"Look, Aunty Anna," she said to the old woman when she returned home during a cloudless evening. "The mountaintop is beautiful, isn't it?" Georgia exclaimed and pointed at the snow-covered peaks. It was late afternoon and the sun was still reflecting a pink color off the white snow.

"They are majestic," Anna said drily.

"What lies behind them?" Georgia asked apathetically.

"Oh … beyond these peaks is your country. There is a terrible war going on up there between the men of your king and our freedom fighters," Anna murmured. "On a sunny day, I used to see airplanes swooping over the land, dropping bombs at the men who are entrenched on those peaks. When I was attentive enough, I could hear the earth-shaking rumble of the bombs exploding. I don't think the freedom fighters have a chance of winning the war. The airplanes are gone." Shuffling her feet on the bare floor, she left the veranda and entered her house. Georgia stayed there a little longer to absorb an idea that popped-up in her mind. Later, when the two sat at the dinner table after supper, Anna took a serious look at the young woman and said.

"I feel guilty having you sleep on the floor at the entrance to my house like a watchdog. You only have an old blanket to keep you warm and comfortable. Why don't you use the spare bed? Heck, beds are made to sleep on," Anna concluded with her unbecoming smile and a dry cough that lasted several seconds.

"If it pleases you to have me use your free bed, I welcome your generous offer," Georgia responded with humility. For the first time since she met the old lady, she walked over to where Anna was sitting and hugged her tenderly. Anna returned the hug and asked Georgia to go ahead and change the old bedding with fresh blankets and pillows. The new bed was soft, warm, and comfortable. Anna's frequent trips to the toilet at night did not bother Georgia. She became accustomed to normal sleeping and enjoyed the luxury of a comfortable bed.

Later that night and every night thereafter, Georgia took time to tuck the old lady under her bed covers, thanked her for allowing her to use the spare bed, kissed her on her forehead, just above the empty eye socket, extinguished the kerosene lamp that illuminated the room, and crawled under the covers on her new bed. Sleeping in a normal bed was an experience she had forgotten.

Tonight, she could not close her eyes. She was counting her blessings meeting Anna. She stared at the darkness around her for hours. She did not even toss around in her bed, for she was careful not to make noises and wake up her snoring roommate. In the stillness of the night, the thought that she could scale the mountain to the other side made her mind go around in circles. *As soon as the shooting is over and the snow melts, I'll climb up there and find my way back home,* she said to herself. That positive thought made her fall asleep.

*

Fotis, hiding in the cave by the seashore, fell into a deep slumber, also. His youthful energy was drained and the young lad went to sleep way past midnight. In the pre-dawn darkness, two young men, wearing sleeveless shirts and Greek fisherman's caps, climbed the rocky precipice and like cats entered the cave where Fotis was sleeping. Fotis heard nothing, as the persistent slapping of the waves covered any noise. Suddenly, a poke in his ribs forced him to open his eyes. In the dim moonlight, he saw two shining daggers inches away from his jugular veins. One of the sunburned men whispered, "Are you Ulysses?"

Fotis' brain leaped into gear.

"No, I am a hermit crab."

"Devil you! I was about to put a crimson string of pearls around your throat," the other sunburned man commented and inserted his dagger back in its leather sheath. "Wake up and let's get out of here before the day breaks. We must be out of Albanian territory before the new day is here."

The three men tiptoed out of the cave and, one behind the other, they walked to another hidden nook where a dinghy was anchored. With the agility of mountain goats, all three jumped in the vessel and took their seats. The two fishermen grabbed the oars and sped quietly toward the mother ship that waited in deeper waters, several yards away from the rocky seashore. Finally, all three climbed aboard the larger boat, lifted the dinghy up to the deck, and walked over to where the captain and two other husky seamen stood. The captain stepped forward, shook Fotis' hand, and said in his authoritative voice, "We do not have to know your name and your whereabouts and for reasons I cannot explain to you, you will not know our names either. You will only know me as captain, and you can call my men friends or comrades. The first rule in the business I am in, is absolute secrecy. Welcome aboard, son."

He walked away and the other four men followed on his heels, leaving Fotis on deck by himself. Fotis paced the small deck several times and, noticing that piles of fishing nets were everywhere, he concluded that he was aboard a small fishing boat. Moments later, the engine roared and the boat inched forward, away from the rocky shore. Fotis walked over to one of the piles of fishing nets, sat on it, and turning his face toward the east, saw the sun rising as if it were coming out from the waters. Minutes later, one of the four fishermen returned to the deck and told Fotis that the "rags" he had on his back were not clothes for a Greek fisherman.

"Here," he announced and threw a pair of slacks, a sleeveless black shirt, and a fisherman's cap to him. "Put them on and donate your Slavic attire to Poseidon," he thundered with a laugh. Fotis smiled at the other man's sense of humor and followed his instructions. He removed his old clothes and, one at a time, tossed them overboard. He put on the fisherman's uniform and decided to descend to the lower level of the ship, where the captain and three of his men went. The fourth seaman stayed at the wheel.

The lower level of the boat was not what Fotis was expecting to see. He envisioned a refrigerated area with loads of boxes topped with ice. Instead, he saw several wooden boxes, stacked neatly, one next to the other in one of the corners. At the moment when he came down, the captain and his men were covering the boxes with layers of worn-out fishing nets and piles of tarpaulins.

"These boxes contain the cargo that you will use when you become an active member of the revolutionary army," the captain said to Fotis. "I understand you are very good with the bazooka, aren't you?"

"I fired a few of them, during my training, with a high degree of accuracy, I may add."

The sun was up. The fishing boat kept sailing southeast toward the southern Peloponnesian coast of Greece. The crew dropped some of their nets in the water and kept only a small prize catch. Obviously, they were not commercial fishermen. Their mission was to deliver Fotis and the bazooka somewhere. Occasionally, they pulled into a fisherman's harbor to buy gas, food, water, and alcoholic beverages. After two days at sea, they met another boat in the open sea, early at night. The two boats exchanged their crews and Fotis, with only two new, hardened seamen, sailed toward a remote seashore and dropped anchor a few feet from land. The other boat turned back and disappeared north toward the way it came from.

Fotis was welcomed by several freedom fighters who stood on land. Another group of men transferred the wooden crates from the boat to dry land, loaded them on the backs of mules, and drove away. Fotis and his welcoming company shook hands and took a goat path toward the mountain ahead of them. After an hour hiking through remote passages, they reached the camp of one of the few revolutionary armies that was still active in the Peloponnese. About seventy young warriors were sitting around on a flat plateau surrounded by a thick pine forest. Most of them were just lying around. Others were cleaning their weapons, and still others were either playing cards or were engaged in casual conversations. The commander and his subordinate officers were huddled under an old pine tree, studying a map in front of them. Fotis introduced himself to a group who stopped playing cards and came over to meet him. Each one of them shook hands with the new man and bombarded him with questions about his name, his place of birth, his rank, and his age. As soon as Fotis answered all the questions that were directed at him, two of the fighters settled down and began to narrate details of actual battles. Fotis sat in their company listening to their gory stories of destroying human life indiscriminately. He began to wonder, once again, if joining them was the right thing to do. *Joining these cut-throat characters is not what I should do, but is there an alternative?* he asked himself in a soundless voice that only his brain registered.

"Eh, you! You fresh guy, come with me," another man said to Fotis. "The commander wants to talk to you."

Fotis jumped off the rock he was sitting on and followed the other man to where the commander stood. The impressive leader took a careful look at the eighteen-year-old Fotis, extended his right arm, and welcomed him with a firm handshake.

"The file that came with you tells me that you are good with the bazooka. Is that true?" he inquired.

"I scored high with it during my training. I was able to consistently hit a target as big as a large watermelon, two hundred feet away," Fotis responded with pride and self-confidence.

"That's very impressive, boy! I will have a need for you in a few days," he continued and turning his attention to one of his subordinates, he ordered him to give Fotis a uniform and a light rifle, and have him ready for action before the end of the following week.

When the subordinate went away to fulfill his commander's order, Fotis took a close look at the captain and saw a ruthless man with a thirst for action. He was a short guy with broad shoulders and oversized hands. His uncombed hair hung several inches below his cap. The cap itself was decorated with three brass stars, fixed one next to the other just above its brim. Most of his face was hidden behind a full beard that was trimmed short. Underneath a furrow of thick eyebrows were the most peculiar green eyes Fotis had ever seen. They were big and glittered like the eyes of a Siberian tiger. They radiated authority and demanded unquestioned obedience. His uniform was nothing special, just military attire, and his boots were dusty and worn out. A 45mm revolver with a shining ivory handle rested inside a canvas holster. The holster itself was attached to a wide leather belt that he had strapped firmly around his waist.

"Are your parents still living?" he asked Fotis.

"No, commander, they are not. They were killed by a band of fanatic Macedonians."

"I'm sorry to hear that, comrade Fotis," he responded. "Any siblings? I mean, do you have any brothers and sisters?" he added to clarify the meaning of the word "siblings."

"Yes, I have a twin sister," Fotis said.

"Let me brief you on a job I have for you," the commander said. "There is a stronghold in a town close by, which is defended by a band of well trained, heavily armed ex-policemen. We attempted to take the place in the past, but we were repelled with considerable losses of men and ammo. When they heard us coming, they barricaded themselves inside a hole with five-foot concrete walls all around it. The closest we can get to this place is the school, which is two hundred feet away. Small-arms firing power does not do us any good to break through their concrete wall, and that's when you will come in handy. You will blow holes at the damned wall for our fighters to rush through them and behead the bastards of the king. Do I make myself clear, son?"

"Yes, you do, comrade commander," Fotis responded.

"You are dismissed. I'll call you when the time is ripe for your participation."

Fotis withdrew to the area where the other men were loitering around, sat on a protruding boulder, and reconsidered his ability to hit a target the size of a watermelon two hundred feet away! The things that he did not know were the penetrating power of the bazooka the commander had in his hands and the thickness of the concrete wall. The scenario that bothered his mind the most was the aftermath of a successful attack. He envisioned young Greeks slashing the throats of other Greeks with their daggers. He saw with the eyes of his imagination some of the young men, who were resting around the camp to be dead or dying on the ground between the school and the concrete wall. He also saw blood gushing out of the throats of the defending ex-policemen, and the whole thought made him sick to his stomach. He gagged several times and managed to keep down the bitter bile that gurgled up to his esophagus.

"Okay, comrade, here is your rifle and your uniform," he heard the voice of the subordinate coming from behind him. He took his place on the rock next to Fotis and explained that the rifle was clean and ready for action. He handed over to him the weapon and a shoulder bag with fifty rounds of ammunition, packed in clips of six. Lastly, he asked Fotis if he knew how to aim and fire it. The rifle was a bolt-action World War II weapon with a retractable bayonet. It was short and light, and Fotis knew that the thing was designed for close action. Fotis told the subordinate that he had seen it before. He placed it in his lap, removed its bolt, aimed it toward the sky, and looked inside its barrel. He placed the bolt back in its place and told his comrade that the weapon was in excellent condition, considering its age. Fotis felt uncomfortable talking with a fellow whose name he didn't know. He knew that everyone was going by a new, revolutionary name, but he asked the other man for his rank and his name anyway.

"All of us go by names given to us when we volunteered in the revolution. My name is 'Kostas.' I am the deputy commander."

"What is all the fuss about the target we plan to hit?" Fotis casually asked.

"That place has been a thorn in the commander's ass," Kostas whispered. "We lost ten men the first time we attempted to take the place. The enemy barricades inside an above ground, unfinished cistern and calls for reinforcement from the big city which is only seven miles away. We must be fast getting to them, clean them up, and get out of there in fifteen to twenty minutes. Otherwise, armored vehicles will show up. Keep this conversation to yourself. This plan is top secret," he added, and walked away. Fotis sat there for a while longer, thought about the information he obtained from the assistant commander, and let his imagination wander aimlessly about the impending waste of human life. He felt his heart pounding hard and placed his open palm over it to stop it from bursting through his rib cage and flying away. In doing so, he felt the charm that Grandpa hung around his neck and the words of the gracious old man came to his mind. *It is blessed by the Patriarch.* Fotis repeated Grandpa's words and retrieved the charm from its hidden place. He brought it to his lips and kissed it with divine respect. He did not know what he expected the thing to do for him, but he kissed it, several times, with reverence. The full moon was directly over his head and he thought that his mother's smile was engraved on its equatorial line. The rest of the camp was quiet like a cemetery; not even a leaf was moving. Fotis moved to a grassy, flat spot, put his head on the canvas bag with the ammo, took his rifle in his embrace, and went to sleep.

Human commotion woke him up early the next morning. The entire camp was up in arms and he saw the rebels running in the forest with their weapons in their hands.

"Airplanes!" a voice shouted through a loudspeaker, and screeching sounds of airplanes filled the air. Fotis grabbed his sack with the ammo in one hand and the rifle in the other and attempted to reach cover. Instantly, he realized that the airplanes were over his head. He dropped behind a big oak tree and heard the deafening sound of a bomb exploding nearby. He was lucky. The bomb landed on the other side of the tree. A mixture of soil, stones, and branches filled the air and a three-foot-deep crater appeared at the spot where the bomb landed. Fotis dived into the crater and plugged his ears with his index fingers. The terror-spreading iron birds made several passes over the camp. They dropped more bombs, riveted the ground with rapid firing of machine guns, and, one behind the other, flew away, not to return again. Minutes later, a voice announced that the airplanes were gone and the freedom fighters began to come out of their covers.

"Comrades assemble here in two minutes," the voice of the imposing commander was heard though a loudspeaker. As soon as everyone regrouped in the clearing, he stood on an elevated spot and told his men that someone had betrayed their hiding place. He ordered that every man should be ready to move out of there before noon.

"We cannot afford a battle with the regular army in open grounds like this," he growled. "We choose the place where we meet them, not where they want us to face them. They might have better weapons, but we have the heart to fight and we will win. Long live freedom and justice for all," he declared at the end, and the fighters repeated his salute in one voice.

It was almost one o'clock in the afternoon when the entire force formed three groups under three leaders. Loaded with weapons and supplies, they moved out of the camp following different paths in three different directions.

There were forty-four men in Fotis' group, and the company was led by the commander himself. Kostas, his top lieutenant, was in the same group, for he was to be the commander should something happen to the leader. Fighters and officers from Fotis' group meandered through narrow passes in the forest for two hours until they reached the place where they were to rest during the night. They chose a friendly village tucked away in an isolated gorge and upon their arrival, they took possession of the school building. The local people appeared to welcome the group with open arms and ran to serve them. Men and women brought food and wine and catered to them throughout the evening until the next morning. In the meantime, Kostas drilled Fotis on the impending attack. Hour after hour he went over the plan of attack. Kostas was to supply the bazookas to Fotis, and he was to fire them at the wall as fast as he could, until he was ordered to stop. He went over the exact spot where Fotis was to be concealed during the firing action several times, pointing on a map.

"Fotis, this plan has to work, if you and I value our lives! Otherwise …" The lieutenant pointed with his index finger at his head above his ear. "Pow, the commander is not joking. You must blast that wall to bits."

Fotis looked at the other man with self-confidence and assured Kostas that he would do the job effectively. Every time Kostas reminded Fotis that everything depended on his ability to blast the wall apart, Fotis nodded to show that he understood him. Deep in his heart, he felt guilty about giving an opportunity to Greeks to kill other Greeks. He knew that the very same young men who were looking forward to killing the men behind the wall were innocent country boys. They were just brainwashed to believe that to be a communist was patriotic and that communism was the solution to their poverty. Yet, when he examined his predicament, he felt like a man trapped between an advancing fire behind him and a deep cliff ahead.

Hours before the attack, all the fighters spent their time cleaning their rifles and sharpening their daggers to razor-sharpness. Everyone was on high alert when they assembled for dinner. You could see it in their faces and their mannerisms. After dinner, the commander stood in the center of the gathering and delivered a fiery message to his fighters.

"Comrades, they tell me that the war is over, up north, but not here in Peloponnese. You are the future of Hellas! You are the chosen children of our mother country! You are destined to deliver justice tomorrow. You and I will scale the water-retention wall and we will cut to pieces those who are behind. Our new comrade," he barked and pointed at Fotis, "will blow that wall wide open for us to rush in and cut the throats of the king's boys. The events of tomorrow will enter in the pages of our history. They will remind future generations that your deeds were the turning point for freedom and justice for all Greeks," he thundered in his harsh voice. "Go and get some rest now. We must be there before dawn."

Two hours before dawn, the group marched away and before the sun came up in the morning, the commander's group sneaked into the village that the ex-policemen had occupied. Unnoticed by the villagers and the policemen, they concealed themselves inside and around the school building. Fotis and Kostas hid behind a pile of rocks close to the northwest corner of the school. Still undetected by their enemies, they brought up several bazookas and pilled them close to the spot Fotis chose as the place offering the best view to his target. As soon as the light of day illuminated the wall, Fotis removed the safety pin from the trigger on the first bazooka, aimed at the wall, put his finger on the trigger, and told Kostas that he was ready. The assistant commander signaled to the commander that he and Fotis were ready for action. A few seconds later, they received the "go ahead" signal from the commander. Fotis aimed the weapon at the wall, pulled the trigger, and the first deadly projectile hit the wall and exploded. The ex-policemen, who were previously informed about the impending attack, were barricaded behind the wall, waiting for the attack. The deafening explosion created havoc among their ranks. Several more bazookas followed the first one, and a section of the concrete wall crumbled to pieces. The shelling continued in rapid fashion until the voice of the rebel leader came through his loudspeaker.

"Hold fire," he ordered, and at the same time his fighters rushed toward the broken wall with a rifle in their hands and a dagger held between their teeth. Fotis stopped firing his deadly bazooka at the wall, put his palms on his ears, and buried his head behind the pile of stones in front of him. A pandemonium of rapid firing from both sides of the wall followed. Screaming of men ensued for ten minutes. At last, the shooting quieted down and only agonizing, human moaning filled the air. The ex-policemen were ether dead, lying wounded on the ground, or throwing their weapons away, putting themselves at the mercy of their attackers. The bloodthirsty commander arrived at the scene after the shooting was over. He retrieved his revolver from its holster and executed, in cold blood, all the prisoners and any other enemies on the ground, moaning or just breathing. Those of the freedom fighters who were not hurt were drenched in human blood. Apparently, they had used their daggers in close combat with the ex-policemen to express their primitive, animal instincts. The other two groups of freedom fighters did not take part in the fight. They arrived at the scene when the action was over. They came to carry away any wounded comrades and haul away the spoils of their victory. Thirty minutes after the first bazooka exploded on the wall, the rebels were gone. The morning sun saw a group of victors running away from the scene and dozens of lifeless bodies littering the crimson-spotted earth on both sides of the crumbled fortification.

Fotis, running away in the company of the victors, felt shocked beyond description. His stomach was tied up in a huge knot. He wanted to throw up but he couldn't do it. The churning in his stomach worsened when he saw one of the rebels carrying the head of an ex-policeman. He cursed the moment he joined this ruthless group. At that instant, he made the biggest decision in his life. *I must get out of this awful life, at any cost,* he thought, and kept walking next to Kostas at the tail of the group.

"I am sick to my stomach," he said to his walking partner and stepped off the path to vomit in privacy. He kneeled behind a thick clump of shrubbery and attempted to relieve his stomach from that uncomfortable feeling. When he finished spitting his guts out, he lifted his head and noticed that the rest of his comrades were out of sight, around a sharp bend in the path. He retrieved the charm from his chest, kissed it once, and whispered solemnly, in desperation. "God! This is the only wish I will ever ask you to grant me. Please help me get away from these people." Without calculating the risk he was taking, he took off toward the direction from where he came from He kept running like a wounded jack rabbit until he came close to the village where the battle took place earlier. He crawled under a cluster of thorny wild rose bushes, covered himself with leaves and grass and cocked his ears for any calls coming from Kostas.

CHAPTER THREE

G eorgia, after a few weeks in Anna's company, found herself and her ambition to go on living come alive. Today, she woke up rested and with a positive attitude that the worst part of her odyssey in a strange land was coming to its end. She had a pleasant dream last night. She dreamed that she met a handsome young man who was crazy about her.

The sun was shining in the eastern sky and most of the snow on the mountain peak was gone. She started the fire in the fireplace and brewed fresh mountain tea.

"Aunty Anna! Are you up?" she called politely. "I made fresh tea. Would you like me to bring it over to your bed, or do you wish to join me at the table? I feel good today!"

"I think I will join you at the table. You sound cheerful and I like to know the reason of your exuberance," Anna said and broke into a prolonged, whistling cough. While the tea was simmering on the fire, Anna put her socks on her bony feet. Holding on at the edge of her bed, she managed to walk over to the table and threw herself in her favorite chair with a "ha" sound that came out of her toothless mouth with effort. Georgia filled two cups with the hot tea, added a spoonful of clover honey to each one of them, placed one in front of the old lady and placed the other on the table in front of her chair. Before she made herself comfortable on her chair, she went over to Anna and greeted her with a kiss on her wrinkled forehead. The old woman took a noisy sip from her cup and focused her single eye directly on Georgia's youthful face.

"Now, tell me what makes you so vivacious, this morning? You sound like you are in love." Her annoying cough returned to interrupt her speculation, but she tried to hear Georgia's answer.

"The snow is gone up at the mountain, and the nightingales around us sing their spring songs," Georgia said poetically. "I'm ready to move on with the last leg of my adventure, here in Macedonia. I made up my mind to return home and, hopefully, find my brother, back in my village."

"Dear girl, the war is still raging up there," Anna responded, and her concern for Georgia's safety echoed in her statement. "Stay with me a little longer, until the shooting stops. It's risky for a girl without experience to venture in a place where bullets fly in all directions and all kinds of bombs turn the earth upside-down. Stay until it is safe to travel! I'll miss your company." Anna's trembling voice was interrupted by a deep sigh. "Stay, dear, and we will find a good young man for you, here in town," she whispered and paused to hear Georgia's answer.

"My most precious Aunt Anna! My destiny calls me elsewhere," the girl managed to say and walking around the table embraced the old lady as if she were her own mother. "I have to go, but as soon as I establish myself back home, I will return to visit you."

Anna drew several deep breaths, regained her strength to face the unpleasant news and responded in a faint voice that betrayed her disappointment for losing the girl. Georgia meant so much to her.

"Sweetheart, I cannot stop you from doing what your heart calls you to do. I only offer my advice. I feel for you! Remember, dear, that the door will be open for you, as long as I'm still dragging around my beat-up, old self." She wiped her eye with the heel of one of her hands and delivered a painful smile to her listener. Georgia was shaken to the core hearing Anna's plea for her to stay, but she had made up her mind to go. Her instinct to chase the dream she had last night told her that her future was in some other place, not here with the gracious lady. She had made up her mind to climb the mountain ahead of her, descend over to her country, and follow her destiny, whatever it may be. She thanked Anna again for being such an understanding person, but she was convinced, beyond reasoning, that she had to venture home. She spent the rest of the day keeping company with Anna or doing things that had to be done around Anna's house. Early the next morning, she wrapped herself with her old blanket and walked away from Anna's house without even waking her up to kiss her goodbye. She did not have the strength to see her one eye crying. She just took the road that led toward the mountain and kept going. *Lord, give me the strength I need to start living again,* she pleaded to God who was watching her from above.

The climbing was difficult, but not impossible for a young woman like Georgia. At times she had to crawl on all fours between rocks and junipers that blocked her way. Yet, she kept moving upward toward the summit. Occasionally, she had to stop to catch her breath and to listen for unusual sounds that might signal danger. She heard nothing alarming and kept going onward. Late in the afternoon, she arrived at the foot of the summit and, like a serpent, crawled to what she assumed was Greece. Ahead of her was Macedonia that belonged to Greece, and behind her was Macedonia that was a part of Yugoslavia. She spread the old blanket on a flat spot on the ground and lay on it to catch her breath. Moments later, she stood up from her reptilian position, wrapped her worn-out blanket around her body to prevent the chilled mountain breeze from reaching her bones, took several deep breaths to restore the oxygen in her bloodstream, and with a heart filled with new hopes for tomorrow, she came out into the open. She had only taken a few steps on her motherland when the blast of a machine gun broke the silence. Several bullets crashed on the rocks next to her and splinters of rock and lead flew in all directions. Georgia fell on the ground and managed to crawl behind a massive rock next to her. Instantly, she felt a stinging sensation in one of her thighs, just inches above her knee. When she lifted her dress high enough to see what was wrong with her leg, she realized that she had been hit. A trickle of blood, originating from a hole in her thigh, was advancing downward toward her knee. The girl became frightened and started to cry aloud, seeing blood oozing out of her leg. She placed her thumb over the wound, pressed it a little, and noticed that the flow of the blood stopped. But as soon as she took her finger away, the blood gushed out with new vigor. "Now, what do we do?" she shrieked and applied pressure back on her wound.

"Stay calm, girl," she heard a command in her language and saw a young man in military attire crawling behind her. The soldier grabbed her by her shoulders and, like a wolf, dragged the helpless girl away from the firing line. Once on safe ground, he pulled up her blood-stained dress and declared, "Chicken-pecking. Keep pressing on your wound with one of your hands and rest the other on my shoulder. You and I are taking a little walk together." He lifted her off the ground by her waist and carried her back toward the direction she came from. "Girl, you should know better, not to venture up here. Did anyone tell you that life is cheap, up here? There is a war going on!" he exclaimed.

Georgia was lost for words and became speechless. The man's sarcasm about the seriousness of her wound made her assume that she was not in any imminent danger. Furthermore, hearing him speaking her native language fortified her hope that she was in good hands.

"Are you Greek?" she managed to say. "You spoke to me in Greek."

"Hell, no! I am not Greek. I'm Macedonian. My father is Greek and forced me to learn Greek, when I was a child. I heard you expressing your agony and fear in Greek, and that's how I knew that you are Greek."

Just several yards away from where she was wounded, the man found an opening on the side of the rocky summit, stooped his shoulders toward the ground, lifted her off the ground completely, and carried her through the opening as if he was taking his little girl to her bed.

The setting inside the place was an emergency hospital. There were sick people on beds and medical staff hurried about earnestly. Pungent odors of iodine and alcohol were everywhere. The faint humming of a generator was discernible in the farthest corner of the room. The man deposited Georgia on an operating table and a young doctor rushed to her help with a nurse at his heels. The doctor took a brief look at her thigh, diagnosed the injury as superficial, and asked the nurse to hand him surgical tools.

"Does it hurt a lot?" he asked his patient and pressed at her thigh around the bleeding spot.

"Just a little," Georgia responded courageously.

"Good, because it will hurt more, when we get in there to take out a piece of metal which is lodged on your thigh bone. You will be uncomfortable for a second or two, then everything will be okay. Your bone is not fractured, and you will walk without a cane in no time." He slipped a pair of plastic gloves on his hands and with the composure of a poker player, he asked, "Ready?"

"Anytime you are ready, doctor," Georgia responded and promised to herself that she would be brave during the procedure, regardless of how uncomfortable the surgery was. The nurse brought a tray with surgical paraphernalia and the soldier held Georgia's injured leg flat on the operating table.

"Ouch, it hurts," Georgia exclaimed when metal forceps were inserted in her wound. Seconds later the doctor pulled the forceps out, deposited it on the tray, and walked away. The nurse dressed the injury with white gauze and assured Georgia that she would be okay. "Yay! It's a big one," she exclaimed and showed Georgia the forceps, holding a bloody piece of metal.

Georgia stayed at the underground hospital for about two weeks. During her recuperation, she became friendlier with her Macedonian savior. She narrated to him the story of her life from the beginning, and she was not shy to tell him her ambitions for her future. He, in turn, told her that his name was Alex Bookas and that his father was born in a Greek village close to the borders of the two countries. Regarding his relations with his parents, he expressed love for his mother, but not for his father. He told Georgia that the old man was the product of "old Greece."

"He does things his way, not necessarily the right way."

Finally, he asked Georgia if her father was dogged like his old man.

"I am not sure," she responded. I was in diapers when he was killed," she answered with a deep sigh.

Alex was a robust, well-proportioned fellow. He was about five feet, eleven inches tall and weighed around 180 pounds, with bushy blond hair. His face was elongated and light in complexion. His nose was Mediterranean-looking, his lips full, and his eyes as blue as the cloudless sky. A well-arranged row of white teeth popped into view when he smiled. His overall appearance was not Grecian at all, but his manner with other people was authoritative, just like her brother, Fotis. He was not a commoner, Georgia could tell from the way he conducted himself in front of women. He gave the impression that he had been raised by a well-to-do family.

"You should reconsider your plan of returning home at this time," Alex advised Georgia. "The security thugs back in your country will have a file on you, several inches thick. You are marked as a communist and as soon as you show up, you will end up in a holding area until they bring you in front of a judge, and if my sources are reliable, you will spend years waiting for your trial. Here is my suggestion: stay in Macedonia until the war is over and until order is restored in your country."

He assured her that she would be safe with him until the war came to its end and he admitted that the communists would be the losers of the conflict, for they had not received the promised help from Stalin. "Come with me, back to my parent's home. I am sure I can mend things with my father and you can stay there until it is safe for you to return to your country. You have no family waiting for you back home, and as far as your brother is concerned, you don't know where he is or if he is still alive!"

Georgia mulled over Alex's advice for a few days and tried to identify his motives for asking her to stay. A new trickle of hope traveled from her head to her heart.

I kind of like this young man, she thought and for the time being she dismissed the rest of the questions that flooded her mind. As the days went on, the shooting and bombing became less frequent and freedom fighters were seen retreating into Slavic Macedonia. The king's army had taken control of the borders and the Greek flag was raised at the highest peak of the mountain. Gradually, doctors and nurses disappeared from the underground emergency hospital and patients were taken away.

Alex took a risk waiting for Georgia to make up her mind. Finally, he packed his belongings, wired a huge pile of ammo with dynamite inside the hospital, and ordered Georgia to get out of the place. "I am ordered to destroy this place," he told her. "You must either walk toward the line where the Greek soldiers had established their defensive position or come with me, for this place will go up in smoke shortly. Afterwards, he bent over the pile of explosives and activated a timer that was connected to the pile. He took several steps away from where Georgia was standing, then he momentarily stopped. He took another look at Georgia, who was standing at the entrance like a salt statue of Gomorrah, then renewed his walking away from the place.

"Wait! I'm coming with you," he heard Georgia calling and saw her hobbling behind him. He retrieved his pocket-watch, checked the time, and chose a rock formation that provided protection from flying rocks. He dragged the girl under it. He took another look at his watch and started counting to ten backward. At zero, a muffled, earth-shaking rumble shook the mountain and seconds later, a rain of stones poured down from the sky. Alex held the girl close to his chest for several seconds while the flying debris was coming down from above. Georgia felt uncomfortable in the arms of a man she had met only days before, but the feeling of being away from harm's way overpowered her emotional discomfort. Finally, the ringing in her ears and the dust in the air gradually returned to normal. She wiggled away from Alex, shook her head to get rid of the dust that was deposited on her thick hair, looked directly into her companion's blue eyes and asked, "Now what? What do we do next?"

"Now, we walk toward our new beginning. Unless you have a better solution to our impasse, let's pay a visit to my parents. I know my father will welcome you with open arms. I hope he will open the door for me," Alex said and began to walk in the direction from which Georgia had come two weeks before. The thought of abandoning Alex and returning to Anna crossed her mind several times, but the feelings she experienced in his embrace during the explosion prevailed. She kept her walking pace next to a young man who was not even her friend. He was just an acquaintance whom she met under stressful circumstances. Alex was in deep thoughts for another reason. He was ashamed of returning home defeated. He couldn't bear the thought of facing his father as a soldier of a defeated army, but he had no choice but to swallow his pride and return home humiliated. He knew that his mother would welcome him, but his old man was something else. He would corner him and tell him that "fathers know best, boy!" He had to take his father's criticism standing erect, like a grown-up man. Georgia noticed Alex's state of mind and attempted to cheer him up.

"There is something that bothers your mind, Alex," she said firmly. "I hope it has nothing to do with me and my presence in your life. If I am a burden to you, please tell me. I can walk a different path. I have been alone before!"

"Nothing of that," he emphatically said. "I cannot get away from thinking about the sacrifices we, as Macedonians, made to make our country bigger. If that Bolshevik Stalin had honored his promises, I would be in Salonica today. My country would have been twice its present size, from Albania to European Turkey. Instead, I'm returning home like a whipped dog with my tail between my legs."

"I feel bad for those who did not have the chance to return home, not for those of you that returned, even defeated," Georgia said. "In any contest, there is a victor and a loser. It just so happened that you are on the side of the losers."

"You are right, I guess, but it hurts to be betrayed," Alex lamented and kept walking. At the end of the day, now better acquainted, they arrived at a village where Alex had friends. He knocked at the door of one of his buddies and the friend invited them in. He offered them supper and gave them separate rooms to sleep. Georgia retired early, but Alex disappeared with his friend until three o'clock in the morning. A country breakfast of smoked ham, scrambled eggs, home-made bread, and mountain tea greeted them at the kitchen table the next morning.

Georgia had a difficult time understanding the language spoken at this house. She ate her food, drank her tea, and just stood there trying to guess the subject the two friends were discussing. Later in the morning, Georgia and Alex thanked their friend and took the road toward the town where his parents were living. Georgia had difficulty walking next to him, for the road was narrow. She sauntered behind him wrapped in her own thoughts. The fact that she was the companion of a stranger crushed her self-esteem and her ethical values were decimated. All her life, she had been the subject of someone's authority, and now she was following a defeated soldier to a home where he was not sure he was welcome. Alex kept striding ahead of her in dead silence, with his chin buried in his chest and with his hands in his pockets. His self-esteem was low for a different reason. He was a soldier of a defeated army, a member of a group of young patriots dreaming to make their country bigger and more powerful. Worst of all, he was about to face his father who had advised him not to enlist in the guerrilla army and march against the Greeks.

"Boy, you don't know Greeks," was coming back to haunt him. "They are brave and cunning in battle. Don't underestimate them. I saw them fighting the Italians in 1940." Thus his father had tried to convince him not to join the Greek rebels against their king.

"Macedonians are the descendants of Alexander the Great," Alex told his father. "You will see whose flag will fly in Salonika by next year." And now he was on his way to face him and to admit that he was wrong about the supremacy of the Slav Macedonians over the Greeks. His lengthy debate with his father on the issue of

Alexander the Great being a Greek or a Slav reverberated in Alex's mind for hours. He knew that he would debate the same question with him when he returned home and he was mentally preparing for the moment.

"My dad came to Macedonia from Greece with a big flock of sheep at about the same time the Turks were forced out of here," Alex said unexpectedly. "Dad claimed big tracts of land from the retreating Turks, and he built his home where it stands today. He met my mother, the daughter of a local landlord who was in cahoots with the Turks for years. My old man is a good guy, don't get me wrong! We only disagree on the issue of Alexander and the thinking behind the recent revolution in Greece."

It was late in the afternoon when the two of them arrived at Alex's home. His father was not there, but his mother answered the knocking at the door.

"My dear son! My dear Alex!" she cried and ran to Alex with tears in her eyes. He opened his arms and buried his mother in his embrace, lost for words to phrase his emotions. He kept her in his arms until the sobbing subsided. Still holding her by her hands, he took another look at her, and said, "Mother, you look as beautiful as you were, the first time I saw you."

His mother recognized that her son was trying to tell her that she was still a lovely lady, but said nothing to express her emotions. She blushed slightly and pinched his cheek.

"For the time that you were gone, this house was a mausoleum without you."

Then she turned her attention toward Georgia.

"Tell me, dear, who is the charming lady that is with you?" pointing at Georgia with the open palm of one of her hands.

"Oh, I almost forgot!," and turning toward his companion, he introduced Georgia to his mother.

"Georgia, this is Lady Sofia Bookas, my lovely mother," he said, and pointed at his mother.

"Welcome to our home, my dear," lady Sofia responded and extended her hand for a handshake. Georgia stood there dumbfounded, for she did not understand anything spoken by Alex and his mother. They spoke a Slavicized Greek dialect that Georgia couldn't speak or understand.

"By the way, mother, she is Greek. She doesn't understand our language," and he began to translate his mother's remarks to Georgia into Greek. Georgia stood there like a marble statue, speechless and motionless, wearing a fake smile on her face. She was pleased to hear that the lady of the house was delighted meet her, but she felt like a fish out of water. Here she was, a stranger among strangers and in the company of people who had a long dispute with the Greeks over the nationality of an ancient hero. The general mood became lively, though, when the father walked in and faced his son.

"Welcome home, son!" he said in a trembling voice and threw himself at his son with open arms. "I mean just what I'm going to say, my only son! My house was a graveyard without you," he continued and releasing Alex from his embrace, he wiped his wet eyes with the oversized palms of his hands and added in an unnatural, emotion-stricken voice. "Let me take a good look at you, young man!"

He walked around his son, voicing his satisfaction. "There you are, young man. It looks to me that we brought into this world the second Alexander the Great."

"May I ask who this lovely young lady is, who brightens our house with her presence and her whole-hearted smile?" His grin forced his bushy moustache to part in the middle and exposed several of his upper white teeth.

"Dad, I met this lady two weeks ago, under dire circumstances. Her name is Georgia, and she is from your country. I found her bleeding, badly with a shrapnel lodged in her thigh. She has no place to go and no relatives to turn to for help!"

"Oh, you are Greek!" the father exclaimed and hugged the girl with fatherly passion.

"Who said that you have no place to go? Friends of my son are always welcome in my house. Welcome home, dear!" He thundered and released the shaken girl to allow her to catch her breath. Georgia thanked him and his wife for giving her a place to stay and entered a lengthy conversation with her host. She told him all about losing her parents at an early age and narrated her experience of being forcefully expatriated to Macedonia with other children.

"Them god-damned Bolsheviks in Moscow! They managed to divide the Greeks and put them to fight each other, like old times," he said bitterly.

This was Georgia's introduction to Alex Bookas, Sr., and his wife, Sofia. Breakfasts and dinners were plentiful for the weeks to come and their aimless chats during the days and the evenings were pleasant and harmonious. The father left every morning to care for his sheep and to oversee the cultivation of some of his land. Alex visited friends and relatives. He was trying to get back to civilian life and decide what to do for the rest of his life. The lady of the house spent her days like a princess from the past. She spent her idle hours beautifying herself with cosmetics, trying on new dresses, and gossiping with her friends who came over to have a cup of tea with her. Georgia couldn't believe her good fortune. For the next two weeks, she kept company to the hostess and did all kinds of chores around the house. She scrubbed the wooden floors of the house with soap and water, cleaned the windows, and wiped the glass panes with vinegar until they were squeaky-clean and spotless. She tilled the garden and planted a variety of vegetables for both the summer and the coming fall season.

Frequently, she had to skillfully evade passes she was getting from Alex, Jr. She needed more time to decide what she should do with him. She knew that his mother adored her, and that she stole the heart of his father. Yet, she was not convinced that Alex was available for her. Something, deep down in her heart, was telling her to delay her decision with the young warrior. His mannerisms and his behavior did not make him trustworthy, in her eyes. He was the product of a different culture. Every time he passed by her, he did not express an interest in her as a total person; his eyes were only fixed on her protruding chest and her slender hips and thighs. She was getting the impression that he sought only sexual fulfilment. In her estimation, Alex was not the man for a lifelong relationship.

"You like my Alex, don't you, dear?" Sofia said to Georgia one day in her broken Greek. "He is a gorgeous and charming man, ready to make a woman happy."

"Yes, who doesn't like Alex? He is a cute young man with a bright future," Georgia responded and avoided making further comments.

The days went by aimlessly and Georgia kept thinking of her predicament with Alex. She knew that the status quo must come to an end. She either had to force the issue to come to its conclusion or walk out of his parents' house with just a sincere thank you for their hospitality. Forcing some sort of decision was as risky as getting up one day and announcing that she was leaving. At night, when everyone was sound asleep in the house, she retrieved her charm hanging around her neck, kissed it repeatedly, and asked God, for help. *Dear God, show me the way out of this quandary! I don't know what to do.* She would go to bed, retrieve her charm from its hiding place, and talk to it endlessly. But the next morning she was disappointed at having no answers from above. She often had a premonition that something good would come down from above, and that glittering hope kept her going on living.

One day, lady Sofia and her husband were getting ready for some social event. The man took his time to shave clean, comb his hair, and put on his newly pressed formal attire. A pair of polished black shoes went well with his dark blue suit. His wife, assisted by Georgia, fixed her hair in a smart style, brushed a little rouge on her nose and cheeks, put on a chiffon dress with flowers printed all over it, and inserted her feet into a new pair of bright red shoes.

"You'll be here with Alex today," the lady of the house told Georgia. "My husband and I have a social event to attend. We plan to be back late in the evening. There are eggs and salted ham in the cabinet and green peppers in the garden. You can make omelets when you get hungry."

While the couple was gone, Georgia noticed that Alex was being nicer to her. His unusually cordial behavior frightened her and she thought the worst. He kept smiling at her, as if he wanted to say something, something very important, but he did not know how to say it.

"Alex, there is something that bothers your mind today," Georgia ventured to say. "I am your friend, you remember! You can trust me." The face of the young man lit up like a Christmas tree, hearing that she was ready to hear his secret. Here was the opportunity he was waiting for. This was the moment for him to express his feelings and bring everything to its end. He got off his chair, took a serious posture, cleared his throat several times, and, looking like the key speaker at a public gathering, began to speak.

"Georgia, the thing that keeps me on edge, day and night, has something to do with you. We met in such an unpleasant moment, and from that day on, you have been on my mind in a way I have never experienced before with any other girl I met. So, there you have it," he said humbly.

"I like you," he added, and grabbing her by her arms, he brought her close to him and kissed her tenderly, several times. She melted in his arms. Unable to resist him, she stood there like a lifeless object. She wanted to say, "No, please go away," but an inner voice dictated otherwise. Alex felt her indecisiveness and let her get free from her precarious position.

"Are you sure this is what we should do? What do your parents have to say about this?" Georgia managed to ask.

"Don't worry about my parents. You are their choice, to begin with. They are crazy about you."

Georgia placed the palms of her hands on her pounding head, just above her earlobes, and quickly considered the proposal. *I have no other place to go, and Alex has been nice to me,* she thought to herself, then she opened her mouth and said softly, "Before we do anything else, I would like to hear the opinion of your parents about it," and allowed him to kiss her, this time on her mouth. The rest of the day went by with exchanges of "sweet talk" until his parents came home in late evening. Alex asked his parents to sit down, for he had something very important to tell them. He went around and around with disjointed sentences, but he could not phrase his thoughts clearly. Georgia came to his rescue. She rose to the occasion and told Alex's parents that she and their son were in love and wanted to get married.

"God be with you! You have my blessings," the father said. His mother reacted differently to the news. She rose from her chair, walked around the table, and placed a "smacker" on the cheeks of both Alex and Georgia. Meanwhile, the father brought out a bottle of ouzo and four empty glasses. He poured some of its contents in each glass, handed one to everyone, and wished Alex and Georgia happiness and a long life. He jingled his glass with the glass of everyone and for the first time, Georgia felt the tickling of his bushy moustache rubbing on her cheeks. They spent the rest of the evening in good spirits, full of laughter, until they retired to their own bedrooms. Georgia crawled under her bed covers, kissed her charm twice, closed her eyes, and tried to make sense of what took place during the day and the early evening hours. Her commitment to marriage was the turning point where she cast off misery and sprinted toward happiness. Or was it? Alex's inability to announce the great news to his parents, and their decision to let him stay with her all day long, pointed to some well-orchestrated plan. The possibility that Alex was forced to commit himself to this marriage without his full consent kept Georgia up. That very possibility kept rolling in her mind like a dice wheel in a gambling casino.

*

Fotis, in his hiding place was camouflaged under dead leaves. For the rest of the day and all night long, he lay flat on his face, smelling the moist soil beneath him. He occasionally heard people's steps going by and heard their conversations, mostly about the massacre of the defending ex-policemen. The church bell rang out its monotonous tolling of death, all afternoon and most of the night. His hair on his arms rose to goosebumps when he heard the ear-piercing wailings of women from the village where the men had been brutally killed, and his self-esteem sank to its nadir. He cried softly and wished he could find the courage to load his riffle, put its muzzle under his chin, squeeze the trigger, and blow his head apart. He felt guilty for what he did with the bazooka, but he had no choice. He had to do it. It was an order from his superior officer.

When nature was engulfed in the blessing of sunlight and the wailing from the village no longer came to his ears to remind him of his deed, he pushed the camouflaging debris away from his face, rose to his feet, and directed his gaze upward. He saw the gyrating clouds looking down upon human misery. The morning sun in its arc smiled at him no more. All that remained was a great sea of hopelessness on which he was floating forever. As soon as the obstructed sun came out of a puff of dark clouds to claim the sky, he felt that all time ended. Desperation and hopelessness shrouded his being. But still inside him, in the deepest place, was a kindling flame of hope, the eternal hope, telling him that he would not perish like a serpent.

As soon as the new day was on its way– thirsty, hungry, exhausted, and stiff from the chill of the night – he managed to get up and stand erect. He shook the leaves off his head and clothes, left his rifle and his ammo bag where he was hiding, and came out in the open. He raised his hands high above his head and began to walk toward the village. On his way there, he expected to hear a rifle shot disrupting the peaceful morning and feel a bullet making a hole in his head. He did not care anymore whether he would stay alive to see the end of the day. Still inside him, in the deepest folds of his heart, the eternal flame for a miracle was not extinct – not yet. His hope to live through this ordeal came alive once again and he regained his courage to keep walking. The attitude that "there is still hope even in the direst moments" kept his feet sturdy and sustained enough energy to keep his hands pointing toward the sky. When he was within earshot of the first house in the village, he heard a man's voice ordering him to stop.

"Drop to the ground and put your hands behind your back," the voice commanded. Fotis did exactly what the voice ordered him to do. Seconds later, a rope secured his hands behind his back, and two armed men in military attire lifted him off the ground, frisked him thoroughly, and escorted him to their leader without uttering a word to him. Fotis was about to faint from fear and exhaustion when he faced the leading officer. The one-star officer standing in front of him, with his status-symbol baton in one of his hands, conveyed the image that he was about to separate the boy's head from the rest of his body. Instead, he spoke in a fatherly voice.

"Okay, young man! Tell me who are you and how you came to be here. Remove the rope that keeps his arms behind his back."

Fotis took several deep breaths, rubbed the part of his wrists where the rope had dug into his skin, and wiped a trickle of blood coming out of his nostrils, the result of a blow he received on the face from one if his captors. He took the chair another man placed in the middle of the interrogation room and began to narrate his life story from the beginning. Occasionally, the military officer interrupted him, gave him a cup of water, and asked for clarification on points that were not clear or were contradictory to his previous statements. The interrogation was brief.

"You said earlier that you are not a communist and that you were forced to join them. I don't understand why you did not attempt to get away earlier. What, suddenly, made you run away from them, yesterday?"

"I did not participate in the actual fighting," Fotis said with emphasis. "I was a good distance away from the firing line, guarding some of their supplies. But when I saw Greek blood on the hands of other Greeks, I realized I was in bad company."

"Let me get your story straight," the officer said and snapped his baton on the side of his leg. "You are not a communist, lost your parents at an early age, were taken away to a country outside Greece for several years, resisted the indoctrination to be a communist, joined the rebels willingly, then you realized that you were in bad company. Finally, you surrendered to the authorities this morning. Am I correct?"

"I did not join them willingly, sir," Fotis declared. "I was forced to follow them."

"Okay, young man, I'll make a note of that. The preliminary search for the truth about you and your doings is over for now." Turning to one of his men, who stood there taking notes of Fotis' testimony, the officer ordered, "Put him in regular handcuffs and take him to headquarters for a future court appearance."

Two civilians, apparently with authority to act as bailiffs, shoved Fotis out of the room and cuffed his hands in front of him. Landing several kicks on his behind, they threw him in a dark and musty holding basement below the interrogation room. There was no light and Fotis could not see the faces of his new roommates. He could only hear the moaning of someone who was in pain. Fotis stayed where he fell and did his best to be comfortable. He was a captive of questionable loyalty to the king. Contrary to what he had in his heart, he was labeled as "a traitor and a communist."

He spent five days in this hellhole, inhaling air saturated with the smell of human excrement and sweat. Worst was the pain caused by his handcuffs digging into the skin of his wrists. Once a day, two men visited the holding place and gave a piece of bread and a glass of water to each of the detainees. That was the only time when the men took away the plastic bucket that contained human waste and replaced it with an empty bucket.

The opening of the door to give the prisoners their daily allotment of food and to take away the bucket with human excrement provided an opportunity for the inmates to see each other's faces. Eight unshaved faces stared at one another. The faces of two of them were badly bruised. Two other men had lacerations all over the exposed parts of their bodies. A moaning man at the far end of the room complained that he had difficulty breathing. The other three sat at the farthest end of the room with their faces toward the wall. Fotis' face was still unmarked.

Early one morning during the start of his incarceration, a man came to the door and asked for Fotis Liakos.

"Come with me, bud," he sneered with a smirk on his face and left the room with Fotis behind him.

"Tomorrow, you will go in front of a panel of three judges who have the power to either set you free or send you to face a firing squad. In any case, you must be presentable when you appear in court. You will wash your clothes and dry them before morning. You must shave, get a haircut, and take a bath. I'll take the handcuffs off your hands to do the things I said. Attempting to escape, between now and tomorrow, will be the last mistake you make in your life, a painful mistake indeed." He directed his prisoner to an enclosed area where soap and water were available, removed the prisoner's handcuffs, and asked him to get undressed and start the cleaning.

"Here is a bedsheet with a hole in its center. Run your head through the hole and let it drape over your body to cover your nakedness," he instructed. Fotis followed directions and minutes later his clothes were washed and were hanging on a rope to dry. Using a facecloth and the same bar soap he used to wash his clothes, he scrubbed his body from head to toes. He wiped the water off his skin with the bedsheet, threw it over his nude body again, and asked his guard for the barber.

"Barber? You are looking at your barber," the other man responded, and took out from one of his pockets a razor and a pair of shears. The boy felt relatively secure hearing the clicking of the shears around his ears and neck, but he panicked feeling the razor blade gliding down his face. He couldn't get away remembering one of the rebels carrying the head of a policeman in his hands. That scene gave him the creeps just thinking about it, and he felt chills penetrating every part of his body.

When the preparation for standing in front of the three judges was over, Fotis put on his damp garments and his shoes without socks. His guard handcuffed him as before and brought him back to the holding room.

"What's that thing hanging around your neck?" the guard asked while Fotis was trying to put on his wet clothes.

"Memorabilia," Fotis responded. "My grandpa gave it to me when I was a baby. I keep it around my neck to remember the good old man."

As the door of the holding room opened, enough sunlight illuminated the space for Fotis to notice that only four of the prisoners were seated on the floor. The other four were gone. The door slammed shut and total darkness prevailed, once again. He fumbled around for a second and as soon as his vision was adjusted to the darkness, he found a clean spot to sit down and make his bed for the night. He had not eaten anything all day, but he was not hungry for food, anyway. He was hungry for precious freedom. He was yearning to return home and search the world, from one corner to the other, to find his dear sister. He imagined her to be a full-grown woman, if she was still alive and well. The alternative of her being dead was frightening, and he did not want to think about it. He only needed positive thoughts to face the tommorow, which might be the last day of his life. He envisioned himself free, walking north all the way to Vivitsi, finding the home of his parents, settling down for a new beginning, and starting a vigorous search for Georgia. The image of him standing against a wall with twelve rifles aiming directly at his heart made his mind stop dreaming, for there would be no future anymore. Everything would come to an abrupt end when the rifles spat fire and lead. Pondering these possibilities, he heard two of his roommates talking about the future of the civil war.

"I hear that the war is at its end," one of them said to the other, "and if we are lucky, the king will stay in power and extend clemency to all of us who opposed him."

"Yeah, he is a generous man," the second fellow responded. "It sounded to be like a clever idea bringing communism in this country, but I realize now that the Russian system will not work for us. Did you hear what them bastards did with children up north?"

"No," the first man said.

"They sent our children to countries outside of Greece and put them in camps to convert them to communists. Tell me, what kind of freedom and equality is that? That's not what Greece stands for!"

"Don't believe everything you hear. It may be a rumor or propaganda from the other side," the first man responded.

"No, it's true," Fotis interjected. "My sister and I were among the forty eight children from our village who were herded out of Greece like goats going to the stockyard. I cannot talk about the rest of my experience with them for three-and-a-half years. I can only tell you that there are still thousands of abducted Greek boys and girls in countries like Albania, Serbia, Bulgaria, Rumania, and even as far as Czechoslovakia and Poland, who are waiting for someone to bring them back home."

"Tell us, young man, about you and the place of your birth," one of the men asked in the pitch-dark room. "How did you get mixed up in this mess?"

"I took an oath to keep this information private," Fotis responded, and curling up like a dog on the ground, he put the palms of his hands against his ears to avoid hearing additional questions. He did not want to talk about himself and his past life. The three-way conversation among the strangers came to an end. Discomfort-related sounds of sobbing and moaning suppressed the offensive odors of unsanitary conditions in the room. Fotis cried uncontrollably for several minutes, but eventually the outburst of his emotions came to its end. Sometime in the heart of the darkness and before he fell asleep, he had a conference with his other self.

"Boy," his other self said, "remember what you said in your original confession. When you present yourself in front of these Judges tomorrow, don't lose your cool. Give them the same story, word-by-word. Do not contradict yourself with what you said earlier, and don't get intimidated by their authority."

"But there is something that I did not tell them. I skipped telling them that I was the one who shot the bazooka."

"That's okay to distort and stretch the truth, especially when your life is at stake," his other self responded. "Besides, firing the bazooka at the wall was not your choice. You were forced to do it, weren't you?"

"Yes ... but ..." Fotis attempted to reason.

"Nothing of that "yes ... but ..." stuff will help you. If you want to get away from standing in front of the firing squad, do as I tell you: Be consistent with the things you said before!" The advice stayed in Fotis' mind for a while longer. He knew who his other self was. He could trust it. He had fun conversing with it, many times before. Tonight, his other self was argumentative and dictatorial and for a moment Fotis thought that he was hearing the voice of his late father. He was about to ask where his mother was, but the other self vanished from his imagination. Instantly, when he opened his eyes, he saw perfect darkness around him. Not even a breathing sound was detected in the stillness of the night. At that instant, he broke into a continuous wailing that disturbed the dead silence.

"Bad dream?" one of the prisoners next to him asked, but Fotis was not in the mood to respond. After a while he had enough crying. He wiped his eyes dry, rearranged himself in a fetal position on the ground and spent the rest of the night thinking about his pending court appearance.

Most merciful Lord, help me! Fotis retrieved his charm and kissed it several times with reverence. *Save me one more time. Please do not let them take me away from this Earth yet! I want to see my sister one more time before I die.* He kept listening for some answer, but he only heard a muffled moaning coming from the other end of the room. Finally, a guard opened the door and called for him. Fotis did his best to rearrange his clothes, found the plastic bucket in one of the corners of the room, emptied his bladder into it, and joined the guard who stood at the door waiting for him.

The courtroom was larger than the holding room in the basement. There was a large table against the wall opposite the entrance. Three chairs were behind the table, one next to the other, and the portrait of the king hung on the wall behind. Three chairs stood against the opposite wall that was facing the table where the judges were to sit. No storage file cabinets, impressive collections of penal code books, or any visitor's gallery decorated the room. Justice was delivered quickly by military officers without defending lawyers. A person who was brought in front of the court was guilty of committing crimes, innocent of his accusations, or just a misinformed country person without any human blood on his hands. The punishment for the first class was death by a firing squad. The second was complete freedom and the third was retention on a remote island for a few months.

Fotis and two other men were brought into the courtroom at 8:30 a.m. They took their seats facing the empty court bench until a voice declared: "Court rise!" The three prisoners rose to their feet and three military officers of high rank marched in and took their seats behind the large bench. As soon as they felt comfortable in their seats, the elder of them called for the attention of the defendants and spoke in a crisp, firm voice. He told the three defendants that they were in front of the court because they had been accused of being communists with a criminal history. He pointed out that the court would give them plenty of time to defend themselves and to prove that the accusations were false. He concluded his introduction by saying that the court would render an irrevocable verdict and wished good luck to all three of them. He readjusted his plump body in his chair, took several deep breaths, and motioned to one of the guards to approach the bench. He whispered something in his ear, took out of the guard's hand a sheet of paper, and commanded one of the prisoners to approach the bench. One of the men, who was sitting next to Fotis, rose to his feet and one of the guards escorted him in front of the tribunal.

"Dino, you are accused that you participated in the execution of an innocent man from the village close to your village," the presiding officer said, and dropping on the table the sheet of paper he held in his hands, gazed at the face of the terrified Dino and asked him if he killed that man.

"I am innocent," the desperate fellow managed to say. "We only exchanged a few harsh words over the borderline of some of our lands that were one next to the other. No, sir, I did not kill him." The judge picked up the sheet of paper from the desk, rolled it into a tube, and pointing it at Dino, declared. "Two men from your village told me, right here, that you eliminated the other man because he refused to be a member of EAM, the so-called Hellenic Freedom Front. They also tell me that you were the man who pulled the trigger. Were you a member of the EAM?"

"Yes, sir, I was. Everybody was forced to be part of the revolution, but I did not kill anyone." The prisoner launched into a lengthy monologue about the perils of the civil war. "We all thought we were doing the right thing for our country. We strived to be true patriots and to be remembered as dedicated Greeks. If you want to be remembered, don't carve your name in the sand, by the seashore. Do it on the rock by the cliff."

The three judges exchanged glances and whispered messages to one another's ears. Then the one that sat at the center delivered the verdict of the court.

"Dino, you are lying! You haven't proven that you are innocent, therefore the court takes the accusations against you to be the truth of your activity as a communist. You are guilty," and ordered the guard to take him away. Another guard escorted the condemned man out of the courtroom and a third one approached the other two prisoners.

"You are Fotis Liakos. This is your real name, isn't it?" Before he received an answer, the guard placed one of his hands under Fotis' armpit and guided him in front of the three judges.

"Fotis, by your own admission, you joined the rebels recently and you surrendered to the authorities just days ago. Tell the court who are you and how you came to be a fighting communist." He also ordered the guard to remove his handcuffs.

Good start, his other self said to Fotis.

Fotis felt a warm radiance flowing from the judge. That comfortable sensation gave him courage to start telling his life story from the beginning to the moment when he decided to escape and put his life in the hands of the law. The three judges interrupted his narration, several times, and interjected discriminating questions regarding the truthfulness of his story.

You are doing a marvelous job, his other self said to him. *You are winning the case. Stay cool and control your emotions.* Fotis kept plugging along, telling the court how he felt about losing his parents and his sister. He emphasized the pain and the revulsion he felt at seeing a rebel carrying away the head of a man by its hair. The three military men were not moved by hearing the impact his life experiences had on him, but they listened patiently. Fotis' testimony finally came to an end after two hours. He returned to his chair and the judges conferred with one another by simply exchanging looks and facial expressions.

"Fotis," one of them finally said, "The court does not have enough information on you to reach a verdict. No witness came forward to file anything against you, or in your defense, for that matter. You see, you came from Northern Greece, and the authorities were not able to find anyone who claimed that he knows you. We only know that you were an armed communist fighter who, for some unexplained reason, decided to surrender. To keep you away from getting mixed up with fanatic communists again, you are going to be confined in a concentration camp until the state decides what to do with you." One of the judges ordered to remove the prisoner's cuffs and take him to the lock up area. Fotis, in the company of his guard, just walked out of the room with new hopes for his future.

*

Georgia had difficulties living up to her commitment as Alex's wife. Her decision to be the wife of a man whom she barely knew clashed with her dreams for the future. What she wanted was to return to Greece and make her home in the house of her parents, not in a foreign country trying to speak the local language she hardly understood. Besides, Alex's behavior toward her felt like ice under her armpits. He was "cold like a fish" with her. He talked to her only when he had to do so, or when he wanted something from her. He treated her like a servant, not his future wife. When she asked him about his conduct, he responded, "Sweet lady, you have to realize that you are not in Greece. You are in Macedonia, and Macedonians are different from the men you knew. Just remember that!"

His parents, unaware of the chill that dampened the relations between Alex and Georgia, initiated preparations for the big day. The father hired carpenters to remodel the section of the house that the newlyweds were to occupy after the wedding. Alex's mother had women take a roomy bed out of storage and assemble it close to the fireplace in one of the bedrooms. They dusted it clean, dressed it with warm, sweetly scented beddings, and hung new pink blinds over the windows.

Georgia reconsidered her reaction to the conduct of her husband-to-be, but she came up without any definite answers. She debated whether to wed someone who had not fully committed himself to the marriage or to try to escape back to Greece. She was told that the civil war was over and returning to her country was not impossible. Starting over without the help of someone like her parents or brother seemed difficult. There was no person to help her start her life at the old house back home. Alex told her that she was branded a communist and that her road to entering her former society would be long and difficult. On the other extreme, she could go ahead, marry Alex, and address marital problems as they arose. She knew that she had the full support of his parents and their future appeared to be secure. Alex' father had accumulated a vast amount of land, enough to grow crops for more than one family. Additionally, he had a thousand head of sheep grazing in his pasture.

As time progressed, Georgia made the final decision. She concluded that no marriage came down from heaven. *I will marry him and with the help of his parents, he will learn to be a dedicated husband,* she said to herself. In the evening after she decided to marry Alex, she asked her future mother-in-law to go ahead with plans for the big day.

"It's time for me and Alex to be serious about our relations," she confessed to Mr. and Mrs. Bookas. "Your son and I are old enough to settle down and start a family, with your blessing and help, of course," she said, and pointed at Alex seated next to her, at the dinner table. She walked where Mr. and Mrs. Bookas were sitting on their favorite couch, hugged and kissed them with affection and respect, as if she was their blood child. "You are the parents I barely remember," she managed to say and broke down to a continuous, soft sniffling.

Mr. and Mrs. Bookas rose from their couch, wrapped their arms around Georgia, kissed her several times, and assured her that they will be there to help and assist, in any way they could. Alex stood there motionless, looking at the emotional outburst of his parents and his future wife. Finally, he gave in. He mastered the courage to be a part of the happiness his parents and his future wife were experiencing. He walked over, stretched his arms around the heaving trio, delivered kisses to whoever was in front of him, and with an emotion he never experienced before confessed that he loved all three of them.

A week after that eventful evening, Alex Bookas, Jr., and Georgia Liakos became husband and wife according to the rules of their communist community. No marriage certificates were issued by a judge and no priest blessed the union. A verbal commitment of the husband to his bride was enough. As expected, the young Alex became involved in cultivating his father's land and helped him to manage the business of herding and farming. As time went on, he convinced his father to sell some of his sheep and convert some of his grazing fields to farmland. Georgia became the personal assistant to Lady Sofia. She was trusted to supervise a woman whom her mother-in-law had hired to do things around the house. Georgia's relations with her husband improved somewhat and things seemed to fall into place for them. Alex hired new people from a Greek ghetto to shepherd the sheep and to work the land. Alex Sr. sat back and allowed the young man to take care of things.

Georgia, in her daily chats with her neighbors, learned that there was a considerable number of Greeks living in several Greek ghettoes in town. Informers told her that most of them were young men and women who were fortunate to have survived the same sort of camps she had experienced and the inhumane treatment that followed after the camps were broken apart. Others were the remnant of the guerrilla fighting forces, Greek young men and women who had managed to cross from Greece to Slavic Macedonia to escape the menace of the king's victorious army. Whenever Georgia had the opportunity, she visited some of these ghettoes and inquired about her missing brother.

Living conditions in the ghettoes were deplorable. People managed to erect one-room shacks in which five to ten of them dwelled. There were no beds, electric power, or running water. These dwellings only offered protection against rain, snow, and the scorching heat of summer. Most ghetto dwellers were begging on the streets to survive. A few of them were able to secure food by working as servants. They offered their labor and crafts to local farmers around the area just for a dish of leftover food or a hunk of stale bread.

Georgia knew about human suffering, but she wanted to hear their stories, anyway. She liked hearing stories about people and places in Greece. She had not abandoned the idea of returning home someday, ideally escorted by her husband. Primarily, though, she was hoping to hear something about her brother. The flame of hope was still burning inside her, although she was afraid that he was dead. At times she imagined him dead in some battlefield, torn apart by carnivorous birds. That vision of him tore her heart to pieces. At other times, she envisioned him going from camp to camp, hoping to find her and take her home. The thought that he forgot her and returned home with some other woman crossed her mind frequently, but she knew him better. She was his only sister. *Most likely, he is ill or injured in some hospital and when he gets well, he will search the world over, until he finds me,* she concluded, creating a positive picture for the tomorrow.

She felt a different love for her brother than for her husband. Her husband was a dispensable man in her life, but not her brother. She could have another husband, but not another brother. He was the only brother she would ever have. The same blood flowed in their veins.

A year went by and Georgia was struggling with her relations with her husband. Something was also telling her that her brother was still alive. Lady Sofia and Alex, Sr., began to enjoy a semi-retirement while hoping that Georgia would surprise them with their first grandchild. On several occasions, Lady Sofia hinted that it was time for Georgia to be a mother.

On Sofia's birthday, Georgia went out of her way to prepare a luscious dinner for all four of them. After dinner and the customary "Happy Birthday" singing, Alex Sr., having had several glasses of homemade wine, became euphoric and expressed his yearning to become a grandfather.

"Kids, I am tired waiting to having your baby wetting my lap," he said, and burst into his customary roaring laugh.

Alex, Jr., and Georgia blushed and the younger Alex responded.

"Dad, good things take time. Georgia and I are still young! What's the rush?" and with a broad smile on his face, he changed the subject. He filled his glass with homemade wine and cheerfully declared.

"Happy birthday, Mom!" and to escape the talking about a baby, he asked his mother, "May I ask you, Mom, how old are you today?"

Lady Sofia was not prepared to answer her son's question. She took a sip from her wine glass, swallowed twice, but no answer came out of her mouth. Her husband came to her aid.

"Thirty-nine and counting," he boomed and spread humor and laughter on the face of everyone around the table.

The evening ended in cheers, hugs, kisses, and good wishes. After the kitchen was in order, everyone went to bed. Georgia and her husband, tucked away under their warm covers, kissed each other good night, turned the lights off, uttered their short invocation, and got ready to surrender to the ferries of the night.

"Alex. Are you sleeping?" she asked her husband, after a while. "The things that your father said about us having a baby keep me up."

"The whole thing bothers me too, Georgia. These things are not under our control, you know." A deep sigh echoed into the darkness. After a few seconds, she felt his arms reaching around her body and heard his voice coming softly to her ears.

"Let's go to sleep and leave these kinds of things to God."

*

Fotis, after he was sentenced by the court to serve time in a concentration camp, was escorted to a holding area under the watchful eyes of armed guards. There were two other men in the holding pen. One was an older man in his sixties and the other was a younger man in his early thirties. Fotis was shoved into the enclosure by a guard, like a stray dog, and heard the door slamming behind him. He took a quick look around him and chose to occupy an empty corner, just opposite from where the other two men were sitting cross-legged on the floor. They were quiet when Fotis entered. The only lighting in the place was the indirect sunlight coming in through a small window up toward the ceiling.

"Hello, guys!" he said. "My name is Fotis, Fotis Liakos, from Vivitsi, Macedonia." The younger man ignored his introduction but the other man responded that he had never heard the name Vivitsi. "I know northern Greece like the palm of my hand. I fought the Turks and the Bulgarians for ten years there. I never heard the name of your place. Where, exactly, is Vivitsi?"

Fotis explained that Vivitsi was located close to Albania on the border of Greece with Yugoslavia and went on to tell him that his father was a teacher, born in the Peloponnese.

"Aha," the younger man interjected. "There are several Liakos families in Telos, a village close to mine. Your last name is not common in the area I'm coming from, but rare as it may be, you might be related to the Liakos families I know."

"Both my mother and my father were executed by Slav guerrillas and the only sister I had is missing," Fotis said. The tone of his voice indicated that he was not interested in pursuing his father's origin, for he didn't know the name of the village where his father was born. The older man was chatting more than the other guy and continued the conversation. He told Fotis that he was much too young to be a bona fide, dedicated communist.

"I was taken away from home, trained to believe in communism, and forced to join a fighting force of guerrillas," Fotis responded.

"Yeah," the young man responded from his corner. "In order to save your ass, you claim that you were forced to take arms against the nationals. Don't tell me that you did not have an opportunity to get away, earlier! All of us claim the same thing. 'It's not my fault; the devil made me do it,'" he roared sarcastically.

Fotis and the older man fell silent when they heard the younger fellow fixing responsibility for crimes committed during the civil war. They did not know if he was a mole, poking around among detainees to find hardcore communists among them. Each one of them became mute and crawled into their corners until there wasn't any light coming through the window. The room became dark and only their shuffling noise on the floor was discernible. The silence was suddenly broken. Someone opened the door, and the silhouette of a man entering the room with a flashlight in his hands became apparent.

"Fotis Liakos, where are you? Get up and come with me," he commanded and pointed his beam of light around the confined area to find him. Fotis unfolded himself off the floor, stood erect, and obeyed the order. At the door, he met another burly man, also in civilian clothes. Fotis tried to ask where they were going, but one of them punched him in his belly and growled.

"Walk with us and keep your mouth shut." They descended several steps down to a musty basement and stopped in front of a closed door.

"Where are we going? Where are you taking me?" Fotis asked, fearing for his life.

"There are still-unanswered questions about your role as a guerrilla fighter," one of the escorting men responded, opening the door in front of them. The other guy shoved Fotis inside and turned on the light. He slammed the door and threw Fotis on a metal chair next to a metal table that was anchored on the concrete floor. One of them positioned himself behind Fotis and the other sat on a chair on the other side of the table.

"Tell us the real story, punk! Vomit out the whole truth of your life from the beginning," the sitting man barked and banged a club on the table, barely missing Fotis' trembling fingers.

"I did nothing wrong! I was forced to join them ..." He attempted to defend himself, but he felt the fist of the standing guy land, like a sledgehammer, on his neck. Fotis saw stars floating in front of him and it took him a few seconds to regain his vision.

"That's not what he asked you, little bastard," he heard the man behind him saying. "You are here to tell us the truth, willingly. Otherwise, we will extract it from you, our way. Start from the time you remember yourself until the time you came to us, I believe it was two to three days ago," he screamed at the frightened face in front of him. Then, he swung his huge palm against the face of the boy, striking him on both cheeks mercilessly, several times, while swearing.

"Are you ready to talk, little ass?" the man in front of him barked. "Or I'll have my man continue ..." Fotis felt an uncontrollable discharge of urine wetting his pants and asked permission to use the bathroom.

"Okay, go," the seated man said and motioned the other fellow to escort their prisoner behind a temporary barricade that kept occupants out of view. The floor was wet and a filthy, a plastic bucket stood there, filled halfway up with human excrement. Fotis positioned himself over the bucket, relieved himself, and returned to the interrogation table. He sat on the wet chair and began to tell his life story starting at the age of four.

"Skip that part," one of the interrogators ordered. "Start at the point when you were taken away from home. We are not interested to know all about the marble games you and your friends played before grammar-school days." Fotis began telling his odyssey, starting at the time he and his sister arrived at the grounds of the church at Vivitsi. He was occasionally interrupted to answer pointed questions, especially about the terrain they traversed and the people who traveled with him. Next, he spent two hours describing the settings and the conditions of living in the camps. Finally, he began to narrate the daily sessions the children attended. His interrogators interrupted him several times with detailed questions regarding the material taught during those sessions and facial descriptions of their teachers. It was almost midnight when his interrogators took a brief break to drink a cup of water and confer about the progress of their interrogation. Fotis was not allowed to get off his chair or have any water. He sat in his place until the interrogators returned. Seconds later, the questioning began with a new vigor.

"Okay, kid. Put yourself together and get ready to tell us all about your training to join the fighting forces of the guerrillas." The leading investigator stated and clenched his teeth. "It's important for us to know as much as possible of this part of your life. Go."

Fotis went through specific details, including the number of bullets he used in each practice, the kind of firearms he used, and some of the scores he made on targets with the rifle. He said nothing about his experience with bazooka. He had a tough time convincing his interrogators that he did not know either the names of the places he went through or the names of the men who brought him to the shore of the Peloponnese.

It was three o'clock in the morning when the interrogation came to its last stage. Fotis, worn out from the cruel treatment he had received all night, began to describe the capitulation of the barricade where all the ex-policemen were brutally annihilated. At the point when he started to describe the actual massacre, one of the men interrupted him and insisted on knowing where he was and what he was doing at that instant.

"I was about fifty yards away from the wall, guarding things that were covered under a tarpaulin. When the shooting began, I buried my head behind a pile of rocks, and I couldn't help hearing the firing and the screaming ahead of me. It was the first time I was experiencing war and I was scared for my life," he mumbled in tears.

"Were you behind a rock or were you leading the charge with your dagger in your hands?" the man behind him said, and grabbing the boy's head by the hair, he pounded his face on the metal table in front of him until the other man intervened. Blood burst out of Fotis' mouth and nose. When he lifted his head off the table, scarlet fluid poured down his chest and bathed his charm that was still hanging around his neck.

"Son of a bitch, you lied to us all night!" the standing interrogator barked and released the boy's head.

"That's enough," the seated investigator told his partner. "The kid knows nothing more than what he already told us. Let him go." He handed Fotis a piece of a bedsheet he retrieved from one of the desk drawers in front of him. "There is water by the sink. Use the washcloth I gave you and clean the blood off your face. When you are done with that, clean the table and the piss off your chair. We are done with you for now."

Fotis lifted himself off his chair and, with the rag pressed against his face, walked to the sink. He turned the water on, soaked the rag with running, fresh water and gently, wiped the coagulated blood away from his face. He rinsed the rag several times, then repeated the cleaning process, again and again, until there was no more blood coming out of his lacerations and his nose. Finally, he rinsed the rag several times again and returning to the interrogation table. He wiped clean his chair and the table in front of him. As soon as he felt that he had adequately cleaned his bloody mess, he wiped a trickle of blood that persisted to roll down his upper lip from his nose and stood in front of his two torturers for further directions.

"Okay, you Slav weasel," one of the brutes said to him. "Follow us."

Fotis walked between the interrogators like a tamed tiger until they came to the holding area. The first man opened the door and the other threw him inside the room, just like a bag of horse fodder. They slammed the door shut, locked it, and went away, not to be seen again.

It was early in the morning and a ray of sunlight, coming in from the window high above the opposite wall, brightened the room and made things visible. Fotis rolled on the floor twice and his head rested, face up, at the spot where the sunbeam of light was landing.

"You either kissed a woman that belongs to bigger guy, or you walked too close behind a mule," a roaring voice came from the other corner of the room.

Fotis ignored the sarcasm. He was happy to be alive and still in one piece. Nothing was broken. His nose felt like a pickle and deep lacerations on the inside of his lips made his voice unnaturally, blurred. He was physically hurt and his ego and self-esteem was shattered in a thousand pieces, but his lips, his eyes, and his teeth were still in place. He was humiliated beyond description, and he was mad with everything and everyone around him, including his own person. He hated himself for going along with the guerrillas to blow up the wall, resulting in the death of all those men. He hated himself for not running away at the time he was left alone in the cave by the seashore, or when he had the opportunity to escape when the airplanes bombarded them. He hated the moment he was born. Hate dripped off from every inch of his sore flesh. Hate was all over, inside and outside of him. He wanted to vent his anger away, but he couldn't make up his mind to either scream at the top of his voice or lie down and cry his guts out. *Hold it Fotis,* his other self said. *Who told you that human beings are like angels? You are a mortal; therefore, you are not a perfect angel. You are expected to make mistakes. Endure, buddy! Things will change. The worst is over.*

"Let me see what they did to you," the elder roommate said, bending over Fotis, who was curled on the floor nursing his wounds and his anger.

"You should have seen my face two weeks earlier. The whole thing looked like fresh liver, bloody and black. In a week, your face will look shiny and smooth, just like the monkey's ass," he encouraged and broke out in a prolonged laughter. Fotis found the other man's humor hilarious and a faint smile stretched his lips, but the smile froze instantly, halfway to blossoming. The smile stretched his wounded lips and caused new blood to trickle through one of his lacerations.

The next morning, the sun and his roommates saw a different face on Fotis. His cheeks and his eyes were swollen to the point that his eyes were closed shut. His nostrils were half their original size, and his nose was big, big like the snout of a tracking hound. Eventually, though, the swelling disappeared and the black bruises went away, as the old man predicted a week earlier.

Two weeks went by, and nothing significant happened. Fotis kept stewing in his anger against himself, but he became accustomed to the last week's event and was able to sleep. His previous roommates were taken away and five other ex-guerrilla fighters took their places.

It was fall, 1948, and the war was officially over. Captured freedom fighters overcrowded the prisons and the court system. It took time for a police force to be organized and establish itself in strategic locations throughout the land. In the interim, residents loyal to the king were armed and deputized as police in their own villages. Guerrilla fighters who survived the clashes with the regular army had no place to hide. They surrendered to the temporary authorities and were brought in front of judges and magistrates.

Fotis was not forgotten in his short-term imprisonment. An official appeared at the door of the holding room late one morning and summoned Fotis to come forward. The young man, accustomed to obeying authority, walked in front of the official and identified himself as Fotis Liakos.

"Come with me, young man," the official ordered. He informed Fotis that he did not belong in this rat-hole and that he was going on "vacation" to one of the Greek islands, close to Turkey. While they walked away from the lockup, the official told Fotis that he would be on the island for a while, and if no new charges were filed against him he would be a free man in no time.

"The gracious king is expected to pardon those who were forced or duped to take arms against his royal highness."

He further added that the courts had found him to be one of the innocent victims of the war. Fotis was delighted that he had made the move to get away from the fighting guerrillas, but he was disappointed that he was not a free man yet. He was still yearning to resume normal life and find out what had happened to his sister. *Is she still living, or did she perish in the hands of some exploiting brute? I must know where she is.* His mind kept fabricating scenarios. At times he saw her remains decaying in a shallow grave close to the concentration camp, and his heart ached. At other times, he envisioned her as a servant, even a mistress, to some foreign person, just to stay alive, and that thought humiliated the high-spirited young man. Still, at other times, he saw her forced into a marriage that she did not want, and that possibility enraged him. The positive thought that she was happily married with children and with a devoted and loving husband put his mind at ease. In that frame of mind, he boarded the ferryboat that brought him to the island of his temporary banishment, far away from the village of his birth.

Young and old, men and women, all found by the courts disloyal to the king, were aboard a ferry going to some unknown destination. They were either ex-guerrilla fighters or sympathizers to them. Fear and terror were painted all over their faces, for their destination and their future were uncertain. Rumors circulated aboard that their ferry might be wired to blow up in the middle of the Aegean Sea. Other speculations were that they would perish from starvation at the place of their temporary banishment. How many of them, if any, would ever return home to their loved ones, and if they returned, would they be accepted with the friendship they knew before the war? In the eyes of the winners of the war, these people were the villains and were to pay the price for their uprising against the king.

The ferryboat with its four hundred passengers, packed like sardines, steamed along for two days, bouncing back and forth in the choppy waters of the Aegean Sea. Several policemen, in civilian clothes, were among the detainees to monitor their general conduct and to enforce obedience to the rules of public safety. Fotis became acquainted with one of them, and during the two days aboard the ship, he had the opportunity to tell him all about his experience in the camps of Paithomazoma. The officer was born on the island of Crete and because of the distance between Crete and Northern Greece, he admitted that he never heard anything about Paithomazoma. In awe, he expressed his disbelief that innocent children were indiscriminately taken away from their families and sent behind the Iron Curtain.

"Some people say that we were taken away to be protected from the perils of the fighting. Others suspect that we were there to learn the principles of communism. Who knows the truth?" Fotis said sadly. "I only know that I am in a real mess today. My parents were gunned down like mischievous pups, and my sister, the only sibling I had, is missing. How much harder can my life be?" He felt his eyes getting wet. The compassionate officer embraced Fotis and in a parental tone of voice told him that it could have been worse.

"You could have been one of those officers in the unfinished water cistern. Did you hear what happened there? An entire platoon of ex-policemen was beheaded with daggers. They did not die like heroes in a battlefield. Your friends butchered them with a knife," he intoned and spat on the floor to express his anger and repugnancy for the ghoulish event.

"Yeah, I heard something like that," Fotis remarked. "Civil war is a terrible thing. Only the dead see the end of it. Those who survive continue to live with its outcome and its consequences."

As soon as the ferryboat dropped its anchors at the harbor of its destination, catwalks were extended from the dock to the ship and everyone aboard exited the vessel. Once on solid ground, they were led inside a fenced area where officials took attendance and recorded their age, sex, and place of birth. At the end, one of the officials climbed the podium and briefly spoke to the crowd. He told them that until further notice, they would live under tents, and they would have three free meals a day.

"Occasionally, you will be expected to volunteer your labor to plant pine seedlings at certain slopes of the island. Your chaperones will direct you to your tents now, and they will show you your beds. Starting tomorrow morning, officers will discuss with all of you the rules of living here. We expect your full cooperation to make living conditions as tolerable as possible. Do as you are told, not as you want to, and you will be okay for the duration of your detention here."

A year went by, and most of the detainees returned home. Fotis, age twenty, was to stay a little longer, until the authorities were able to investigate his criminal past. In the interim, he became accustomed to a lazy life of doing nothing, under the blue sky on the serene island. During the day, he walked the sun-bleached shores and collected small pieces of driftwood of unusual shapes. Those pieces of driftwood that resembled a bird or animal, he carved into a statuette. At night, he and his new friend went fishing for octopus in the moonlight with their homemade spears. His new friend, a young female detainee, became his inseparable friend and continued to be his close companion for the duration of the time she was there. Their relations were purely platonic, for any other relation was strictly prohibited by the authorities. Unfortunately for Fotis, she was released two months after they became close friends. She had an old guitar with her and Fotis had fun singing local serenades while she played it. At times, other people gathered around bonfires by the seashore to hear her stroking her guitar and him singing tunes of his birthplace.

"Here is my guitar," she said to him, before she boarded the ferry back home. "It is to serve as a reminder that, somewhere in this vast world, there is a person who thinks of a lonesome man. You can find my address scribbled under its keyboard. I would like to see you again." Handing him the guitar, she placed an affectionate kiss directly over one of the facial scars he received during the interrogation.

For the rest of his stay on the island, Fotis discovered that he was talented as a guitar player and as a singer. When his mood or his moral condition was down in the "bottom of the outhouse," people saw him with his guitar, sitting on one of the highest cliffs by the foaming sea, singing songs that came from the depths of his being. These songs were not sentimental songs that people had heard before. They were poetic stanzas that sounded more like the wailing of an unhappy and hopeless person. They were not songs glorifying love or friendship between people. They were cries of a young man with a deep-seated emotional problem. He was unhappy at being alone in the world and guilty for contributing to the gory execution of Greeks by other Greeks. At times, sitting at the top of this cliff lamenting his dismal future, he felt like putting an end to everything by diving head-first at the hostile rock that was protruding above water several hundred feet below him. His other-self advised him against the idea of jumping to his death. *Your sister might be still alive and may be yearning for her brother! You cannot be a coward and ignore her.* The advice from his other-self came through loud and clear. The lonesome monk at the monastery of profit Elias heard Fotis' wailing and singing. He felt that only the profit can help him. He fired the incent burner, kneeled in front of the profit's icon, and read prayers for his sinner brother Fotis.

Fotis lived in that state of indecisiveness until his name was posted on the blackboard by the dining area. Among six other names, the name Fotis Liakos was listed to be released from custody as soon as the next ferry arrived from the mainland. He summoned his closest friends and handed them his driftwood creations. He only kept one of them that, he said, reminded him of his lost sister. A few days later, the ferry showed up and Fotis, armed with all the necessary documents for his release, boarded the vessel and sailed back to the mainland. Three days later, he arrived at the seaport of Piraeus holding his old guitar in his hands with a huge hope in his heart for a fresh start in life. He still wore the uniform the guerrillas gave him on the day he joined them in the mountains of the Peloponnese. While on board the ferry, he made plans to make enough money so that he could be independent from other people's donations. Granted, he did not have any profession, but he had a guitar, a good voice, and a natural ability to compose lyrics and sing them. Besides, he was healthy and was willing to do anything to improve his life.

During his first week in town, Fotis slept on vacant properties, in abandoned stores, or by the seashore. In the morning, he visited local churches and was content receiving a piece of bread and whatever nourishing food the priest had to give away. Occasionally, he tried out his musical talent on the streets and was encouraged by the attention his singing drew from passers-by. Finally, he made the big decision. He walked over to a tavern and asked to see the leader of the musical group that performed there at night. He did not know what he was expecting to hear from the man, but he mustered the courage to approach him and introduce himself, anyway. He shook hands with the other man and called upon his audacity to tell the other man that he was a talented musical entertainer.

"Let me hear something from your mouth and from this antique guitar you hung on your shoulder," the other man responded. Fotis took his guitar off his shoulder, tuned it gently, plucking its strings, and began to sing a popular song.

"Hmm … not bad! Not bad at all," the musician remarked. "I'll tell you what, young man, your name is Fotis, isn't it? Come over tonight at nine o'clock and I'll introduce you to my group. My leading vocalist came down with laryngitis last week and I need someone to take his place for a while. Are you available tonight? You might have a future with us."

"I have all the time in the world," Fotis responded exuberantly. "Count on me. I'll be here at nine, sharp." *I told you,* the other self whispered in Fotis' conscience. *That's the break we need.* Fotis said adios to the other man, retreated to an isolated spot far away from public interference, tuned his guitar, and practiced playing several of his favorite tunes until it was time to join the music group at the tavern.

"I discovered the new Enrico Caruso," the band director said to his group and introduced Fotis to them. "He bangs that 'old thing' with gusto and has a promising voice. Wait until you hear him playing and singing!"

Fotis was just twenty years old and here was his chance, the first opportunity he had, to prove that his life was not a dead-end street. He played his guitar and sang with the group from nine to eleven o'clock that evening and pocketed good money for a beginner. His confidence of becoming a full-time member of the band soared like an eagle. The crowd applauded him all night long and the rest of the musicians patted him on the back for making the evening pleasant and exciting. After he finished entertaining the crowd at the taverna, he walked directly to a nearby motel, booked a room for the night, and had a belly-bursting dinner at a local restaurant. It was the first time he had had money in his pocket and a comfortable bed to sleep in. As far back as he could remember, he never had enough food to fill his stomach. He returned to the tavern every night after his first appearance, and from this point on, he entertained people with his old guitar and his passion for singing. After a while, he saved enough money to buy a new guitar, a new pair of shoes, and modern clothes. From this point on in his life, he was not just Fotis the orphan without a place to go. He was Mr. Fotis Liakos with a reputation as a musician and with a fat wallet in his pocket. Now, he moved upward in his social circle. He rented a room in a three-star hotel and mingled with people from the higher levels of society. Young ladies buzzed around him like bees around a bowl of honey and, no doubt, he enjoyed the attention he was receiving. Yet, his mind was fixed on his sister's whereabouts. He was dying to venture back to their last camp and track her down like a bloodhound.

A year after he started playing music, Fotis took two days off his job and boarded a train to the nearest town to Vivitsi. He hopped on a local bus and went to the village of his birth. His parent's house was deserted. The old lady's house with the nanny goat was occupied by another senior citizen that he didn't recognized.

The ground where his parents were interred was overgrown with vegetation and bushes. Using a fictitious name, he borrowed a pick and a hoe from the church, went to the burial grounds of his parents, cleared the area of weeds, and re-erected the cross back to its original position. Before leaving, he visited the local flower shop, purchased two bouquets of white roses, returned to the place where his parents were sleeping, and deposited them next to the standing cross. The people he briefly spoke with had no idea what happened to the children who were taken away from the village six years earlier. One of them told him that the International Red Cross was working on it, and another shook his head to express his disdain.

"Who knows ... Anyway, who are you, young man, and why do you want to know about Paithomazoma?"

"Oh, I am passing by. I read about the incident in a newspaper, and just became curious to know something about it. That's all," Fotis said, and kept walking. At the bus station, he had a cup of coffee sitting next to an elderly local man, who knew more about Paithomazoma. When Fotis asked him about it, he was willing to talk about the event and to offer his opinion.

"Friend, I have not been a communist nor do I defend the other side. I am ashamed calling myself a Greek, for we killed each other to serve the interests of Churchill and Stalin. Let's not talk about that subject. It makes my blood boil," he said and took a long drag on a cigarette, he held in one of his hands. Seconds later, he exhaled a small cloud from both his mouth and his nostrils and took a noisy sip from his coffee cup. "All wars are bad and costly, but a civil war is the worst kind. You don't know who your enemy is. It may be your own brother. About Paithomazoma, I bet that many of our children are still alive and well. Most likely, they have adopted the local life and care less if they see their birthplaces, again. They only have bad memories of their villages."

He broke into a deep, raspy cough. "Sleeping in the snow on the Albanian mountains during World War II will do this to you." After pounding his chest with his fist several times, he took another sip from his coffee cup. Fotis started to tell him that he was a musician in Piraeus, but his bus arrived at the station and interrupted his narration. He got off his chair, told the other man goodbye, boarded the bus, and headed back to Piraeus. The other man removed the cloth hat he wore on his bald head and waved it at the bus until it disappeared in the far distance. Fotis was deeply moved, experiencing candid talk from a rural person. He only knew how to obey commands from superiors in concentration camps and how to react to vulgar expressions coming from supervisors and jail guards. It was hard for him to get accustomed to kindness and heart-to-heart chatting with local folks.

He sat next to a man his own age for the four-hour ride to Piraeus. The other guy was a soldier on a short leave of absence from his base. He was traveling to Athens to spend time with members of his family. His parents had moved to Athens from a remote village just when the civil war erupted. He told Fotis that his parents couldn't put up with the constant harassment from paramilitary groups in the area.

"We were labeled as communists for some reason my dad never understood. The entire family was 'red' to them," he told Fotis and bragged that his father was successful in their new environment.

"My father works as a controller for a truck company and my mother is a full-time housewife. All three of my sisters are honor students at their school! Not bad for a guy who was forced to abandon home and start from scratch elsewhere, is it?"

"The story of my family is quite different from yours," Fotis responded. "Rebels took my parents from our house and shot them dead, leaving their twin children to the care of a widow neighbor. The same rebels rounded up all the children from the village, including me and my sister, and sent them out of the country. Have you heard anything about Paithomazoma? And that's not the end of my saga. They forced me to join a guerrilla group in the Peloponnese and take orders from people like those who killed my parents. My sister is still missing," he added angrily.

"Yes, I heard a lot about Paithomazoma," the other man responded. "The issue is quite controversial in nature. I don't know the motives behind the abduction. What shall I say! I'm sorry to hear that you lost your parents during the conflict, but war is war and people perish in the process. What we need now is to forget the past and try to build the future, for the future is what counts for all of us who survived the ordeal of the 1940s. Let's clean the slate of the past and plant the seeds of love in the hearts of all Greeks. I sincerely hope that your sister will show up, someday."

"It's easy for you to say all that priest-stuff. Still though, my parents are prematurely and unjustly dead and no one knows the fate of my sister," Fotis responded furiously.

"What do you think you will accomplish carrying hate in your heart? Do you think that hate will bring back your mama and papa? Will hate speed up the return of your sister?" The other man let Fotis register the wisdom of his statements.

Fotis buried his head between the palms of his hands, sniffed his sorrow for a few seconds, and attempted to make a statement of his own. He took his hands away from his face and opened his mouth to respond, but no words came out. He only motioned with his hands that he had no answer to the things he heard from the other traveler. He shook his head sidewise, several times, and changed the subject of their conversation to soccer events between nationally competing teams.

The rest of their chat was not emotional as before. It became friendly and affable between them. Finally, his new friend shook hands with him and got off the bus in Athens. Fotis continued his trip to Piraeus. The next day, he resumed his appearances in the taverna as the leading guitar player and a new vocalist of the musical group.

On the surface, things looked promising for the young man. He was making good money and was surrounded by good friends. Deep inside, he was not happy, though. During his private hours, he was able to convince himself that being indirectly responsible for the death of the ex-policemen was excusable. *There was a war going on and, as a soldier, I had to obey orders,* he reasoned with his other self. The memory of his sister was eating him up, though. *Georgia might be alive somewhere, and she may be in dire need for help,* he kept thinking. During a lengthy intercourse with his other self, he was convinced that he should keep his work for a while, save his money, and launch an all-out search for his missing sister.

*

Georgia's marriage was not a happy union between a man and a woman. Mr. and Mrs. Bookas were not happy, not with her as a person, but as the wife of their only son. For more than a year now, she was not a mother yet. It seemed to her that her husband was fixing blame on her, and his parents expressed their disappointment of not being grandparents.

"Dear Georgia," Lady Sofia told her during a private conversation when the men were not around. "I love you as a person and as the wife of my dear Alex, but that's not enough to keep the family together. Soon, very soon, the two of you should have a baby to continue the family tradition."

It was not the first time that Georgia had heard derogatory comments from Sofia and from Alex Sr., who had voiced similar concerns in recent days. Georgia was overwhelmed with the indirect accusation that she was to be blamed for her infertility. Her anger took over her politeness and good manners and she replied to her mother-in-law in an unbecoming tone of voice.

"Mom, only God will decide when, if ever, you will be a grandmother. My heart shatters into a thousand pieces every time one of you fixes the responsibility on me. It takes two to make a baby, you know! Have you ever thought that Alex is to blame?" She fixed her angry glare directly at her mother-in-law. Sofia became angry and responded with a burning comment of her own.

"If that's your opinion about my son, do something about it," she retorted and walked away, steaming with anger. Georgia had enough of that talk and made up her mind to put an end to these accusations.

To hell with this talk. If God ordered for me not to have a child, who is going to change it? It's not my doing. Blame God for it, not me. She tried to forget the argument. When she brought up the subject to her husband, when they were alone in their bedroom, he ignored her concerns and avoided discussing the rift between her and his mother. He reacted as if he did not give a damn about the impact his mother's concern had on his wife. His apathy made Georgia assume that their marriage was coming to its abrupt end. She began to think of walking away from the Bookas family and forgetting that she was the wife of a warrior. She knew that unless her abdomen began to expand soon, the rest of her life would not be harmonious. Yet, she did not know what to do next. She only knew that she could not live with Alex and his parents under these conditions. She had to leave the Bookas' house to avoid the unbearable friction from her in-laws and the apathy of her husband. Should she return to hobo living or try to find her way back to Vivitsi? Returning to her birthplace was more attractive than walking to one of the Greek ghettoes and starting her life from the beginning. But if she tried to go home, she had to cross the borders, be detained as a communist agent, endlessly interrogated by police, and if she was lucky to reach Vivitsi, would her house be there for her? Would she be branded as a communist for the rest of her life, thus being unable to secure decent employment? Staying in one of the ghettoes, she only had to worry about finding a job and, eventually, a man of her kind, a Greek who spoke her language and laughed at the same jokes with her. In the final analysis, she decided to stay with Alex if possible. If living with the Bookas family became untenable, she could walk over to the ghetto. Thinking over her alternatives, a new solution to her problem hit her like a thunderbolt. The picture of the old lady who shared her house before she attempted to cross the mountain over to Greece came to her mind. *What the hell is wrong with you, Georgia?* her other self asked. *Anna said that you are welcome in her house, if you don't have another place to go! Going back to Aunty Anna will give you time to think through your alternatives.* At that instant, Georgia made her big decision. Later that night, she confronted her husband.

"Alex, I will make things easier for you. You and I know that we will not be happy as husband and wife. There are cultural differences between you and me that make your life and mine intolerable. Worst of all is the problem we face having no children.

I don't know about you, but I cannot live that way." She moaned softly and threw herself in a chair. Her cry fell on deaf ears in the house of Bookas, and no one noticed her tears rolling down her face. Alex stood frozen in space, as if he did not care about his marital crisis. When he recovered from his initial shock upon hearing that his wife was about to run away, he attempted to mend things back together to save his marriage. He reached over to Georgia, grabbed her by her arms and attempted to pull her close to him, but his move was useless.

"Please don't try to do the impossible. You must choose either the will of your parents, or my love for you. You cannot have both. Think about it!"

"Georgia, you forget that I saved your life and brought you to my father's home," Alex said in frustration. "Is this what I get, for all the things I did for you in the past?"

"Alex, the past belongs in the past. You saved my life and I gave you myself in return. I became your devoted wife. I cannot help it if we have no children, nor can I change the attitude of your parents toward me. This marriage must come to its end before something tragic and catastrophic takes place. For our sake and the happiness of your parents, we must put an end to it." She pushed Alex away from her face. Alex, facing stern rejection from Georgia, said nothing more. He stood there, looking at her as if he were looking at a woman he had never seen before.

"Alex, come tomorrow morning, your house will be without me. I'm leaving tonight. Tell your parents adios from me, will you? I don't have the stomach to face them!"

"Where are you going?"

"I don't know … I'll take a road, and I'll walk to its end." Georgia walked out of the Bookas' residence without expressing any other remorse. She was mad with the world and deeply hurt and disappointed about the treatment she had received as a wife and a daughter-in-law.

It was still early evening and the sky was free of any threatening clouds. She took the five-mile dirt road toward Anna's house and kept walking, alone in complete darkness. The light reflecting on the surface of the half-moon in the east and the light coming from the evening star to the west was just enough to guide her steps forward, toward the unknown tomorrow. Sometime during the night, her feet refused to obey her will. She found a flat boulder by a creek and sat on it to rest her fatigued body and quench her thirst with fresh, running water.

It was summertime and the vegetation was fully mature, ready to turn to hay. The trees along her way were green. All kinds of nocturnal creatures rattled away in the underbrush. They were spooked by the noise the night traveler was making in her advance toward Anna's house. Georgia sat on the boulder by the running water, took off her shoes, drank some of the gurgling, clean water, splashed some of it on her face, closed her eyes, and tried to reorganize her confused mind. Minutes later, she was in a deep sleep.

A barking dog forced her to open her eyes and she realized that the sun was up. She turned around to look at the barking dog and saw a powerful man with a shotgun strapped over his shoulders, holding the leash of an oversized sheep dog. The man was staring at her as if he had never seen a woman before in his life. Georgia became alarmed at the presence of the strange man with the growling dog and attempted to run away, but he blocked her way and in a gentle manner told her that he meant no harm to her. "I'm after a wolf that killed one of my sheep," he added, and withdrew himself and his dog away from the frightened girl.

"Who are you, and what are you doing in my feeding pastures," he asked with eyes wide open. "I thought for a moment that you were dead."

"I'm on my way to town and I stopped here to rest and have a sip of water," she responded. "Please, let me go! People are waiting for me." Walking around the big shepherd, she started to run. She was frightened to remain standing in front of a big countryman, restraining a mean dog by its leash in one hand and with a big gun in the other.

"I mean no harm to you, young girl! Stop and let me help you with whatever problem you have. Don't run away! I'll share my sandwich with you!" Georgia slowed her run to a brisk walk and turned her face toward the shepherd.

"Thank you for your offer, good man, but I need to get to town, as soon as possible."

The shepherd was almost certain that the girl was mentally disturbed and said nothing more. He only stood there, holding the leash of his dog in one hand and his shotgun in the other, until Georgia disappeared from his sight, over the hill ahead of her. An hour later, Georgia reached the town where Anna was living and asked her memory to guide her steps toward Aunty Anna's home. As soon as she approached the old house, a chain of chilly thoughts paraded through her mind. "Is she still alive, and if she is, will she open the door for me?" she asked herself. Amid these frightening thoughts, she mustered the courage to lift the door knocker and announced her presence. The screeching voice of the toothless, one-eyed old woman echoed in the distance.

"Go away ... this place is contaminated with a deadly form of leprosy. For your own safety, do not enter. Go away ..." she repeated from somewhere in the house. Georgia understood the bogus nature of Anna's warning and responded with a distinct vitality in her voice.

"Aunty Anna ...This is Georgia! Do you remember me, dear?" Several seconds passed in dead silence. Then the front door cracked open and, ever so slowly, the face Georgia knew well appeared though the partial opening.

"My dear Georgia! You are back. Please come in," Anna said softly. "I was worrying about you, since you left, more than a year ago! Come in and tell me what's going on in your life, girl." She reached over to where Georgia was standing, took her hand, and guided her toward her favorite room with the worn-out recliner. Georgia followed the old lady like an obedient dog on a leash and sat on a chair that Anna pointed at with her bony hand. She took several deep breaths, put the events of her recent life in chronological order and mustered enough composure to narrate her life events from the time she left Anna's house to this morning. She was as honest as she could be, including her brush with death and the saga of her marriage with Alex Bookas. Anna sat motionless in her chair and listened to Georgia's story. At the end, Georgia wiped her tears off her face, fixed her gaze on Anna's face, and took a prolonged, deep breath to subdue the sobbing that bubbled up.

"What are you planning to do now?" Anna asked with a serious expression on her face.

"I'm not sure, yet. Can I stay here for a few days, until I figure out which direction I'm heading next?"

"Dear Georgia, I had similar experiences in my life. In some cases, they were worse than yours. I understand what you are going through. Don't you worry about having a roof over your head, dear. You are welcome to stay with me for as long as you wish. I confess that I missed your company for the time you were gone. I liked having another woman with me to keep me company, and you are the best companion I could ever wish to have. I feel secure with you around here – believe me, I do." Georgia was elated to hear that she was welcome in Anna's house. With fresh tears in her eyes she walked over to where the old lady sat and embraced her with a subdued "thank you, thank you."

Georgia was mentally and physically exhausted. Every drop of energy had drained out of her body. She felt guilty abandoning her husband, as if he were just an ordinary boyfriend. The fear and insecurity she recently felt, when she woke up by the brook and saw a huge man standing over her head, holding a gun and a restrained dog, were still clear in her mind. She had no idea what happened to her while she was sleeping, and that uncertainty was eating her up. *Did I pass out from fatigue or was I experiencing an epileptic seizure?* Sitting across from Anna, she could not hide her exhaustion. Her eyes were flickering uncontrollably and Anna noticed Georgia's discomfort.

"Take a nap, dear. I promised my neighbor that I'll be over in fifteen minutes. She wants to ask me for something. I must keep my promise. Lie down and rest." Anna picked up her walking cane and waddled out of the house. She wanted Georgia to be by herself to regroup her thoughts and to unwind. Georgia welcomed the opportunity and as soon as Anna was out of the room, she wrapped herself in a plush quilt and lay on the floor next to the bed. In a minute, a purring snore broke the tranquility in Anna's room. Two hours later, Anna tip-toed into the room with a shopping bag in one hand and her cane in the other. Anna's steps made the boards of the floor squeak and Georgia woke up.

"After my visit, I stopped at the local store and bought a few things for dinner. I assume you are hungry, my dear," she added and placed the shopping bag on the floor next to the table. Georgia folded the quilt neatly, placed it back where Anna kept it, and suggested that Anna should sit down and rest. The old lady misunderstood Georgia's proposal as being a move to take over the affairs in her own domicile and turned down Georgia's suggestion. She lifted the package off the floor, placed it on the table, hung her walking cane on a hook next to the fireplace, and returned to the table. She took everything out of the shopping bag, retrieved two dinner plates from her antique cabinet, and garnished them with thin slices of sausage, ham, preserved fish, and canned peaches and pears. She placed a hunk of fresh bread to the left of the dinner plate and a fork and knife on the other side. As soon as she was done with the formal part of their dinner, she declared that dinner was on the table, and asked Georgia to sit down. Before they began to eat their dinner, they thanked God for allowing them to meet again. At long last, they made the sign of the cross, and Anna recited a short invocation she knew by heart. The two lost friends ate their dinner in peace and tranquility.

The evening was quiet and pleasant. Anna did all the talking and Georgia did the listening. The old lady spoke about her youth in a big house with her parents who descended from royal stock. Her marriage was a disaster, she told Georgia. Her husband was a decorated military officer, but he did not live long enough to enjoy the glory of his accomplishments as a military officer.

"He was assassinated by a radical group before we had the chance of having children," she said, sobbing. When she regained her control to continue, she told Georgia that his family did not make an attempt to locate her and she lamented that she was forced to live all by herself. She adopted a monastic life and locked herself away from the rest of the world until Georgia showed up.

"I will never tell you what to do, dear, unless you solicit my advice," she said to Georgia and commented that the woman was old enough to choose what she wanted to do for the rest of her life. She pointed out that Georgia was still young and beautiful. "You see, dear, God made angels and human beings. Angels are infallible, but not humans," she added, philosophically. "Keep your chin up. You are only twenty years old and have my support."

Georgia felt ten feet tall hearing Anna's encouraging comments and her confidence for a better future shot toward the stars. She walked over to the old lady, wrapped her arms around her benevolent supporter and, in genuine tears, thanked her for being generous and understanding.

"If there is something that I can do for you, even if you may think that it is out of my grasp, please ask me," Georgia declared. "Meanwhile, I need to find a job, any job, that will generate income to support myself. I want to be independent. Do you have any ideas, dear aunty?" Anna, scratching the front part of her white head, thought for a moment and responded that nothing came to her mind for the time being. A few seconds later she suggested that her neighbor, next door, might be of help. "Let me ask her tomorrow."

The two newly reacquainted friends went to bed, immediately after Georgia cleaned the dinner table and put things away. Anna's snoring did not disrupt her night meditations. Her mind was running in circles with other things, and the monotonous purring that was coming from the other bed did not interfere with her thinking process. Her mind was assessing the wisdom of abruptly walking away from her husband and the potential for finding a job to start life anew. She felt guilty for flushing Alex out of her life, just like that. Maybe, if she had allowed a little more time, things would had been okay with her marriage. She might have been pregnant shortly, and things might have been different in the Bookas domicile. Alex could have taken her side and his parents would have accepted her as a person, not to perpetuate the Bookas legend. All these maybes were just ifs in her contemplations for her future. *Anna might pull a rabbit out of the hat tomorrow and things wouldl fall into place.* Eventually her thoughts drifted to her brother. She refused to accept the possibility that he was dead. Something in the labyrinth of her subconscious was telling her that he was well and was searching for her. The magic charm, still hanging around her neck, was either mute or did not want to reveal sad news about her brother. Enigmatic dreams tortured her mind at night. It had been more than two years since her brother disappeared, as if the earth opened and swallowed him. No word of him, or about him, had reached her to this day. She wished to walk the entire Earth and find him, either dead or alive. She couldn't live with the uncertainty of his fate. She had to know, at all costs.

Georgia made every effort to be pleasant while she was living under Anna's roof. She never poked her nose into Anna's past and never expressed her curiosity to know the secrets behind the door of the locked room. She kept active with things that were neglected, things that had to be attended to around the old house. Someone had to scrub the floors, clean the windows, and till the garden. One lovely afternoon, when Anna returned home from a brief visit with her neighbor, most of Georgia's concerns came to a pleasant end. The old lady asked Georgia to join her by the table, for she had something very important to tell her. Georgia came down from the ladder where she was cleaning a window and sat on a chair facing the other woman. Her heart was pounding, for she did not know what was in Anna's mind. The thought that the old lady had decided to sell the house and move away to live with one of her forgotten relatives crossed her mind. Anna focused her one eye on her, wiped her lips with the palms of her bony hands, and announced that there was a pickle-canning factory in town and her neighbor was related to the owners of the place. She told Georgia that her lady friend was willing to introduce Georgia to the manager in hopes that she could be employed at the place. She explained to her that curing and packing pickles was a seasonal activity and at this time of the year, and they needed all the help they could get.

"Do you want to give it a try?"

Georgia rubbed her hands against her thighs and with an overwhelming, emotional expression on her face, gave Anna her answer.

"Of course, I'll go to work as early as they need me." She exuberantly grabbed the bony hands of the other woman and kissed them with affection. "You are an angel from heaven!" Now that faith sprang open the gate of hope, Georgia saw a brighter tomorrow ahead of her.

"That's okay, dear! No need to cry. Come tomorrow morning, you will meet my friend. The cannery is only a walking distance from here and if things go as I expect, you will have your first employment."

As time went on, Georgia had a challenging time comprehending the good things that holy providence had steered her way. She started to accept the thought that a good life could be possible away from Vivitsi and far away from the oppressive atmosphere at the Bookas' house. She began to think that things could be promising in this country after all. She began to think that she will learn the Slavic version of the Greek language. The memories of brushing with death at the mountain and the fiasco of her marriage took a back seat in her voyage through life, for she had the support of gracious Anna. She gave her free shelter and as recently as two days earlier went out of her way to find a job for her. *If I can only find Fotis, I'll be the happiest girl in the world,* she said to her other self, every night, before she closed her eyes to go to sleep.

Georgia had a peaceful and dream-free night. She woke up before Anna the next morning, ready to tackle the new day with vigor and vivacity. She washed her hands and her young face with soap and water and put on the only dress and the only pair of shoes she had. She combed her hair and arranged it in a simple bow on the back of her head and before the sun was up, walked outside and sat on the patio of Anna's house to welcome the first rays of the July sun. Birds of all kinds and colors chirped in the tall trees to the northwest. A stray cat, who kept the chair warm all night, was spooked away and vanished in the dense foliage on the other side of the house. To the northeast, the view was unobstructed and at the far distance, the mountain, without snow at its peak and just lit by the brilliant rays of the morning sun, brought memories to her mind. She remembered the agony and the fear when something pierced her thigh. She drew a deep breath and a feeling of guilt surfaced in her heart. She felt that she betrayed that brave soldier, who picked her up and carried her into the underground hospital. Drawn to that memory, she did not notice that Anna stood behind her for several minutes. An intentional hissing sound that came from Anna's throat brought Georgia back to reality.

"I sit out here often to see the sun announcing a new day," Anna said and suspiciously cleared her throat, as if she meant something else with her comment. Georgia acted as if the other woman's statement did not contain an allegoric meaning and simply responded.

"It's beautiful to see the sun peeking at us through the snow-free mountain top, isn't it?"

"Yes," Anna responded. "It gives you the impression that the mountain top and the sun have a love affair going on!" The old lady giggled and changed the subject of their conversation.

"I see that you are all dressed up, ready for work! Let's have our tea, then go next door and meet Olympia. She will be waiting for us."

After the two women had their traditional morning refreshment, Georgia, holding the old lady by her free hand, walked with her next door and met Olympia at the doorstep. Anna introduced Georgia to Olympia and after the formalities of two people meeting each other for the first time, Olympia asked, "Are you ready to pack some pickles? You need a waterproof coverall. The pretty dress and shoes you have on are not the thing you wear when you work on the line putting pickles in jars. I still have a used outfit I can spare. You can have it," and took Georgia into the house. Minutes later, Georgia appeared at the door dressed in a one-piece, black, waterproof coverall that covered her from the neck to the ankles.

"They have gumboots for everyone at the factory," Olympia said to Georgia and handed Georgia's dress to Anna. "This dress is only good for dancing, not working in a pickle-packing line. Let's go, dear."

Anna returned home happy and content, holding Georgia's dress in her free hand. She felt great that she was able to find a job for desperate Georgia. Likewise, Olympia felt rewarded paying back some social debts to her long-time neighbor, and Georgia was delighted for the kindness she received from both ladies.

Six months went by. Georgia put her heart into her job. She was there every day and never objected to working overtime. She stashed away her money and made many friends from the Greek ghettoes. Several of them were displaced by the civil war but five of them had been abandoned in camps, just like her. During her socializing with them, a man told her that her brother was shipped to mainland Greece, right after he received additional training on guerrilla war tactics. This piece of information ignited new hopes in her mind, hopes that her brother was still alive, somewhere in Greece.

During weekends, when Anna and Olympia had nothing for her to do, Georgia visited the Greek ghettoes to gather pieces of information about her lost brother. One day, she stopped at a traditional *kafenio* and became acquainted with its owner and with some of the customers. The kafenio was the place where primarily idle Greeks gathered on weekends to play cards and exchange information about their motherland. While she was talking to the owner and holding a cup of Greek coffee in one of her hands, she noticed that another customer kept looking at her intently. She felt that she knew him too, but she couldn't remember his name or the occasion where she met him. Presently, a new customer came in the store and with a friendly gesture, slapped the other guy on his back.

"Hey, Demos! What are you doing here? Rumors are going around that you went back home."

"Yeah, I did," Demos responded and gestured with his hands that his trip home was not pleasant. The two men moved to a separate table on the other end of the shop and resumed their friendly talk. Judging from the expressions on their faces and from the motions they were making with their hands, Georgia suspected that the two were engaged in some friendly conversation. They were out of earshot and she couldn't hear their voices, but she could guess the subject.

The enigma man kept stealing glances at her, and that was when the light went on in Georgia's memory. *By God, that's Demos Prasinos from Vivitsi. He is the one who was taken away from the village, like me!* She rushed over to the men and abruptly interrupted their conversation. Demos rose from his chair, opened his arms, and Georgia threw herself between them. Their emotional outburst was brief and when it was over, Demos saw that his friend's chair was empty. The other man was courteous and walked away for the two lost-and-found friends to be alone and talk in private.

"Sit down," he said to Georgia. "We have a lot of things to talk about. You went through the ordeal of living in the camp unhurt, I see."

"As you can see, I came through okay except for getting a hole in my thigh," she responded. "Fotis, my brother, is still missing. I haven't seen him, or heard from him, since the time they took him away from the camp." She sighed deeply.

"An old lady, back in the village, told me that there was a young man walking around your house several months ago. The guy refused to identify himself, and that's what made her suspicious. Do you have any other relatives? Or ..."

"I don't have any other relatives, to the best of my knowledge, who would be interested in our home at the village. If he was Fotis, why would he hide his identity?"

"Those of us who were taken to the concentration camps are suspected of being indoctrinated, fanatic communists," he responded. 'That's why I came back," he emphasized with bitterness.

"Are you saying that the mystery man could be Fotis?"

"I wouldn't exclude the possibility. He might have a 'tainted' past. He was a guerrilla fighter, wasn't he?"

He might have participated in some bloody encounter with the king's army and wants to conceal his identity." Demos expressed his ambiguity by flipping the palms of his hands in an upward gesture. He added that her old house was in dire need of repair. Demos sat back in his chair, took a sip from his water glass, and told Georgia that the walls and the roof of the house were still there and the old woman with her goat was gone. He began to talk about his assessment of political life in Greece, but his listener did not register a word of what he was saying. Her mind was fixed on the possibility that her lost brother was well, somewhere in the motherland.

"Georgia!" Demos exclaimed. "Judging from the fact that you are alone here, and that there are no rings on your fingers, I assume that you are still single. Are you?"

"Yes, I'm single," she responded with modesty. Demos' eyes lit up and suggested that they should see each other more often, for they had many things in common. Georgia took her face between the palms of her hands and said to her other self, *Many people recognize your face, some remember your name, but no one knows what is hidden in your heart.* A deep sigh escaped from her mouth.

"Did I say something that offended you?" Demos said, surprised by Georgia's sudden mood change. Reaching over to her, he took her hands away from her face.

"You will never understand the pain that dwells in my heart. I lost my parents as a child and my brother as a young adult. I am living the life of a parasite for all my adult life, without any hope for betterment," and wailed softly. "I want to see all this misery change, change to a happier life. Do you understand that Demos?"

"Let me do my part," Demos responded with compassion and gentleness. "Don't place Fotis with the dead, yet. Remember that the flame of hope is eternal."

Georgia sat there, speechless. She had difficulty grasping what Demos had just said: "Let me do my part."

Their conversation drifted to something more cheerful. They reminisced about their grammar school life and laughed at their occasional mischievous deeds in Vivitsi. Georgia did not remember his parents, but he remembered her father well. An hour later, they stood up and embraced. Demos said that he wanted to see her again. Georgia considered his invitation for companionship.

"Thank you, Demos, for being a real friend. Yeah, let's do what you suggest. Gee, I'm late returning home." As she left, Demos took her in his embrace and whispered softly.

"Let's meet here on Sunday, say, around one in the afternoon, shall we?"

"I'll try to make it," she responded. "As I told you earlier, I'm taking care of an old lady who is Ill. She is in need of my help. I'll try to come." She gave Demos a hug and took the road toward Anna's home.

Demos stayed around the kafenio for a while. He wanted to shake hands with some of his old cronies and find lost friends from his past life in the camp. Besides, he was homeless and was looking for some friend who would give him a free dinner and a place to sleep. He was penniless and unemployed, for he was just back from Greece, broke and in desperate need of help.

On her way back to Anna's home, Georgia mulled over the things Demos said. She already had a warm feeling about him, but she was not convinced that he meant anything he said to her. Was he looking for a girl to keep him company or was there a hidden message, something leading to a long-lasting friendship? *Will his attitude toward me change when he finds out that I was married before?* Her half-hour walk back home came to its sudden end. She was in front of Anna's door.

Months later, Anna's health took a downturn. Her cough became worse and because of that she couldn't sleep at night. Recently, she lost her appetite and mumbled meaningless words in her bed. All day long, she sat on her plush chair and kept her eye fixed at the ceiling above. To make matters worse, Georgia lost her employment at the pickle-packing place. No pickles to pack meant no employment for her. Luckily, Olympia was willing to share some of her resources with Georgia until the next pickle-packing season commenced. Suddenly, Georgia became a full-time helper for Anna and a part-time housekeeper for Olympia. She cooked and washed clothes for both women and cleaned their houses as needed in return for free meals and a warm bed. Anna lingered between life and death another six months and Olympia kept providing money to buy the bare necessities for all three of them.

"Georgia, dear," Anna called early one evening while she was resting peacefully on her chair. "Come and sit next to me," she gurgled, and pointed with her bony hand at an empty space next to her chair. I have something very, very important to tell you. Move your chair here and sit close to me.

"I am accustomed to you living with me all this time, and I see in you the daughter I never had. I feel that the Almighty will call me to His kingdom shortly." Her bothersome cough came back and interrupted her intention to emphasize what she had to say. She fainted for a while and when she regained her strength to continue, she reached under her shirt and came up with a worn-out key and a small leather, wallet-size pouch.

"This is the key to the room next to the dining room, and this pouch contains a diagram for my secret pot. I have hidden an earthen pot inside this room with money in it. The pouch contains a diagram that shows the exact spot where I have the pot. When I'm gone, and only when I am dead, you can open the room and help yourself to whatever you would like to have, including the money. I kept things in there that I consider valuable, including this money for a 'rainy day.'"

Georgia put her hands over Anna's aged hands and felt the key and the pouch held firmly in Anna's fists, but she made no attempt to take them away from her grasp. Instead, she kissed Anna.

"Precious Aunty Anna! I'm indebted to your kindness, beyond description. I hope that God will reward you for being such a kind person. The only thing I possess that I can offer you is my immense and boundless love. You will be in my prayers for the rest of my life."

Anna was breathing regularly, but she did not respond to Georgia's acknowledgment of her generosity. Her one eye was closed shut and a peculiar expression covered her face. Resting peacefully on her pillow, she resembled an African mask of some kind.

"Dear Anna, may I make a cup of mountain tea?" Georgia asked after a while, when the old lady rolled to her side and opened her eye.

"No, dear. Just give me your hand and help me be comfortable in my bed. I'm tired ..." She extended her hand toward Georgia. The other woman sprang off her chair, took the begging hand in hers, gently helped Anna to reposition herself in her bed, and tucked her under her favorite quilt. Anna seemed comfortable and Georgia decided to leave her alone for a while.

It was cool, not cold, outside. Georgia decided to move to the veranda for a breath of fresh air and think about the things Anna had said. It was stuffy in the house, and she needed to inhale the breeze that swept through the valley, coming down from the mountain in the distance. She sat on an old chair, placed her feet on another one, took several deep breaths from the pine-scented, fresh air that penetrated everything around her, and sank into deep thought. She mulled over the hope that a small fortune was behind the locked door. A thousand ideas paraded through her mind, when she considered all the things that she could do with the money, once Anna was gone. *Before I do anything else with the money, I'll go to a store and buy new clothes and new shoes,* she promised herself. She was tired of wearing the same dress and the same pair of shoes that Alex bought for her a year and a half ago. The idea of spending some of the money to find out what happened to her brother came and went through her mind like a barn swallow. She reasoned that finding her sibling was her paramount obligation, but a disheartening thought was coming back to haunt her. She was torn between spending her money, finding Fotis and cultivating a meaningful relationship with Demos. She was in her early twenties and finding someone to her liking had occupied her mind lately. *My life is like a tornado. It swirls around from place to place, leaving destruction behind.* She was tired of the uncertainty of her future and wanted to change things. "If Demos meant what he said, he and I can get married, move back to Vivitsi, and with the money I'll have acquired from Anna, we can start our life anew," she said to herself in a whisper. The uncertainties of how sincere Demos was, and the amount of money to be found in Anna's hiding place, dampened her dreams. The only thing that she was certain of was that she had to change her life. Bouncing from place to place clashed with her expectations for herself. Things had to change and the appearance of Demos in her life offered an opportunity.

After a while, the mountain breeze turned from refreshingly cool to uncomfortably chilly. Georgia felt goosebumps popping up on her exposed legs and arms and she started to shiver. Darkness began to engulf nature and tree frogs stopped sending their love signals to other frogs from every tree around. Georgia slipped her feet into her shoes, walked back in the house, closed the door behind her, and decided to check on Anna before she retired for the evening. She turned the lights on, tip-toed to Anna's bed, and took a close look at her. Anna had repositioned herself in her bed and was purring like a kitten. Georgia rearranged the quilt to cover Anna's back, silently said good night, turned off the light, and walked to the other end of the room where her bed was. She skipped her evening tea tonight for she did not want to make noises that could awaken her roommate. She just curled up under her covers and went to sleep. No dreams, pleasant or frightening, came to wake her up during the night.

The morning sun was mischievous that morning. Without warning, it whirled its golden rays at her from the peak of the mountain, entered through a window, and kissed Georgia on both cheeks.

Georgia woke up, rubbed her eyes with her bare knuckles, placed her feet in her shoes, and walked over to Anna's bed. Her beloved Auntie Anna was lying there, peaceful. She was unnaturally peaceful! She did not respond to Georgia's calls and her hands and face were cold to the touch. Anna was dead!

Georgia wept over her lifeless Auntie Anna for a few seconds, but when she overcame the initial burst of grief, she opened the hand of the lifeless woman, retrieved the key and the tiny pouch from her grasp and secured them in one of her own pockets. Next, she did the sensible thing. She opened the secret room and, using the hand-drawn map, she located the treasure pot.

The pot was a one gallon earthenware jug. Its lid was sealed with red wax. Georgia took the vessel out of its concealing place, left the room, locked the door behind her, and hid the pot under her own bed. Finally, she hurried over to Olympia and, between genuine sobs, told the other woman that Anna was with her beloved husband in heaven.

"Anna was my truest neighbor and friend, all our lives," Olympia said in a hushed voice. "She helped me when I needed help, and I did likewise when she was in need for my consoling and support.

"There are rules and regulations that must be obeyed even after death," Olympia added. "I will take care of all the 'red tape' regarding the mumbo-jumbo to bury a dead person. You don't have to worry about anything. You can stay at Anna's house until the authorities come and ask you to vacate the property. It may be a month from now, or a year. It depends on how busy they are. I'll call them, and in a few hours, someone will show up to remove Anna's remains."

Georgia was relieved that Olympia was there to help, for she did not know where to start. Taking the money and walking away like a thief was not in Georgia's character. She felt that it was her ethical obligation to see that the remains of her dear Anna were handled with dignity and according to local tradition. She returned to Anna's home, closed all the doors, and sat close to her lifeless and benevolent friend. She wept for a while but said nothing. She had nothing more to say. All the expressions that came in her mind, were those she articulated, when Anna was still alive.

It was almost noon and Georgia had enough grieving over Anna's death. She left her alone on her bed and walked over to where she had hidden the pot with the treasure. With the edge of a knife, she scraped away the sealing wax. The lid gave way and she saw paper money bound together with strips of newspaper. A small roll of gold coins was at the very bottom of the pot. In her excitement, she dropped the lid on the hard floor and the thing broke into several pieces. She had no time to count her trove at this time. She was expecting someone to come and take away the remains of her benevolent friend. She placed the money in a pillowcase and shoved it under her mattress. Then she crushed the lid and the pot in tiny pieces and scattered them among the vegetables in Anna's garden. Having nothing else to do, she took a broom and swept the house one more time. Two hours later, the undertaker arrived at the front door. He was a large man with a goatee and a well-trimmed mustache. He placed Anna's tiny body in a black bag, flipped the bag over his shoulder and returned to his horse-drawn hearse. He deposited the bundle on the floor of his open-top vehicle, mounted it, and with a "hsst" command, the horse with its burden trotted away. Seconds later, Anna was no more.

Georgia returned to Olympia's house and spent the rest of the afternoon talking about Anna's past. She was curious to know if Anna and Olympia were related. Most of all, she wanted to know if Anna had any descendants who would show up to claim the house and her personal belongings.

"No. She told me that she did not have any children, and that her husband arrived in Macedonia with a military attachment from Poland, when the Cossacks chased the Turks away from the walls of Vienna," Olympia said earlier. She had two brothers and a sister, back in Herzegovina, but she did not know if they were still living. The house and its belongings will become the property of the city, according to our new laws. All of us work for the government, and the government feeds us and takes care of us," Olympia said dubiously. "My husband was anti-Tito, and he paid for it with his life," and broke out sobbing.

"He was a good man, Georgia! He did not have to die so soon!"

Georgia made no comment, for she did not know Olympia that well. For all she knew, she could have been placed there to spy on the people for the government.

"What are you planning to do now that Anna is gone?" Olympia asked.

"I'll try to find a job to support myself, and if this plan fails to be a reality, I'll take a road and walk to its end. It will not be the first time I did this sort of thing."

"Hang around, girl," Olympia urged. "We will find food for you until the pickle-packing season comes around."

"I need something more than food. Lady Olympia, I'm tired of living the life of a parasite. Can you help me find my way home? That's what I really need. I want to get back to my own country. Can you do that for me? I'll eat grass to survive until I get there."

Olympia was moved by Georgia's determination to return home and attempted to ease her homesickness. But she came up with nothing encouraging and, out of the blue, she changed the subject and asked Georgia if she ever fell in love.

"The hell with love," Georgia responded. "I had my fill being a wife! I am starting to believe that it will be better to be a nun or simply stay single for the rest of my life than getting tangled with another man."

"Take it easy, girl," Olympia responded. "All of us have had our ups and downs in life. You are not the only one who made the mistake of marrying the wrong guy. Do you mind telling me your experience with your marriage? It will help you to get it off your chest." Georgia thought for a few seconds and finally felt bold enough to reveal the circumstances under which she met Alex Bookas and her unpleasant experience as his wife.

"Georgia, you are still young, and certainly you are a beautiful girl. Go and buy some good clothes and shoes, fix your hair, and start all over again. You underestimate your worth, young lady. Come tomorrow morning, and you will go with me to the store and fix yourself. Don't you worry about who will pay. I'll pay for everything.

"No, Lady Olympia. Anna gave me a little money that she had stashed away for 'a rainy day,' as she put it. I'll use it."

"As you wish, dear," Olympia responded, "but let me go with you to help you make your selections. I know what things will look good on you. Besides, I know the storekeepers in town. I'm an 'old fox'; they cannot cheat us on the prices." Her last statement stretched her lips in a broad smile and exaggerated the wrinkles around her mouth and down her throat.

Georgia returned to Anna's house early in the evening. She locked the doors, lit the kerosene lamp in the kitchen, retrieved her "loot" from under her mattress, and sat at the dinner table to count the money and assess its worth. She had never seen that much money in her life. There was a small roll of gold coins, wrapped in plastic film, and two wads of paper money. She took apart one of the wads and attempted to count them, but she lost track of the numbers. She was agitated and confused, and at the same time, her mind was cluttered with a thousand thoughts. In that state of bewilderment, she remembered that she had seen a backpack in the secret room. *That's what I need to store and carry around my money and all my other belongings,* she reflected and without giving it a second thought, she returned to the secret room and came back with a worn-out, dusty, leather backpack. The thing looked more like a soldier's knapsack than a young lady's hiking pack. She wiped it clean with a towel and placed her modest fortune in one of the inside pockets. She only kept in her pocket a handful of bills to shop with. She hid the backpack with the rest of the money in the secret room, locked the door, and returned to the kitchen. She made herself comfortable in Anna's chair and took her time to count the money she had for shopping. In her estimation, she had more than enough cash to pay for everything she had in mind to buy. She even had enough money to get some cosmetics for herself. Later in the evening, exhausted from the intense activity of the day, she made a cup of mountain tea, drank it alone, threw herself on her bed, and allowed her mind to wander at will. After a while, feeling chilled, she reached over and pulled the blanket over herself. In doing so, her charm came out of its hiding place and landed in her left hand. She was so accustomed to wearing it around her neck that she was not aware that she had the thing still hanging there. She gently brought it to her lips and, with divine respect, kissed it several times.

"Thank you, oh merciful Virgin Mary, thank you! Thank you for not forgetting your humble servant. Thank you for steering me to the door of compassionate and understanding people. Thank you, thank you," she repeated, and took another look at the shining charm. The engraved message of *do not lose it or do not give it away* was still discernible on one side, but the face of the saint, on the other side, was almost gone. It was reduced to the silhouette of a human face. She squeezed it between the palms of her hands a little longer. As she was counting the miracles it performed for her, her eyes closed, and she went to sleep. A large, warm-looking moon appeared in the eastern horizon and ripped across the standing clouds, just like a dolphin will cut through the foaming waves of a turbulent ocean. People returning home late at night heard the monotonous call of a barn owl perched somewhere in the foliage of an ancient pine tree in front of the house. Georgia saw and heard nothing of that. She was sunk in a dream-free and restful sleep until a rainstorm accompanied by lightning and earth-shaking thunder woke her up the next morning. She rolled off her bed and, while waiting for the rainstorm to subside, prepared for her shopping excursion with her neighbor.

Olympia was very helpful during the shopping, assisting Georgia to get the things she wanted and bargaining with the storekeepers. Georgia selected three dresses of assorted colors and styles, three white shirts, a red and a green wool pullover, several pairs of socks, and two pairs of shoes. One pair was for mountain hiking and the other a formal pair that matched the colors of her dresses and her hair. Returning home that afternoon, she tried on each of her dresses, one more time, and modeled them in front of Anna's full-size mirror. It was only then that she realized that she was a beautiful woman. She had a round face with big, dark eyes, luscious lips, and flowing, black hair, things men would dream to caress. A generous bosom, a thin waist, curvy hips, and long, well-shaped legs gave her the look of an ancient Greek goddess. *Georgia, you are ready to start a new page in your life.* Looking at the reflection in the mirror, she felt her esteem soar like an eagle. Her confidence in her abilities to accomplish things expanded like the blue sky above her head. She realized that her misfortunes were not her doing, after all. The failure of not having a baby was, most likely, the result of some injury that Alex suffered as a guerrilla fighter. Her suspicion of Alex being incapable of fatherhood was substantiated by his behavior and the conditions under which she met him. He was a nobody guerrilla at the hospital without a special assignment. Was he there for some medical treatment? Furthermore, when they lived as husband and wife, he would occasionally vanish all night long. Was he under some medical treatment for sterility? Making her assessment of who she was and what she could accomplish in her life fortified her desire to return to her birthplace.

"I'll fix the place, find a man who will truly love me, and I will initiate a methodical search for Fotis," she said to herself.

The picture of Demos popped up in her mind and a foreign thought invaded her mind. Could Demos make her dream real? He knew his way around the mountain and he was a master at sneaking over to Greece from Slavic Macedonia. Additionally, something in the deepest maze of her heart was telling her that he was not a bad fellow, after all. With these assessments of herself and her ambitions, she took a brief walk to the little store in the neighborhood and bought provisions for the evening and the next day. Returning home, she saw Olympia going out and exchanged a few words with her.

"Lady Olympia, you look marvelous tonight. Anything special?"

"Ah, nothing of substance dear. I have to chair the local chapter of the women's sisterhood."

"I just want to thank you again for going along with me this morning," Georgia said.

"Do not even think about it, dear! That's the least I can do for you," the other woman said and disappeared around the corner.

Georgia returned home, fried slices of potatoes and sausage and ate dinner alone, without Anna. She re-examined the leather backpack and found it to be big enough for all the items she had bought earlier. The next day, she decided to visit the kafenio. She was hoping that Demos would show up, for she wanted to talk to him about returning to Vivitsi. It was early afternoon when she walked into the place, wearing one of her new dresses and her new shoes. Her long hair was neatly combed and was hanging down her shoulders, halfway to her waist. Demos was not there at that moment. Two other men interrupted their conversation and acknowledged her appearance with their customary whistling. She ignored the compliment, approached the proprietor of the place, and asked him if Demos had been around recently.

"Sure, he comes around here every day, say around three to four o'clock in the afternoon. He'll be here, soon. Anything to drink, lady?"

"May I have a glass of water and a regular Greek coffee?"

"That's the only coffee this place serves," he responded sarcastically, and went behind his counter to make and fetch the coffee for his new customer. Georgia walked to the far end of the place, pulled up a chair by a small table, and sat down facing the street, away from the gaping young men. Her coffee and water arrived shortly. The place was not busy at the time and the owner attempted to initiate a conversation with her.

"New around here, sweetie? I don't recall seeing you before."

"It all depends on what you mean by 'new'" Georgia said flatly. "I'm one of the children who came here during the paidomazoma."

"Oh, you are one of the *forgotten,* like me," the owner said. "Most of my customers are the remnants of that era." He pulled up a chair on the other side of the table and sat down facing her.

At that moment, Demos walked in and with a cheerful tone in his voice cried. "Aha, coffee-maker, lucky dog, you! You found a new girlfriend!" To verify his humor, he slapped the other guy on the back with a friendly gesture. The coffee maker stood up and asked Demos, "What's for you, pal?"

"The same thing." Demos turned his attention to Georgia and expressed his admiration of how beautiful she looked in her new attire.

"What brings you here so early, and what's the occasion for being dressed to kill! Are you getting married, or what?" Georgia blushed, but she held her emotions under control.

"I came here to talk to you about a daring plan I have in mind. I plan to go back home, and I need your help. The last time I saw you, you said that you had just returned from Greece, which means you know your way around the mountains."

"For the last two years, I crossed the border to Greece more than ten times helping people go back home. I know the places that are not guarded by either the Macedonian army or the green-beret, Greek security commandos," he whispered. "There is another guy who wants to go back. If he comes up with the cash, you can come along and split the expenses of my fee. You might even get a free ride. It all depends on how much money the other guy has in his pocket."

Taking her hands, he asked, "Once you are there, what are you planning to do?"

"I'll go to Vivitsi, fix the house up as much as I can, and start looking for Fotis."

Their conversation was interrupted by the coffee shop owner, who brought Demos his coffee. As soon as he went away, Georgia and Demos resumed their conversation.

"Georgia, you need money to put the old house back in its habitable shape. In addition, you must find some way to support yourself. You should know that it is not easy to find a job in the old country, especially for people like us."

"There is a little money somewhere to fix some of the essential parts of the house. I'll manage to find something to do for a living. For example, I'll work as a pair of helping hands harvesting and drying tobacco for one of the growers in the territory. I have had it with camp life and serving others. Greeks are not destined to be slaves!"

"Let me think about it for a couple days," Demos responded. "I want to talk to the other guy too. Let's meet here in two days, right here at this kafenio and at the same hour, yeah?"

"Demos, I'm serious about it. I'm going, with or without you. I'll give you only one day to straighten up your affairs. I expect a definite answer from you tomorrow, no bullshit! Until then, goodbye." Before she walked out of the kafenio and disappeared down the road toward Anna's house, she planted a sisterly kiss on his left cheek. Moments later, Demos remarked to the owner, "Man, this broad is dynamite!"

"She is a heck of a nice girl, I can tell. She will make a fine wife for a lucky guy," he mumbled under his breath and rolling up his sleeves started cleaning a pile of coffee cups and water glasses he had in the sink filled with soapy water.

Demos walked out of the place with mixed feelings. He was confused with the things he heard from Georgia's mouth. "There is a little money to fix some of the essential parts of the house," she had said. Besides, her attitude was positive about her future. She was not afraid to go out and get a job once she made her house suitable for human occupancy. *Hmm. I'll take her back home and see if I fit in her life,* he whispered to himself, while he was walking toward a friend's shack. He knew that going back and forth over the border was a risky business and settling down in Macedonia was not for him either. He was born a Greek and wanted to live his life as a Greek citizen and a Greek Orthodox Christian. He couldn't stand hearing the Muslim invocation from the top of the minaret, next to the Greek ghetto, three times a day. It sounded like a bellowing bull with laryngitis.

Georgia returned to Anna's home, entered through the back door, and sat on the veranda to think through her conversation with Demos. It was the first time she felt attached to a man in an unexplained way. As she sat in her chair across from him at the coffee shop, she felt a quivering sensation in her stomach and realized that she could not take her eyes away from him. The more she looked at him, the more she saw a handsome, sweet, and gentle man in the person of Demos. Was she in love with a man she hardly knew? How could she love a man who was nobody? He was just a drifter without a profession or even a respectable job. He was just a human smuggler. But to Georgia, he was a perfect companion for now and for the future. Thinking about her new experience with him, she found nothing wrong in liking a man whom she remembered as a child. "Obeying the calling of your heart is the beginning of falling in love," she said softly. Her contemplations about her new relationship with a strange man was interrupted when she heard Olympia knocking at the door and heard her voice calling her.

"Georgia, are you home?

"Yes, Lady Olympia," she responded, and hurried to the door.

"I was cooking all day today, and I made eggplants stuffed with ground goat meat. Come on over and have some. You will like my cooking."

"Thank you for the dinner invitation. There is something else that came up." Georgia put on her shoes and, one next to the other, they walked over to Olympia's house.

"Sit here," Olympia said to Georgia, pointing at one of the chairs by the table. "Before you tell me what is 0n your mind, you eat, first." Olympia walked to her wood-burning stove and returned with two stuffed eggplants on a dinner plate. She placed the dish in front of her guest and in her customary polite manner, added, "Would you like water or tea with your dinner?"

"Water will do, Lady Olympia." After a bite, Georgia exclaimed, "Delicious! Your cooking is out of this world!"

"I'm flattered to hear that you like it. Would you like to have bread with your dinner? I heard that the Greeks always eat bread with their meals."

"No, Lady Olympia. I like eggplants the way you prepared them. Thank you. I have enough here to feed two." Her hostess brought a tall glass of water and placed it in front of her dinner guest and while she was organizing her kitchen, Georgia consumed both eggplants.

"Now, tell me my dear. What is on your mind? Who is the lucky guy who conquered your heart? I can see 'I am in love' printed across your forehead," Olympia whispered in a playful tone.

Georgia blushed for a moment and struggled to find words to express her predicament to the other lady. She was not convinced that she was in love with Demos, but Olympia knew better. Georgia was speechless. Olympia came to her aid.

"Sweetheart, don't feel uncomfortable admitting that a young man stole the key to your heart. I remember the day when I stood in front of my mother admitting that I was in love with a handsome young officer, who became my husband later. It's only natural for a woman to fall in love with a man. Your first marriage was a desperate move to survive. It was not an emotional bond to a man."

Georgia finally gained strength to talk about Demos and about her plan to return home with him. She said that he was a handsome and polite man with the potential of becoming a devoted husband.

"I cannot help it, I like the guy, Lady Olympia! I will try my best to make him happy."

"Whoa, girl!" Olympia exclaimed. "Is he committed to this relationship like you are? 'It takes two to tango.'"

"I hope he is. If things go sour, he goes back to where he came from and I'm safe at home."

"The Neighborhood Committee pressures me to tell them when Anna's house will be available for auction. Do you know when you are getting out of there?" Olympia asked. "Don't misinterpret my question, honey. There are rules and regulations set forth by the state regarding delinquent properties."

"I agree, Lady Olympia. Rich and poor are obliged to obey the same rules in our society, for otherwise order cannot be maintained. Don't you worry. I'll be out of here, at the most, one week from now. Besides, the place feels claustrophobic without Anna around. I want to get out of there as soon as possible."

The rest of the evening went by with random chatting. Georgia's spirit was lifted knowing that gracious people still existed in the world. Olympia was spiritually fulfilled to see that someone, in desperate need for human passion, was helped.

At some hour in the early evening, Georgia thanked Olympia for the dinner and her counsel, said good night, and walked back to Anna's house. She was tempted to snoop around the house but found it indecent to dig deeper into the life story of her benevolent Aunty Anna. Instead, she withdrew to her favorite spot of the house, the outside veranda. She took her shoes off, made herself comfortable on the old chair, and fixed her eyes on the faraway mountain. It was dark now, but the silhouette of the twin peaks projecting against the starry sky was majestic. The pine-covered slope of the lowland in front of the mountain appeared black, hostile, and uninviting. The immediate area between the base of the mountain and the house was flat, with houses planted at random among the trees. Narrow roads, crossing each other haphazardly, sliced the area into uneven but geometrically regular plots. Life was serene in the far and near creation of God, just as in a pleasant dream. Georgia was mesmerized by the scene, as though seeing it for the first time.

If Demos is the man that he lets me believe he is, I'll be on the other side soon, Georgia thought. She was determined to leave soon, with him or without him. She would put on her hiking boots, shoulder the old military knapsack with her belongings in it, and march forward to a new adventure. She was homesick.

She was prepared to spend time in a Greek prison as a suspected communist rather than live the rest of her life as an expatriate. Slavic Macedonia was a prison for her, for it placed restrictions on her life. The communist system did not allow her to own a home and she could not accept the local life and customs.

Most of all, she wanted to find her brother. Rumors circulated at the kafenio and in the ghettoes that he went back to Greece as a guerrilla fighter. Her subconscious was telling her that he was somewhere in Greece, alive and well, and she was committed to go and find him. She knew the language of the land and she could read old newspapers and military records filed by both sides. She was planning to travel through the land, to interview people, even at the most isolated villages, and follow leads to find him. She had to put the issue of his whereabout behind her before she did anything with the rest of her life. If he was dead, she wanted to locate the place where he was buried, dig out his remains, and inter them with dignity. If he was in prison, she wanted to visit him and explore all options for his release. If he was mentally ill, roaming the streets, she was prepared to assist him with everything she had. But if he was well and had forgotten her, she was ready to humiliate him in public and forget that she ever had a brother.

Two days later, she went back to the kafenio and found Demos looking for her. He gave her a bear hug and spoke confidently.

"The deal with the other guy, who was to travel with us, bombed out. Are you ready for our perilous voyage back home?" He placed his index finger on her lips. "Remember that we take a risk of being shot or ending up in prison for entering another country illegally. It never happened to me before, but there is always the first time."

"Now you tell me ..." she responded sarcastically and laughed. "I was ready for this trip two years earlier, when I went as far as the summit, before I received a slug of steel in my thigh. Nothing can stop me now. I'm like the relentless waves of the sea that keep coming back to pound the shore, until the rocks break to small pieces to form sand. We are leaving tomorrow. Are you ready?"

"No, we leave tonight," Demos whispered. "We must cross over in darkness, ideally around two to three o'clock in the morning, when everyone pays less attention to their job. Go and get your belongings and meet me at the school grounds in four hours from now. Can you make it?"

"You bet your last dime, I'll be there waiting for you," she emphasized and hugged him passionately. "Don't make me wait for you." Turning around, she disappeared down the tree-lined street. He stayed there a little longer, then went to his friend's shack. He put on his mountain climbing attire and shouldered his backpack with his spare clothes. His friend was not at home, but his wife was outside watering her garden. Demos told her that he was making another trip to Greece.

"If things go as I plan, my smuggling profession will come to its end. You might not see me again in Slavic Macedonia. Please give this message to your husband," Demos said, and walked away, not to be seen in the town again.

CHAPTER FOUR

I t was dark when Georgia said her last adios to Lady Olympia. She handed over the key to Anna's home with tears streaming down her youthful face. She took a last look at Anna's deserted house, waved goodbye to Olympia, and disappeared into the night. She was mentally and physically geared up to face the perils of the voyage. She wore an old dress Olympia had given her earlier and her new hiking boots felt good on her feet. The leather military knapsack, bulging with her belongings, was securely strapped on her back. In one of her pockets she had a four-inch buck knife Anna had kept in the upper drawer of her night table. A few minutes later, she arrived at the schoolgrounds and concealed herself in an inconspicuous corner between two buildings. She placed her back against the outside wall and fixed her sight toward the direction from where Demos was expected to show up.

"Look who is hiding here," a teen-ager's voice whispered in Georgia's ears. "Come out and show us your tits," another youngster's voice came from her other side.

"You don't want to get hurt, boys," she calmly said, and flashed her vicious knife in the moonlight. "Go away, kids. My boyfriend will show up soon, and your little peckers will become fish bait." Before she even had finished her warning, she saw two shadows disappearing in the dark, around the corner of the building. Georgia put her knife back in her pocket and giggled at the unpleasant incident. Moments later, she began to get impatient waiting for Demos and started to consider her contingency plan. *If he does not show up within the next hour, I will go without him.* Pulling out her good-luck charm, she said in a subdued voice. "Oh, most powerful creator of everything visible and invisible! Help me go through this impasse. I want to go home! Is that too much to expect?" At that moment, a faint whistling and the reflection of a flashlight, coming from the other corner of the building, put an end to her conversation with her creator.

"Here! I'm here!" she said loudly enough for the whistler to hear her. "I'm over here!" she added and came out of her hiding corner. Demos appeared in the open and began to walk toward the place where Georgia's voice came from. He had a flashlight in his hands and kept walking toward her at a brisk pace. She met him in the open space between the gym and the administrative buildings, embraced him with tension, and heard him whisper, "Let's go. We have no time to waste with sentimental stuff."

Demos took Georgia's hand in his and like children going to grandma's dinner invitation, began to walk toward the mountain. She felt his hand squeezing hers, and the feeling of being secured in his company made her steps sturdy on the uneven path. A strange feeling began to inundate her heart. It was a feeling of belonging to one another, a feeling of wanting him, something she never experienced before in the company of any other man. Her hand felt good in his grasp, and she realized that she was drifting closer and closer toward him, as they advanced forward. Holding hands, they followed the beam of the flashlight in an eerie silence. At times, they momentarily stopped to catch their breath or to swat insects away from their faces. During these brief intermissions, she felt his arms wrapped around her and an unexplained rush of blood traveled throughout her body. She sensed his warm breathing sweeping her ears when he asked her if she was okay. Walking in the darkness became perilous when they began to climb the mountain slope. The path became narrow and stones and shrubs hindered their forward advancement. After a while, they abandoned holding hands, for they had to use them to push tree branches away from their path. Often, they had to crawl on all fours to go through tight spots along the way. Halfway to the summit, Demos called a stop.

"There is a small cave, a half of a mile up from here. The sun will rise soon, and we must be out of sight before the day breaks. Besides, I see you are exhausted. You need to rest. We will spend all day in the cave, and when darkness returns, we will descend the other side of the mountain to cross the border. Just hang on for another hour and you will get your rest." Georgia's mind was elsewhere, though. She was not thinking of getting her badly needed rest. She was struggling with the emotional state of her mind. She was afraid that she was in love with him, and that thought frightened her. She had enough of that "love stuff" from Alex.

"Would you like me to carry your backpack?" he asked her.

"No, that's okay," she said. "I can handle it."

She repositioned her knapsack on her shoulders, balanced its weight on her sturdy back and legs, and said. "Lead the way, partner! I'm behind you." Demos resumed climbing toward the cave with Georgia close behind him. The eastern horizon was getting pink and birds started to send thanks to their creator for allowing them to live another day. Several additional minutes of tenuous climbing brought the travelers to a rocky cliff. An opening, partially obstructed by a dense bush, led into a cave in the towering rock formations. It was deep, but barely wide enough for two people to lie down, one next to the other.

"Let me go in and look around. Sometimes, snakes and scorpions find these places comfortable and secure, away from their predators," Demos said and, with his walking stick in one hand and his flashlight in the other, entered the natural grotto. Seconds later, he came out and told his companion that it was safe for her to enter and make herself comfortable for the day.

"Get in there and make yourself as comfortable as you can. I don't think both of us will fit inside. I'll make my lair outside, in the thick foliage. The weather looks fine; it will not rain today." Demos kicked some loose stones away from the ground to create his temporary bed. Georgia obeyed his command and, crouching in the cave entrance, crawled inside it, like a serpent, feet first. Once inside, she placed her backpack on the ground under her head. She stretched her legs toward the deep end and realized that the place was roomy enough for both.

"Demos," she exclaimed. "There is plenty of room in here for both of us. I don't want you to be in the direct sun all day long. You can sneak next to me." Demos scuttled inside the cavern, feet first. He placed his backpack under his head and positioned his body next to hers. The radiating heat from their bodies felt good, and the urge to make direct contact exceeded its limits. After a few attempts to become more comfortable inside the confinement, she felt his hands exploring every part of her body and she sensed the urge to do likewise. It was inevitable that a normal woman in her twenties and a young man of the same age would not resist the desire for each other. When the sun disappeared behind the west horizon, Georgia and Demos found themselves sleeping in the arms of each other. They slept intermittently all day until the bright sun gave way to darkness again.

"Get up," Demos said to Georgia and gently poked her in the belly. "It's dark already and we must reach the crossover point before the sun comes up. The sentries from both sides do not hesitate to open fire on strangers who cross their borderline." Sliding out of the grotto, he pulled up his pants and washed his face with some of the water in his canteen. Georgia rubbed her eyes with the heels of her hands, pulled her dress down, shouldered her leather knapsack, and accepted the canteen from Demos. She refreshed her mouth with two gulps of water and used the rest of its contents to wash her hands and face.

"Ready," she declared. Before departing for the next leg of their adventure, they embraced and kissed each other with a new passion.

"Follow me. For the next hour, the path is uneven. We must exercise caution, especially in the dark." He led the way uphill toward the twin peaks of the summit. The climbing was treacherous and downright dangerous. Every now and then, Demos stopped and offered his hand to his companion to climb over rocks and other impediments that blocked their path. Two hours of exhausting climbing brought them to the foot of the mountain peak. He called a halt one more time and instructed Georgia to sit down and get her rest.

"I'll check below. I'll be right back. The sentinels send out patrols every three hours to check the canyon that we plan to traverse. I just want to see what is going on down there."

"How can you see what is going on? It's already dark!"

"Ah. They use flashlights!" he retorted. "Stay put. Don't you worry, I'll be back in a few minutes," he whispered and disappeared like a cat in the darkness of the early evening. Georgia moved around the immediate area, found a suitable spot to place her backpack, and sat on a flat rock next to her belongings. She had confidence that Demos knew what he was doing. He had turned out to be a hardened mountaineer, and he said that he had an outstanding ability to judge things at night, just like a fox.

Georgia thought about the things that took place in the cave all day long, but she did not feel ashamed or regret her experience. She felt a strong bond holding them together. Demos returned soon, picked up his pack, strapped it securely on his back, took her hand, and motioned with his other hand for her to get up.

"Everything is clear down there," he whispered. "It seems that we will go through without a hitch." He gave her a bear hug and a smack on her nose. She responded with the same passion by wrapping her arms around his waist and pulling him close to her, kissing him on the mouth. Minutes later, she was on his heels down the east side of the mountain. One of her hands was holding his shirt that was sticking out loose from his belt. Going downhill was easier but more dangerous than walking uphill. A slip of the foot could have resulted in tragedy. Around an hour before sunrise, Demos' alertness made him freeze in his tracks and motioned Georgia to stop by squeezing her hand in his. A boulder became loose to their far left and tumbled into the ravine below with a loud crashing sound. At the same instance, the voice of a man echoed in the twilight of the morning.

"Be careful, man! You should know by now that this pass is dangerous." Apparently, a patrol was going through some narrow pass at the time, and someone kicked a loose rock downhill. Georgia and Demos sat quietly beside a rock formation that kept them out of view. When everything became quiet again and no sounds of human footsteps disturbed the silence of the darkness, Demos and Georgia resumed their treacherous walk. The stars and the half-moon above their head shed enough light for them to find their way downhill. At times, Georgia had to let Demos' shirt go and slide down on her buttocks to reach the next flat spot to set her feet. Demos moved like a mountain goat. He planted his mountain boots securely from one spot to the next and descended the slope effortlessly toward the canyon. Finally, the downhill walk came to its end. They came to a creek. Only the trickling sound of fresh water that rolled between rocks disturbed the perfect quietness.

"Let's take a rest for a few minutes," Demos whispered. "Let's drink water from the creek, wash our faces, and catch our breath, before we resume walking. We timed our trip to perfection. Daylight will break soon, and the sentinel commanders will be busy writing their reports and assigning daily duties to their soldiers. That will be the perfect moment to sneak through their territory. We are almost there, love."

Georgia's heart jumped into her mouth when she heard the word "love" coming out of Demos' mouth. Her mind flew into the future and she envisioned a happy life at the side of her new-found man. The glittering morning star was well above the eastern horizon and the smiling half-moon was playing hide-and-seek with a puff of dark clouds on the western horizon. Demos and Georgia resumed their walking, now on Greek soil, and kept moving with new vigor, away from imminent danger in another nation's territory. The end of their odyssey was in sight. Just after daybreak, they found themselves on a paved road with signs written in their native language. A half a mile behind them was the last military post. Ahead was a total mystery.

"Love, it will be safer if we claim that we are husband and wife," Demos announced. "If a person of authority asks us questions about us, I'll show them my ID card and I'll tell them that you are my new bride."

"Do you think that such a white lie will get us through, or will it get us in hot water with the law?"

"Nothing is certain in life, except death and paying taxes," he exclaimed with a jovial laugh. "Knowing my cunning abilities and our simple-minded patriots, I bet my last penny that it will work. Besides, what other choices do we have? Do you have a better idea?"

Georgia shrugged her shoulders to indicate that she had no better suggestions to offer and continued walking in silence next to him.

In deep thought about the future, they kept walking on the shoulder of the road. It was early in the morning and Demos' eyes were fixed on their surroundings, looking for signs of human activity. A cigarette butt on the ground, an empty beer bottle in the grassy area by the road, or a paper cup flattened on the pavement would be an indication that the road was frequently used. When the sun was way above the eastern horizon, the surroundings became clear, and Demos noticed that the road was frequently used by motorized vehicles. Fresh tire scuffs were all over the road, especially on tight turns. At some point during their walk, he also noticed a goat watering trough by a well, a sure sign that a goat pen should be close by. When the sun was well above the horizon and its rays became unbearably hot, the desperate travelers reached the top of the inclined segment of the road. From there, it was Georgia who spotted a sprawling village in the valley ahead of them.

"Look," she exclaimed, and poked Fotis on his arm to get his attention. "It's a village down over yonder! Let's get there and find a place to buy food. I'm starving. Who knows, we may be lucky and get a free ride to Vivitsi."

It was late morning and they noticed that smoke was coming out from some of the house chimneys, but from that distance they could not see a soul on the streets.

"My God!" Georgia exclaimed. "Demos, dear! We celebrate the Assumption of the Virgin Mary today. Everyone went to church."

With high hopes to get something to eat, Demos and Georgia increased their walking pace toward the village, holding each other's hands. Thirty minutes later, their path brought them in front of the church, at the entrance of the village, and they heard the voice of the chanter reading invocations from some holy book. They smelled the burning incense coming out of God's house and their spirits were lifted. It was the first time since they left Vivitsi that they heard the call "Lord bless your kingdom" coming from the mouth of an Orthodox priest.

"What do we do now?" Georgia asked her companion. "Should we stand here like beggars or keep walking until we find a place to buy food? I'm really hungry. Certainly, we are not dressed properly to go inside to receive the communion and the offering from the hand of the priest!"

"I say, we park there," Demos responded, and pointed at a wooden bench across the entrance to the church. "When people come out, they will notice us, and we may be able to strike up a conversation with someone who will tell us where to buy food, and in which direction our village is located. You are right! Going inside will create havoc in the congregation, and it will interrupt their mystic communication with our Lord."

The two of them took their places on the bench, one next to the other, and made their appearance as pleasant and as natural as possible. Demos took both of Georgia's hands in his, and she rested her head affectionately on his left shoulder. In this posture, they gave the impression that they were in love, ready to take their vows of marriage. They sat there for a while, until the human commotion inside the church subsided. Children poured out of the church and flooded the area with their presence and their cheerful voices. Men and women came out of the church with smiles on their faces, for they had fulfilled their obligation to their Christian faith. They hurried past Demos and Georgia with their heart full of bliss. Some of them said "good morning" to the strangers, but everyone went on to their destination. When all the faithful were gone, the priest and two elderly men came out and stopped by the entrance to lock up the place. The priest spotted the two young people sitting on the bench, motioned to his companions to follow him, and walked over to meet them. Demos and Georgia got off the bench and, before the priest had the chance to utter a word, took his hand and kissed it to express their respect to the representative of God.

"Good morning, children of God. Where are you coming from? I haven't seen you around here before," the priest said compassionately. "Are you passing by, or are you lost? Can I help you?" He placed his hand on Demos' shoulder. Georgia stood next to Demos like an obedient servant, motionless and speechless. "I am Father Constantine," he added and placed his hand on her head to infuse heavenly peace and deliver his blessing to her.

"Father," Demos declared. "My name is Demos Prasinos and this is Georgia Liakos, my bride-to-be. We are on our way to start our new life in the home of her parents, in Vivitsi. Is there a place in this village to buy something to eat? We haven't eaten for twenty-four hours."

"Of course, my child. Follow me," the priest responded. "Better yet, my blessed *Presvitera* will be able to prepare something for all of us. Come along," he commanded, and led the way toward his house. On their way, people stopped to kiss the hand of the priest and to inquire about his companions. He, in turn, responded with the same expression, "God be with you, my dear Christian," and made the symbol of peace to everyone. Once at Father Constantine's home, he introduced the couple to his Presvitera, (his wife) and offered chairs to them.

"My dear," the priest said to his wife. "These two young people are going home to get married. Meanwhile, they are hungry. Can you prepare something for them?"

"There are fresh eggs, smoked sausages, and plenty of fresh, homemade bread," the kind woman responded and taking his hat from his hands, she placed it on top of a night table in the corner of the room. Returning where Demos and Georgia stood, she pointed at a couch and asked them to sit down and to be at home. Before Georgia took her place next to Demos on the plush couch, the gracious lady reached over to Georgia and spoke with a pleasant voice.

"My, me! You are so young and so beautiful," and lifting Georgia's face upward by putting two of her fingers under her chin, added. "Don't be bashful girl! Be happy! The holy spirit is upon you." Georgia blushed for a second and did not respond to the compliment. Finally, she regrouped herself and said awkwardly, "Thank you, madam. You are gracious."

Demos took the initiative to tell them that they were two of the victims of Paithomazoma and that they were on their way back home. He felt uncomfortable lying to the kind priest and his gracious wife.

As the lady of the house was getting ready to put something together for her guests, a messenger knocked at the door and informed Father Constantine that the sergeant of the police wished to talk to his visitors.

Father Constantine did not take the rude demand kindly. He went to the door and using the power and the authority that God and the king gave him, angrily responded.

"These two people are my guests. If the sergeant wishes to talk to them, he knows where he can find them," and slammed the door in the face of the messenger. Returning to the table, he was still agitated. "I don't approve of this kind of conduct. He is not the German Gestapo, or some secret agent from Russia. This country fought a bloody civil war to be a free nation. The blood of the fallen is still warm." Taking his handkerchief out of his pocket, he wiped the perspiration away from his forehead. An hour later, after all four of them had finished their brunch with candid talking and in a civilized manner, the police sergeant showed up at the door.

"Please, come in, captain," the lady of the house said and opened the door for him. She escorted him to the veranda, where the priest and his guests were sitting, and she asked him if he cared for a cup of coffee or a glass of water.

"No thanks," he responded, and turning toward the priest, added, "I did not mean to be disrespectful, father," and taking the priest's hand in his, he bowed to express his respect to God's representative.

"It's okay, son," the priest said calmly. "All of us have a job to do in this life. Can we offer you a shot of ouzo?"

"Thank you, father. No alcohol while I'm working. Do you object if I talk to these two in private? It's my responsibility to know who passes through my territory."

"It's your prerogative to talk to them in front of me, or in private. God hears what we say and sees what we do."

The police officer changed his mind, accepted only a glass of water, and began his questioning. He wanted to know specific details about their route and the timing of their escape from Slavic Macedonia to Greek Macedonia. He was not interested in hearing anything about life in the concentration camps or in the Greek ghettoes. He said that he knew all about it from interrogations he conducted earlier with other escapees. After an hour asking questions about their escape route, he got off his chair, thanked Father Constantine for allowing him to fulfill his duties as a law enforcement man, and walked toward the door.

"You can stop at the station, on your way out of the village, and get a written permit to travel. You might need it, in case other authorities stop you on your way to your destination."

"What are you planning to do next?" the priest asked Demos. "You are welcome to stay with us for the night. You may consider joining me for our vesper tonight."

"No, father. We must respectfully, decline your offer. We must be on our way," Georgia responded. "There are still several hours of daylight ahead of us. We may be lucky and flag down a good Christian before dark to give us a ride home. If not, we are accustomed to sleeping under the stars."

Despite Father Constantine's urging to stay at his home for the night, Georgia and Demos shook hands with him and his wife, thanked them for their hospitality, and took the street that led toward the expressway to Vivitsi. On their way out of the village, they stopped at the police station and received a written permit to travel through the territory, unmolested by other police authorities. At last, they reached the main road that ran from west to east along Greece's border with Serbia and Bulgaria, all the way from Albania to European Turkey. They chose a wide place, took off their backpacks, and motioned at passing vehicles for a ride. An elderly man driving a Mercedes came along, slowed down momentarily, looked at the standing couple, and then sped away. Another vehicle, with adults and children, quickly sped by without even waving a hand at them. Demos and Georgia glanced at each other, smiled, and repositioned themselves closer together. This way they appeared friendly and harmless. Luck finally smiled at them. A big, roaring, military truck came down the road, slowed down, and made a complete stop in front of them. The driver stuck his head out of the window and yelled with gusto.

"Hey, lovebirds! Which way are you heading?"

"Vivitsi," Demos yelled back at the driver of the noisy vehicle.

"I have twenty recruits sitting under the canvas roof of my truck." The driver pointed at the back of his truck with his free hand. "I think there is enough room for two more. Come over and climb in." Getting off his seat, he opened the rear gate of his truck and let his new passengers climb aboard. "Hey, you guys. Make room for two more," he hollered and returned to his driving wheel.

Demos assisted Georgia to get in first, then he climbed up behind her. She sat next to a young recruit and Demos found space on the bench across from her. The roaring engine became louder again and the truck inched forward, first at a snail's pace. Eventually, it accelerated forward, leaving behind the village of the kind priest and the not-so-friendly police officer. An hour later, the truck slowed down, came to a complete stop, and the driver announced, "Hey, you two lovebirds! We are home. We are at Vivitsi."

Demos and Georgia jumped out of the rear gate of the truck, walked to the front, shook hands with the cheerful driver, thanked him for the free ride, and began walking toward Georgia's old house. The truck, with its human cargo on board, rolled downhill and, seconds later, disappeared into the distance.

CHAPTER FIVE

F otis' life was unpleasant and turbulent, to say the least. Since the time he joined the music group as a vocalist and guitarist, people began to call him "communist" and "an agent of the Russian KGB." He was arrested and interrogated by the secret service of the local police in Piraeus several times. Worst of all, he was verbally harassed by his audience and members of his own band.

His private life was not any better. He attempted to restore his friendship with the woman who gave him her guitar, but this turned out to be a total nightmare. There was a new man in her life, who ordered her to stay away from Fotis. This triangular relationship ended up in a violent fistfight late one night when Fotis was returning home from a brief walk in town. When the police arrived at the scene, they let the other man go free but arrested Fotis. They charged him with disturbing the peace, but in reality he was booked because he was branded as a communist. A prolonged interrogation followed his arrest, then he was locked up for a week. Finally, he came in front of a magistrate, was found guilty as charged, and thrown in prison for six months. Worse yet, his name and his address appeared on the watch list that the authorities kept on suspected "reds." When he was released from jail, he came back home jobless, penniless, and listed as a dangerous enemy of the state. His job was given to another singer and his apartment was considered abandoned while he was serving his jail sentence. His possessions were auctioned off to pay the rent and the place was rented to a chimney builder. Desperate, Fotis took a job as a helping hand in a goatskin rendering place, but the stink was unbearable for him. At this point in his life, at the age of twenty-two, he thought that leaving the area of Athens was the best thing for him to do. His life was in shambles and his future was uncertain as a musician. With the few drachmas he still had in his pocket, he took a train to Salonica and hitchhiked to Vivitsi. He wanted to get away from the social smearing of his name in Athens.

When he arrived at Vivitsi, he found his parents' house completely ransacked. Beds, bedding, kitchen utensils, furniture, and everything that could be removed were gone. Only the four walls, the roof and most of the doors and windows were still in their places. He swept a part of the kitchen floor with his bare hands and made his bed with dry weeds he picked from his late father's uncultivated garden. There Fotis lay down like an abandoned dog and did his best to sleep at night, hungry and thirsty. The next morning, having nothing to do, he decided to take a walk around the neighborhood. Wandering down one of the streets, he noticed that the mink farm, which his late mother used to do business with, was still there. The desperate fellow decided to pay the owner a visit and see if he needed a pair of hands. He had a brief experience rendering goatskins and he thought that he would be qualified to handle the job of rendering mink pelts. He approached the place and saw the owner sitting by his desk bending over the local newspaper.

"Good morning Mr. Aaron," Fotis said to him. "I'm sure you remember Fotula Liakos, don't you, sir?"

"Do I remember Mrs. Liakos? Of course, I remember that fine woman," Mr. Aaron responded. "Who are you that ventures to check my memory?"

"My name is Fotis Liakos, Mr. Aaron. I am her only son."

"Don't tell me you are George's boy!" Aaron responded. "Come in and sit down, son! What happened to your sister? You had a twin sister, as I recall."

"She is lost somewhere behind the Iron Curtain," Fotis said sadly.

"Sorry to hear that, young man, but tell me, what things are you doing nowadays?"

"I am without a job, Mr. Aaron. Things did not go the way I was planning them. My last job, in a goatskin rendering plant in Athens, was terminated a week ago, and I came home for a while."

Aaron's eyes opened wide, hearing that a man with experience rendering skins was standing in front of him. He needed a person with some experience in handling his valuable mink pelts.

"Mr. Aaron, I'm looking for a job, any job. I want to hang around Vivitsi for a while. Do you have anything for me around here?" he said with humility. "I'll do anything, anything to earn a drachma."

"If you are anything like either your mother or your father, I will put you to work tomorrow. You claim that you have experience in rendering skins, and I am looking for someone who is not afraid of making his hands dirty. How soon can you start?"

"Is now early enough?" Fotis responded with a faint smile.

Aaron grinned broadly, folded his newspaper and responded.

"Tomorrow will be just fine. Step in my office for a second. Let us have a sip of ouzo," and called out his daughter. "Leah! Bring the bottle with the ouzo here and get ready to meet a stranger from the distant past."

Fotis walked into a neatly organized room and sat on an empty chair. Aaron put the newspaper aside and repeated his inquiry about Georgia's whereabouts.

"The last time I saw her was when they took me away from the camp, three years ago," Fotis said, and launched into a detailed description of his experience in Slavic Macedonia. A young lady, younger than Fotis, came in the room and interrupted his narration. She held a bottle of ouzo with two empty glasses in one hand and two glasses of water in the other. She placed the bottle and the empty glasses in front of her father, put the glasses with the water in front of the two men, and took an inquisitive look at the stranger.

"Fotis, this is Leah, my only daughter, and this is Fotis Liakos, the son of George Liakos, the teacher," he said to her. "Do you remember Fotis?"

"I heard of him and his sister," Leah responded. "I was only two and a half, when the children were taken away from here. My pleasure meeting you, Mr. Liakos." They shook hands and she left. Mr. Aaron poured some ouzo in the empty glasses, lifted one of them in his hand, and said, "Welcome back home, son. I hope you will leave your unpleasant experiences behind. You are a young man and the productive part of your life lies ahead of you. Make the best out of it." Fotis took the last sip from his glass, got off his chair, thanked Aaron for the drink and the job offer, and walked out of Aaron's office to go home. On his way out, he heard Aaron say. "I'll see you tomorrow at eight o'clock, yeah?"

"yes Sir," Fotis responded and kept walking.

On his way back home, Fotis stopped at a local delicatessen and spent his last drachma buying bread, cheese, olives, and a single, smoked chub. He returned to the deserted house with a positive feeling for a better tomorrow. He took the bread, cheese, and olives out of their paper wrapping, sat cross-legged on the dusty floor, and had his scanty dinner, all alone. The odors of mold and mildew that prevailed around the entire place did not deter him from dreaming of a better tomorrow. Swallowing the last mouthful of his dinner, he thought of his parents and promised himself to pay them a visit soon. His mind sailed far and wide, bringing memories of his brushes with death as a guerrilla fighter. The time he spent on the island was almost forgotten, but his brief glory as a musician was unforgettable. Bending over to pick up the last crumb of bread, he felt his charm dangling from his neck. At that instant, he thought of Georgia. His eyes became wet and a rivulet of warm tears streamed down both of his cheeks. He retrieved the charm from under his shirt and holding it at arm's length, declared with his inaudible voice.

Tell me, blessed thing, where is my sister? The little charm, with its enigma engraved on one side and the face of a saint on the other, did not answer his question; his heart did, though. *Your sister is still alive. Go and find her,* a mysterious voice said. Fotis was shaken to his foundations thinking that this ethereal message could be true. He only wished to have the money and the time to backtrack to where he left her years earlier. "For starters, I should try to find out if she is here somewhere in Greece," he said to his other self. "Public records should be available. If she is dead, her name should appear in the records of some hospital. If she was the victim of the civil war, someone should know about her demise." It never occurred to him that she was in Slavic Macedonia asking the very same questions about him.

Don't be that positive that records were kept for everyone who perished during these turbulent years, his other self said in its silent voice. His conversation with his other self continued without reaching an agreement. Later in the night, nature prevailed and Fotis went to sleep.

A bright sun woke him up the next morning. He got off his temporary straw bed, threw some water on his face with his hands, rearranged his clothes on his sore body, put on his shoes, and went to work, hungry but hopeful for a better tomorrow.

"Good morning Mr. Aaron. I'm ready," he said to the mink farmer in an eager voice.

"Good morning, young Liakos," Aaron responded. "Did you sleep well last night?"

"Yes, just like a well-fed lamb," Fotis responded.

"The first thing we do, this morning, is to clean the cage and feed each one of the animals," Aaron began. "As you can see, the animals are isolated in their cages. They attack each other if they are in the same cage. Here," he said, and handed Fotis a pair of leather gloves and an empty, clean cage. "Put the gloves on, transfer the animal from its soiled cage to a clean one, give it a scoopful of food, and hose down the dirty cage. Be careful. They are swift little devils, and their teeth are razor-sharp. I will take care of the cages which house mothers with babies. They need special handling."

Fotis did not waste a minute. He put his gloves on, reached inside the first cage, grabbed the restless animal by the neck, transferred the squealing little beast to a clean cage, gave it its portion of food, and using the hose with pressurized water, hosed the dirty cage clean. There were 72 minks to be fed and transferred to clean cages. Fotis finished his task at four o'clock in the afternoon, received his pay in cash, and readied himself to return home.

"I hope I'll see you tomorrow, at the same time, yeah!" Aaron said. "We will do some skinning and rendering, all day, tomorrow."

"You bet! I'll be here. I need the job," Fotis responded and walked away to go home. He was hungry and exhausted, working eight hours without a break or food. As he was passing by Aaron's house, which was attached to the place where he had his mink farm, he heard guitar notes coming from the adjacent garden. The notes sounded like they were made by the hands of a beginner, and he surmised that Aaron's daughter was learning to play the instrument. He stopped for a second, stretched his neck over the wall that separated the garden from the public street, and saw Leah sitting under the shade of an apricot tree, with a guitar resting on her lap. A branch of the apricot tree, loaded with yellow fruit, was hanging in front of her and was blocking the view of her face. He could only see her long, black hair hanging over her chest. One of her youthful hands was moving up and down upon the strings of the guitar, and the other was plucking them with a plastic pick. Her movements looked natural but some of her notes were not harmonizing with each other. Fotis stood there for a few seconds, hoping to get her attention, but Leah was absorbed in her practice. Seconds later, he lowered his head below the wall and, unnoticed by Leah, went away.

It was August and the afternoons were hot and muggy in Vivitsi. On his way home, he stopped at a natural spring by the road and washed his hands and his face with fresh, clean water. On second thought, he removed his shirt, washed it with the same spring water, put it back on and leisurely went home, whistling a popular Greek song. At home he ate his smoked chub, the rest of the cheese, and his dried-out bread. Rested and somewhat refreshed, he took a hike to the place where his parents had been interred years earlier. The weeds, which he had uprooted the first time he was there, had grown again, and the wooden cross marking the burial spot was flat on the ground. He spread his arms over the ground where his parents were buried, and with a trembling voice, he said quietly, "I miss you, Mother and Dad," and broke into a continuous heaving and sniffling. Eventually, he rose to his feet, sat on a big boulder across from his parents' grave, and let his mind wander far and wide. He clearly remembered the fun he had with them playing hide-and-seek. He smiled, remembering the instances when his father drew faces of children's heroes on his slate-pad. This evoked the aroma of bacon and eggs his mother made in the morning before he went to school. He thought about the havoc he and his sister made, resenting going to bed at nine o'clock, and an endless cloud of melancholy spread over his being.

"Oh, dear Georgia. Where are you? Are you above, or below grass?" he said between uncontrollable sobbing that disturbed the tranquility of the evening. His focus on where Georgia could be was interrupted by a faint noise coming from the dried-up grass under the foliage in front of him. His mind changed gear and his attention was focused on the direction from where the noise came from. A little land turtle came out, lumbering along, looking for juicy weed sprouts to satisfy its hunger. The silvery moon was over his head and the constellation of the Pleiades was as bright as ever. The North Star was partially covered by a lonely cloud. A symphony of cicadas punctuated the murmuring of the leaves caused by the gentle northerly wind. His shirt was dry now, but the young man felt cold. He stood up, rubbed his arms with the palms of his hands to warm them up, and wondered if his parents heard his voice or any of his thoughts. He stood there for an instant longer, looking at the ground that covered his parents, but he received no vibrations from them. Finally, he took the path back home with a heavy heart and a satisfied conscience. At home, he lay face up on his straw bed and went to sleep, satisfied that he had contacted his parents. The next morning, he woke up early and having nothing else to do, walked outside and inspected the garden, the water-well, and the shed where his late father kept his garden tools. The garden was a jungle, covered with a knee-high assortment of dried weeds. The well that supplied the drinking water for the family was still full of water, but the shed resembled a poor man's barn. Only a hoe with a wooden handle stood in one corner to testify that a garden-loving man was living there. With sadness in his heart looking at the condition of his father's garden, he returned to his sleeping spot. He had recharged his energy and was ready to kill and flay minks.

"You may not have the stomach to look at me when I kill the animals," Aaron told him before they started the day. "If so, look the other way," and taking one of the animals out of its cage, he grabbed it by its rear legs, hung it upside-down, and whacked it with a wooden mallet between its head and neck. The animal quivered several times, then it became immobile. Aaron placed the dead animal on a chopping block and, using a hatchet, severed the head and feet from the rest of the body.

"I'll do the killing and the flaying, until you learn how to do it. Watch," he commanded, and with his razor-sharp knife made a skin-deep incision between the rear legs of the lifeless animal, from one thigh to the other. "It's easy to do this, once you get the drift of it." Grabbing the skin with his fingers, he pulled it away from the flesh, like removing a wet sock from his foot. He turned the skin inside-out, scraped away any fat and flesh that was stuck on it, dusted the pelt with a chemical powder, and hung it to dry. "The final treatment to make the skin soft and flexible has to wait for another day," Aaron mumbled. The rest of the carcass was mixed with scraps of fish, milled to a paste, and dried. Eventually, the mix was pressed to small pellets and became food for the next generation of mink.

Fotis had a problem clubbing his first mink, but eventually he became proficient in killing and flaying the furry animal. At 11:30, Aaron called a break from work and asked Fotis to wash his hands and join him at the table for lunch. Fotis did as Aaron said and when they took their places at the table, Leah appeared with two fat sandwiches and two glasses of wine on a tray. She placed the tray on the table and before she went away, Fotis said, "I couldn't help hearing, yesterday afternoon, that you play guitar."

"Yes, I'm learning," she said modestly and stopped to receive any encouragement he might have to offer her.

"I did it for a living." Fotis picked up his wine glass and took another look at the young lady.

"Then you should show me some of the intricacies. I love playing my guitar," she commented with the finesse of a self-confident young lady. Fotis noticed Leah's positive character and the provocative swing of her hips when she went away.

"She is the only one I have," Aaron said sadly. "My wife died of complications during Leah's delivery. What about you, Fotis? Tell me something about your life experience. Did you ever get married?"

"I'm so sorry to hear that you lost your wife so early in life," and tried to assemble the words to answer Aaron's questions. He was honest telling him things about his life, but not everything. He briefed him about the romance he had with the woman who gave him the guitar and narrated the legal mess he got in with the girl's new boyfriend.

"What you were doing on an island? You said that you were born here, in Vivitsi."

"Mr. Aaron, it's a long story," Fotis responded. "I'll need more than a lunch break to explain everything. Leave it for some other time. To your health, sir," he added and lifted his wineglass eye-high.

Aaron did likewise with his wineglass and after they had a sip from the red liquid, they attacked their sandwiches in silence. Aaron suspected some sort of foul play in the young lad's past, and Fotis noticed the leery glances he was getting from the other man. Neither of them pursued the issue any further and the subject was dropped completely for now. The rest of the day, they killed and flayed more minks and preserved their little pelts. At the end of the day, Aaron compensated Fotis for his work and told him that he was expecting to see him back at eight o'clock the next morning.

"Trust me, sir. I'll be right here tomorrow morning, unless thunder comes down from heaven and strikes me on the head."

On his way home, Fotis thought through the events of the day. He relived the brutal handling of the cute little animals all day long. Yet, that experience did not bother his conscience. He had seen dead and dying animals before. He even saw a field covered with bodies of men, some of them calling for help and others for mercy. Clubbing a mink was nothing, compared to the carnage he caused with his bazookas! The thought that Aaron would force him to reveal his life story from the beginning numbed him. The fear that Aaron might fire him, after hearing he was a guerrilla fighter, painted pictures of desperate living in his immediate future. "God knows, if I could find another job in Vivitsi," he mumbled to himself. He felt a strange sensation when he exchanged a few words with cute Leah, but he paid no attention to it. He had more pressing issues to think about.

The hell with everything, he said to his other self. *Someone said that "the past is history and the future is mystery. I can only live the now."* On his way home, he stopped at the local store and bought some sweets and a broom. As soon as he arrived home, he decided to clean the room with the fireplace. He threw away things that looters left behind, swept a portion of the floor next to the fireplace, unhinged one of the interior doors, and laid it flat next to the fireplace. He needed something to keep his back off the bare floor at night. He sat cross-legged at his temporary bed, opened the package with his sweets, and devoured some of his donuts.

"Hey, stranger. Who are you?" Fotis heard a woman's voice at his threshold. Turning around, he saw an elderly woman standing next to the partially opened door. "I'm living next door and I couldn't resist the temptation to know my new neighbor."

Fotis gulped down the food he had in his mouth and said the first thing that came to his mind.

"Hi, I'm a distant relative of Mr. Liakos, the owner of this house. Did you know him?"

"No, my husband and I came to the village five years ago. I understand the owners and their children disappeared during the civil war. God bless them!"

"Yes, and that's the reason I'm here. Do you know anything about their children?" Fotis asked.

"No, I don't. They were taken away, and no one heard anything about them since that time. Son, you need a blanket, you cannot be comfortable on a solid surface like that and without a cover, you will catch a cold! You will get pneumonia, son. Let me get you something to cover yourself at night."

Turning around, she disappeared for a couple of minutes. When she came back, she brought him a warm blanket woven to the shape of an oversized coat.

"This is the sleeping coat my father-in-law brought here from Hungary with his flock of sheep. He was a Vlach (a sheep herder). The thing is made with sheep's wool and is very warm and comfortable. It's a bit worn out, but it can still be used. You can have it."

Fotis thanked the good neighbor for the blanket and after a few minutes of stereotypical chatting between an old lady and a young man, the neighbor returned home. Fotis sat around for a little longer and when darkness spread all over the land, he wrapped himself in the blanket and went to sleep early. It was dark outside and doing work in the garden was impossible. Besides, he felt fatigued and worn out from clubbing and skinning minks all day long. The blanket did the trick. He woke up in the morning, rested and full of energy to tackle the work Aaron had for him.

"Let's finish the killing and flaying, and clean up the place," Aaron said. "It's Sabbath tomorrow and you will be here all by yourself. Leah and I will attend the synagogue most of the day."

Fotis was done with the clubbing, flaying, scraping, and dusting the skins of the last six animals. At ten minutes before noon, Aaron was also done with his clerical work.

"Clean up, and come to the table," Aaron called. "Leah is coming with our lunch." Fotis washed his hands with soap and water, dried them with the edge of his shirt, and sat at a chair by the table. Aaron joined him a minute later, sat in his chair, and said in a happy voice, "God is with us today! Look at this bright sun! It is warming up the earth to produce food for both the sinners and the saints."

"Yes. We are blessed to be alive to reap the fruit of God's blessing," Fotis responded gracefully.

"Tell me, young man, whatever your conscience permits you to tell me, about your life experience, and I will tell you mine," Aaron said. "I'm always interested in knowing as much as I can about my employees."

Fotis sat back in his chair to become comfortable, rubbed his hands one against the other, and began telling Aaron a brief synopsis of his life story.

"I was born in this village twenty-two years ago, the twin child of George and Fotula Liakos. My parents were executed by the communists, when my sister Georgia and I were four years old. I barely remember them. As soon as my parents were gone, the lady that was living alone next door took charge of us. We lived with her until the age of fifteen, and then we became the victims of Paithomazoma. I assume you know all about this chapter of Greek history, don't you, Mr. Aaron?"

His listener nodded, but he kept mute.

"My sister and I, along with another forty-six boys and girls from this village, were taken to a concentration camp in Slavic Macedonia for the next three years, until I was taken away from my group. That was the last time I saw my sister. I was sent to the Peloponnese and was forced to join a band of freedom fighters there. When the civil war came to its end, I was accused of being a communist and was incarcerated on an island close to Turkey. Finally, I was set free, returned home, got in hot water with the law over a woman, and when that misfortune was over, I decided to return home."

"Wow, boy! You went through the mill, so early in your life," Aaron responded with admiration for Fotis' resilience to survive his ordeals. "Do you plan to settle here, in Vivitsi?"

"It all depends on my luck in finding my sister. My immediate plan is to find the means to travel. I want to trace our steps to our camp in Slavic Macedonia and find out what happened to my sister. I cannot live with the thought that she is alive and in desperate need for help. If she is dead, I want to know that too."

"Hello, here you are," Leah chirped, popping out from behind a rose bush covered with red blossoms. She held a package with lunch for her father and Fotis in her hands, and her guitar was strapped over her shoulders. She deposited the food in front of Aaron and, turning her attention to Fotis, said in a sweet and playful voice, "I brought my guitar today. After you have your lunch, I would like to hear you playing a few notes for me. Do you mind doing that for a friend?"

Fotis took a bite from his sandwich, picked up the musical instrument, plucked some notes with his fingers and adjusted the tension on the strings. He took another big bite from his food and began to play a local tune. After he swallowed the food in his mouth, he took a deep breath and started to sing, while his fingers were dancing frantically over the strings of the instrument. Leah's eyes became twice as big and Aaron noticed the change in his daughter's expression. After a couple minutes of singing and playing the guitar, Fotis stopped to take another bite from his sandwich. The ecstatic Leah leaped over, grabbed him in her embrace, and exclaimed, "I love it, I love it!"

Aaron noticed his daughter's reaction. Fotis played several tunes and sang along when his mouth was not full. Then he returned to work feeling exuberant. Aaron noticed those changes in his facial expression, too.

Aaron felt uncomfortable observing the magnetism between his daughter and Fotis. His only child could find a better man than a drifter with a questionable reputation. The young man Aaron had in mind for Leah was a medical graduate, the son of a prominent lawyer he met at the synagogue. For the rest of the afternoon, he devised a plan to extinguish the sparks of mutual interest between Leah and Fotis. Seeing his daughter throwing herself in the arms of Fotis with uncontrolled passion meant disaster for her. Fotis had to go, and go away from Vivitsi, soon, but Aaron did not have the stomach to fire him, just like that. Besides, dismissing him did not guarantee that he would stay away from Leah.

Two months went by and Fotis kept working as Aaron's employee earning minimum wages. His relations with young Leah had not changed, but his interest in her intensified. He began to feel an unexplained desire to lay his eyes on her as often as possible. Aaron noticed Leah's magnetic effect on his employee and activated his plan to send Fotis away. The young lad did not detect any changes in Aaron's conduct and thought that everything was normal at work. Not so with Aaron. The clever father came up with a scheme to permanently get rid of Fotis from his daughter's life. At the end of one month working at the mink farm, Aaron paid Fotis for his daily labor, as usual, and asked him to sit down and hear him.

"You said that you wanted to find your sister," Aaron said to the young Liakos. "Well, here is what I came up with that may help you find her. I met a man who works for the International Red Cross. His job is to find displaced people throughout free Europe and guide them back to their families. He is doing a marvelous job with Jewish people scattered all over Europe. If you are interested, I'll talk to him about you and your quest to find your sister. As faith has it, he is in town."

"God, yes! This will be the rare opportunity I'm looking for. How soon will you be able to see him?"

"Just for you, my son, I'll walk over to his house after work. Better yet, you can come with me to meet the gentleman. He is an important person to know, anyway."

"You know it, Mr. Aaron! I have nothing more pressing to do than finding my sister. Do you think he can help me locate her?"

"Well, we are to find out after work. Why don't you clean up and come with me to his house? It will be supper time when we will finish here, and he should be home for dinner."

Aaron and Fotis cleaned the place, fed the remaining mink, washed their hands with soap and water, made themselves as presentable as possible, and took the street that led to the house of the Red Cross man. They walked in silence with two different objectives in their mind. Aaron was hoping to protect the future of his daughter from getting involved with a guy that was not for her. Fotis was expecting that a strange person would help him locate his sister. When they arrived at their destination, Aaron pressed the doorbell button. Seconds later, a man came to the door and invited them in. All three sat on the veranda and Aaron, with his customary politeness, introduced Fotis to his friend.

"Mr. Angelis, this is Fotis, my employee." He explained their reason for visiting him at that inappropriate hour.

"This young man has a sister, who is lost somewhere in Slavic Macedonia. He is trying to find her and I thought you may be able to help him in his quest."

Mr. Angelis was pleased to see his friend again. Turning his attention to Fotis, he asked him a host of specific questions about Georgia's past, her personal experience at the camp, and her personal appearance.

"My agents investigated several camps in Albania, Serbia, Bulgaria, Czechoslovakia, and Rumania, and they filed reports on their findings. If you wish, you can go through them. I can even hire you as an agent and have you travel with another guy to designated places. It will be difficult justifying the extra expenses for an additional person on my staff, but for Mr. Aaron, it can be done. Are you willing to travel under the supervision of another investigator? You will be required to visit some of God's forsaken places in strange countries and interview people in which you may not speak their language."

"Mr. Angelis. Pardon me for being naïve. How can I ask questions to a person that he or she does not understand my language, and for the same reason, how could anyone understand answers worded in a language they don't know?"

"This guy is a bright young man," Angelis said to Aaron. "I like him. I'll put him to work tomorrow. I'm leaving for Albania tomorrow morning,"

He turned to Fotis. "You and I will be traveling tomorrow morning. Be here at eight in the morning. Can you do it?"

"Yes, sir! I'll be here at 8 a.m. tomorrow."

Aaron and Fotis shook hands with Mr. Angelis and left his house with loads of thoughts in their minds. Aaron had hindered an unwanted relationship between his daughter and a man of low social status and Fotis had secured an opportunity to search for his lost sister. Halfway to town, they stopped at a corner where two streets intersected. Aaron placed his hand on Fotis' shoulder and wished him good luck in his search for his sister. Fotis embraced the other man as if he were his father and thanked him for the things he had done for him.

"I will never forget you and your lovely Leah for the rest of my life," he declared. Finally, the two men walked in opposite directions, not to lay eyes on each other again.

Fotis couldn't sleep in his home-made, oversized sleeping coat. His mind was sailing from Angelis' files to the adventure of traveling in foreign lands looking for his sister. On one hand, he felt the thrill of discovering where Georgia was, hugging her like a big brother and bringing her back home. On the other hand, he felt the chilling thought that he would find nothing in Mr. Angelis' files. While these contradictory thoughts went in and out of his mind, his eyes were fixed at the darkness around him. He wondered if things would ever change for the better. It was well past midnight when his mind shut off and his eyes closed. He finally fell asleep.

At six in the morning, Fotis was up. He folded the blanket the neighbor gave him and placed it on top of a broken table. He washed his hands with fresh water, put on his shoes, combed his hair, and walked out of the ransacked house straight to where he was to meet Mr. Angelis. Little did he know that Georgia and Demos were up, too. They were only 100 miles away from where he was, walking toward the church in another village to culminate their odyssey of returning home.

Fotis and Mr. Angelis met at eight o'clock at their designated place. The sun appeared brighter today and the cloudless sky was a bright blue, endless space. The hilly landscape was teeming with life in all directions and the towering trees looked twice as big in their majestic, green, summer uniforms. Fotis greeted Mr. Angelis good morning and after a reciprocal wish from Mr. Angelis, they boarded a Red Cross Mercedes and took the road toward Albania. They spoke sparingly to each other. Several hours later, they pulled over in front of a gas station, filled the gas tank, and met Fotis' future co-worker.

"This is Vasilis," Mr. Angelis said and pointed at the other man. "And this is Fotis," he added and pointed at Fotis. Vasilis and Fotis shook hands and sat in the back seat of the car while Angelis walked over to the restroom. They started a casual conversation. A few minutes later, Mr. Angelis returned, sat behind the driving wheel, started the engine, and drove away without participating in the conversation of his subordinate workers. His attention was focused on his driving, for the road was in bad shape. There were plenty of potholes and protruding rocks that he had to circumvent. Fotis and Vasilis talked about their places of birth, their families, their experiences during the civil war, and their plans for their future. At other times, they dozed on the back seat of the speeding vehicle. Later in the afternoon, Mr. Angelis pulled over, only a few yards from the border of Albania with Greece.

"We will spend the evening as guests in a private home tonight. Tomorrow morning, we will continue our trip toward one of our centers in Albanian territory. Pending unforeseen problems with either our car or the guards at the border, we will be there in the late morning." He turned to Fotis.

"You will have at your disposal all the documents we have on file. I will give you two days to look through them. Vasilis will help you in your research. After that, you guys will have your regular assignments. I expect a clear and legible report, daily, from each one of you," and he pulled over at a narrow street in the village.

"Let's get in our friends' house, eat whatever they have available, and rest until tomorrow morning. The man and the lady are newly wedded and for that reason, they do not have much to offer. Eat what they will place in front of you and be graceful to the young lady," he cautioned them.

The hostess, a country girl not more than twenty-three years old, went out of her way to show hospitality to her husband's guests. She put an assortment of edible things on the table for them. She had thin slices of preserved meats, goat cheese, hard-boiled eggs, pickled mushrooms, and plenty of freshly sliced homemade bread. Her husband brought a carafe of wine to the table. Their evening hours were dominated by trivial discussions between the master of the house and Mr. Angelis. Vasilis and Fotis sat quietly in their chairs. While the young lady was active doing her household chores, Fotis and Vasilis exchanged glances to convey unspoken messages to each other. At some early hour in the evening, all of them withdrew to separate bedrooms and went to sleep. The next morning, after savoring cookies and coffee, the threesome thanked the man and his wife for their hospitality, entered the Mercedes, and drove away in silence. At the check point, before they entered Albanian territory, Mr. Angelis stopped the vehicle, presented documents to the officer at the entrance and spent several minutes explaining their mission. Finally, they were permitted to enter Albanian soil. After an hour of more driving on bumpy dirt roads, the vehicle entered a military camp. Mr. Angelis stopped the car in front of a brick building with large glass-paneled windows.

"Okay, boys. Here we are. Go to work and remember that the cafeteria is on ground level. Below it, you will find the library with our archives. Offices are on the top floor. If you need me, you will find me in room 210. Good luck."

Fotis and Vasilis walked downstairs and found the section of the library that housed the written reports that were filed by investigators of the International Red Cross. Most of them were scribbled in the Slavic version of the Greek language. Fotis had a difficult time reading and understanding their contents. He and Vasilis spent several hours thumbing through bulging manila folders, looking for any mention of the name of Fotis' sister. At 6:30, disappointed and discouraged from the results of their search, they walked away and went to the cafeteria for dinner. Several young men and women congregated around a long table. They had eaten their dinner and were socializing, exchanging jokes and laughing.

"Hey, Vasilis! Who's the stud who keeps you company tonight?" a plump blond girl said in broken Greek. The entire group broke into a roaring laugh and everyone clapped his hands at the raw sense of the girl's humor. Fotis was accustomed to receiving both complimentary and offensive comments, and he did not react to her rude comment.

"Friends, this fine gentleman is Fotis, our new field investigator," Vasilis said. Walking around the table with Fotis next to him, he introduced the new member to his co-workers. Fotis was conservative in his manners and said little to them. He kept his tongue behind his clenched teeth to avoid misunderstandings regarding the attitude of their newcomer. After the brief introduction, Vasilis and Fotis walked over to the food display counter, picked up a sandwich and slices of melon, and returned to the gathering table.

"There is a band visiting the base tonight," one of the women said to Vasilis. "Most of the performers are Gypsies, but they sing songs in Greek. Several of us are going to see them. You and our new friend are welcome to come along. I hear that they are good instrumentalists." Vasilis looked at Fotis, and Fotis nodded affirmatively that he would like to go with them.

It was eight o'clock when the two newcomers finished their dinner and the rest of them exhausted their social gossiping. Six of them, including Vasilis and Fotis, walked down a dark street to an outdoor nightclub. They took their seats in the front row under the starry sky and prepared for the evening entertainment. Minutes later, the musicians appeared on stage and received a thundering round of applause that disturbed the tranquility of the evening. A Greek-speaking young woman sang verses of passion accompanied by a clarinet, guitar, and violin. Fotis thought the clarinet harmonized nicely with the violin and the vocalist, but the guitarist needed help. The young lad was frequently offbeat, but in general the group was playing good music. Their musical performance was pleasant to the ears and stimulated the desire to dance.

An hour later, the musicians took a break. They moved behind the curtain to rest their aching fingers, smoke a cigarette, and savor water and refreshments. Fotis couldn't resist the temptation of going behind stage to meet the performers. Musicians were people he worked with until his luck turned from bad to worse in Athens. He walked into the noisy crowd, introduced himself as a guitarist and vocalist, and spent a few seconds talking to the director of the group.

"Would you like to get on stage and show us what you can do with a guitar?" the director asked.

"I'd be delighted to play something for you, but I don't have my guitar with me," he responded.

"We normally have two guitar players in the group, but one of them overindulged himself with ouzo last night," the director chuckled. "His guitar is somewhere in the traveling baggage. I'll have someone find it."

"We have another ten minutes before returning to stage," another man said. "He can use my guitar to show us his talents. I'll go and get it" and disappeared behind the drawn curtains. Seconds later, he returned with a guitar in his hands. "Show us how good you are and sing a tune, so we can hear your voice," the band leader said. Fotis took the instrument from its owner, plucked its strings with his nails, and opened his mouth. The jaws of everyone fell to the floor. They had never heard anything so melodious before.

"My God, kid! You have the hands of Segovia and the voice of Enrico Caruso. You belong with us," the band leader exclaimed. "You are wasting your talent doing whatever you are doing for a living."

Time was up, the curtains were drawn open, and the musicians returned to the stage for the last leg of their performance. They took their places in front of their microphones and tuned their instruments to harmonize with one another. Fotis returned to his seat and sat down, quietly. The buzzing noise of people chatting during the intermission quieted down and the band leader took the microphone in his hands and asked for attention.

"Ladies and gentlemen! I want to start the second part of our program with a short anecdote. Back in the distant past, there was a famous guitarist by the name of Arion the Guitarist living somewhere in ancient Greece. During one of his travels to Sicily, his ship was commandeered by pirates. The ruthless buccaneers threw everyone in the Mediterranean Sea and sailed away with the vessel and their spoils. Poor Arion did not know how to swim, but Poseidon, the sea god, sent a dolphin to save him. Arion mounted the dolphin and safely returned to Greece. Centuries later, I found

Arion right here." He pointed at Fotis. "Give Arion a round of applause and ask him to play the guitar for us." He started to clap his hands. The crowd did likewise, and humble Fotis stood up and walked on stage. He took the waiting guitar in his hands and made the instrument sing a love song with him. Halfway into his solo, the rest of the band joined him with their instruments, the vocalist lowered her voice to harmonize with his, and the pandemonium of having fun started. The crowd rose to their feet and demanded more and more from Arion the Guitarist. It was one o'clock in the morning when the dancing and throwing money at Arion came to an end. Fotis, now Arion the Guitarist, went back to the Red Cross sleeping quarters with a fat wad of money in his pocket and an exuberant feeling that not everything was lost. He was pleasantly worn out from singing and playing guitar and abundantly happy. He spent the next day searching the files for his sister and receiving congratulatory comments from his co-workers and Mr. Angelis.

In general, there was a plethora of information about Paithomazoma, but nothing was mentioned about the children from Vivitsi. Several field investigators identified more than sixty camps scattered throughout Bulgaria, Rumania, Hungary, Czechoslovakia, and Yugoslavia. According to the best estimates, these camps sheltered at least forty-five thousand boys and girls during the Greek civil war of the 1940s. In Bulgaria, for example, the records showed that 18,500 abducted Greek children were living in eighteen camps at one time. At the end of the day, Fotis walked out of the record room, exhausted and disheartened. He began to think that finding his sister was just a hope, not a real expectation. He skipped dinner and walked around the grounds without any purpose or direction. He just walked to be alone, clear up his mind, absorb the information he discovered in the records, and map the direction for his next move.

It was Saturday evening, and people could be seen sitting in front of their homes or going somewhere for their weekend.

"Hey, Arion," Fotis heard a familiar voice coming from across the street. Fotis stopped to see who was calling him and saw the band leader walking toward him from the other direction.

"Good evening, friend," Fotis responded.

"Are you going somewhere, or just taking a walk to see the town?" the other man asked. "I mean, can I join you?"

"I have nothing in mind. I just took an aimless walk. Please come along. I need company."

"There is a neighborhood taverna around the corner," the band leader said. "The guy makes fantastic lamb chops and serves the best local ouzo. It's a quiet place. Would you like to join me for a few of his masterpieces?"

"It sounds like a splendid idea," Fotis responded, and took his place next to the band leader. They walked into what seemed to be the large garden of a private home. Tables placed under a dense canopy of grapevines, were covered with white linen. Clusters of red grapes were hanging over their heads and the aroma of sizzling lamb invaded Fotis' nostrils. The two men walked around, selected a table, and sat down. As soon as they took their places, the proprietor appeared, greeted them politely, and asked them to place their orders.

"Twelve chops and a carafe of your special ouzo," the band leader commanded. The proprietor acknowledged the order and walked away. At that moment, the band leader turned his attention to Fotis.

"Fotis, you are a troubled young man. I can see it in your face, and I can hear it in the songs you sing. I will not ask you to tell me the story of your life, nor the place of your birth. That part of you is private. What I'm going to ask you is your plans for your future. You are an outstanding guitarist and a fantastic singer! You can become famous joining my band, man! We will travel all over the Balkans and some of the eastern European countries. With the addition of a talent like you, the group will go places. What I'm telling you is that all of us will make money and you will become famous at the same time. Here is my proposal. You take 20 percent of the earnings and the rest of us will share the remaining money. If you accept my proposal, you must forget the name Fotis and your past. You will be known as Arian, not Arion, the famous mythical Guitarist. From now on, we will call you Arian the Gypsy young lad." His proposal was interrupted by the arrival of the owner, who showed up with a flask of ouzo and two empty glasses. He poured some of the clear liquid in the glasses, placed the flask on the table, and hurried back to his kitchen.

Fotis picked up the glass of ouzo in his hand, took a sip, returned it to the tray, and exhaled with satisfaction."

"Boss, you are offering a deal, hard to turn it down. Let me think about it for a day or two. To tell you the God's truth, I'm here looking for my lost sister," he said and briefed the other man about his experience as one of the victims of the Paithomazoma during the civil war.

"I heard things about the event in my travels, but I never paid attention to it," the other man responded and allowed Fotis to go on with his life as an expatriated man. Moments later, a platter of sizzling lamb chops arrived. The band leader picked up one, took a healthy bite, and declared with gusto, "Mmm, they are delicious, dig in!" Fotis interrupted his narration of camp life and helped himself to the pile of steaming chops.

"With the money you will be making, you can hire a professional investigator to find your sister. Do you have any recent pictures of her?"

"No, I don't. The only memento of her is this." Reaching under his shirt, he retrieved his charm and showed it to the other man. "The last time I saw her, she wore one identical to this one. Our grandfather gave one to me and one to her when we were four years old. I still have mine. I hope she kept hers. Grandpa said that these charms are blessed by the patriarch, and they possess supernatural powers."

"That thing might be the key for an experienced investigator to track her down. For now, eat some of the chops before they get cold."

The two men chatted the rest of the early evening, until all the chops and the ouzo disappeared. Fotis' hopes for a better tomorrow became rejuvenated and the band leader was convinced that Fotis was sold on joining his group. Finally, their cordial get-together came to its end. The band leader paid the bill.

"Arian, it was a pleasure getting to know you better. I hope that we will repeat this get-together soon. Remember, the band needs you and you need us."

"Let me think about your proposal a little longer. Superficially, though, the deal sounds good to me, but give me a day to think it over. Let's meet here on Monday evening, at the same hour. Is it okay with you?" A few minutes later, Fotis followed the other man from under the cozy canopy of the grapevines,and they left the taverna together. Once on the street, the two men wished good night to each other and disappeared into the poorly lit streets of the town. Fotis went directly to his sleeping quarters, took off his shoes and his clothes, and cuddled under the blanket in his bed, wearing only his underwear. He stayed awake for a while, for he wanted to rehash the proposal the other man offered him. To no avail, though, he couldn't concentrate. The ouzo in his bloodstream interfered with his reasoning and in a minute or two, he sailed to dreamland.

Fotis woke up the next day at 8:30. He was thirsty and felt his head pounding. He dragged himself to the restroom, allowed the contents of his bladder to flow freely, washed his face with fresh water, got dressed, put his shoes on, and went to the cafeteria for a badly needed cup of black coffee. Several of his co-workers were still around, but Fotis was not in the mood for socializing with any of them. His sluggish mind was still under the control of the ouzo he drank the night before. He transferred his coffee to a disposable cup and returned to his room. He sat there in perfect quietness, closed his itching eyes, and sipped his bitter coffee to its last drop. Then he dozed on his chair for a while longer. When he returned to his normal self, it was eleven o'clock in the morning. He opened his eyes and noticed that Vasilis was sitting on a chair at the opposite corner of the room.

"You slept like Rip Van Winkle," Vasilis declared. "What's going on with you, partner? We should be out investigating Paithomazoma, not nursing headaches caused by having one-too-many shots of ouzo."

"Sorry, partner, for letting you down. I'm afraid that the job of an investigator is not for me. Before the end of the day, I'll see Mr.

Angelis, and I'll submit my resignation. I'm going back to playing my guitar and singing my Greek songs."

Vasilis was surprised to hear that his partner had changed his mind so abruptly. He thought that a Gypsy spell was cast on him. He wanted to tell Fotis that Gypsies are manipulative, cunning, and deceitful people, but he kept his conviction to himself.

"If that's what you decided to do, more power to you, man! I wish you luck," Vasilis said, and rose from his chair to leave. "Will the musical group stay around here, or are you guys going out of town?"

"I'll be damned if I know where we are going. The group leader makes these decisions. I will be there to play the guitar, sing, and collect money."

"Anyway, good luck to you, friend," Vasilis repeated, and walked out of Fotis' room and out of his life, forever. Fotis spent the rest of the day in seclusion. He wanted to go through the details of the proposal the band leader gave him and put his thoughts together. In the late afternoon, he walked into Mr. Angelis' office and out of the blue sky, he told him that he was leaving the Red Cross organization.

"That will be just fine," the other man said. "May I ask why you changed your mind, just like that, and where you are going?"

"I am disappointed that I found nothing about my sister in your files, and I realize that I'm not cut out to be an investigator. I will join the band that I met two days earlier. I'll be their leading guitarist and vocalist."

"Congratulations, young man! I always admire aggressive people who recognize their limitations and take chances in things they believe they can be successful with. 'Nothing ventured, nothing gained,' someone said. Whatever you decide to do, do your very best," he added and shook Fotis' hand with enthusiasm.

Fotis returned to his sleeping quarters, stuffed his money in his pocket, and walked to the business district of the town. He spent most of his money buying a pair of dark shoes, several pairs of socks, two white shirts, a yellow sweater, a pair of blue jeans, and an inexpensive suitcase which he stuffed with the things he purchased. Monday evening came around, and he was standing outside the outdoor eatery waiting for the band leader to show up.

"Oh, here you are," Fotis heard the familiar voice of the band leader coming from behind him. "Let's get in and finish the conversation we started two days earlier." The two men walked under the grapevine canopy, found an empty table, and sat facing each other.

"Ouzo and fried octopus," the leader hollered at the taverna keeper. "Is the octopus fresh?"

"Fresh from the deep, boss," the keeper responded and disappeared in his kitchen. Minutes later, he came back with a platter of clean, raw octopus.

"Smell it, boss," he demanded. "It came out of the water twenty minutes earlier."

"Okay, it's fresh, I believe you. Where is the ouzo? I am thirsty."

"Coming up," the keeper declared and returned to his cooking area, balancing the platter with the raw octopus on his left hand above his head.

"Arian, you never asked me about my name. You always call me boss. Boss is my title, not my name. My true Gypsy name is Manzoor, but everyone around here, calls me Mazurkas. Do you mind calling me Mazurkas?" He grinned. "Now to the business. Have you decided, or are you still thinking about being a part of our success story? If the deal I offer you is not satisfactory, let's talk about it. I need you, man, and you need me! We are leaving tomorrow for Slavic Macedonia. We plan to perform in several towns there, and these half-Greeks will go out of their minds hearing you singing their traditional songs. Come with me for at least a month," Mazurkas implored.

"No need for all this begging," Fotis interrupted. "My suitcase is packed. I'm ready to hit the road with you. Your offer is acceptable for now. When are we leaving?"

"We have a wedding to do tomorrow in a small village, sixty kilometers from here. The gathering starts at six o'clock in the evening and it will go on until midnight. We will leave from here tomorrow at noon. We will pick you up at the square at one o'clock. Is that okay with you?" Mazurkas lifted his glass of ouzo and declared. "To your health, partner," and clinked his glass with Fotis' drink.

"To your health, Mr. Mazurkas!" Fotis brought his glass to his lips, but he did not drink a drop of its contents. The smell of ouzo made him quiver. He enjoyed the fried octopus, drank only water, and felt secure and comfortable in the company of the Gypsy. Mazurkas was much older than Fotis and projected a fatherly image on the mind of the newcomer. Later, in the early evening, the Gypsy suggested that they should go to sleep, get a good night's rest, and be prepared for the hard ride to the place where they were to play music. Fotis offered to pay for the food and the ouzo, but the insistence of the other guy to pay for dinner prevailed.

CHAPTER SIX

otis, now Arian the Guitarist, boarded a worn-out minibus with the rest of the musicians and started a new life. He sat next to the only woman in the group (another vocalist) and for the first time noticed that she was a very attractive young lady. He initiated a casual conversation with her, for he wanted to be polite and civil. He talked about problems a musical performer faces on stage, and she responded with her own experiences on the subject. When their conversation drifted to their upbringing, she said that she was an unwanted child of a teen-age girl.

"I was raised by my grandparents living on one of the islands in the Ionian Sea. I am a self-starter, with ambitions to be recognized as a singer. My name is Voula."

During the following months, as a musical performer, Fotis enjoyed the fame he received on-stage and off-stage. Secretly, he enjoyed the company of his co-worker, Voula the vocalist. Looking closely at her face during their singing, he felt his heart pumping faster and he thought that his new guitar sounded more melodious than the old one. His voice became one with hers, and the roaring of the audience grew overwhelmingly louder as the weeks went on.

Off-stage, he kept lamenting the loss of his sister. During the day, when the band had no commitment to play music, he visited Greek communities in the towns they played in at night and inquired about Georgia. The crafty Mazurkas, fearing that Fotis would quit the band to follow leads for his sister, did everything within his power to prevent it. He dug out old contacts he had with local communists of the Tito era and found a retired KGB agent who was willing to look for the missing Georgia. Mazurkas introduced him to Fotis.

Fotis met the agent and had an extensive and friendly chat with him. The investigator said that his name was Vladimir Moraska, a Russian. To Fotis' surprise, the man spoke Greek fluently, which disagreed with his claim that he was born and raised in Stalingrad. He spoke perfect Greek with all its idioms and slang expressions. Arian did not care about Vlad's place of birth. He only wanted to find his sister. At the end of their meeting, the old sleuth received a down payment from Arian. Like a tracking hound, he began to snoop around for a woman whose appearance was unknown, who might not even be alive. The only thing he had to go by was her age, her full first and last name, that she spoke Greek, a hunch of what she was supposed to look like nowadays, and an accurate description of an insignificant charm she used to wear around her neck.

Vladimir, the old KGB agent, traveled extensively around Slavic Macedonia, targeting the Greek communities. He concentrated his search in Greek ghettoes that were close to where concentration camps used to be. As his luck had it and his snooping instinct guided him, he came upon a woman cleaning the public toilets in the main square in a town close to a thriving Greek ghetto settlement.

"Yeah, I remember a young girl stopping here some time ago. She told me that she was Greek, and her name was Georgia. It was raining outside, and her worn-out blanket around her shoulders was muddy and wet. The pitiful thing was soaking wet to her armpits, and she confessed that she was one of the girls from the camp. She begged me for shelter in my storage room until she was dry, for she had no other place to go. I felt sorry for her and allowed her to use the space for a few hours to warm up. I gave her an old towel to dry her hair and shared my sandwich with her. Later, she thanked me for everything and left."

"Anything else? Anything that struck your fancy about her?" the sleuth asked.

"Yes, one more thing. When she was trying to wipe the rain away from her hair with my towel, I noticed a glittering pendant hanging around her neck. The thought of asking her for it crossed my mind and I inquired about it. I remember she told me that her grandfather gave it to her when she was a baby and that information extinguished my desire to ask her for it. Shame on me."

At the end of the first month, Vlad reported back to Arian and told him that the only thing he had discovered so far was a woman who claimed she met a young girl by the name of Georgia.

"It's interesting to notice that the mysterious Georgia had a shining pendant hanging around her neck," Vlad said.

"She is the one!" Arian bellowed. "Find her, Vlad," and handed him some more money.

The experienced old detective did not react to the information as emotionally as Arian did. He walked away with the thought that there are hundreds of Greek women with the name Georgia, many wearing some sort of glittering ornament around their necks. He scratched the top of his bald head and reached into the bank of his experience as a detective to plan his next search. Something inside him was telling him that he missed a crucial piece of information from the cleaning lady. Days later, when he was on his way to his hotel, he went back and met the woman one more time. He found her eating a sandwich. She was glad to see him again.

"Do you mind talking about that woman again?" he asked politely. "Is there anything else you can tell me, anything that may be insignificant to you?"

"Hmm … Let me think. She was pretty, black hair, eyes like chestnuts, a noble way of moving her body, and a distinguishing mannerism, as if she were a rich woman. The only other woman

I saw walking like her was a well-dressed lady coming out of the kafenio in the Greek neighborhood about a month ago. She was escorted by a young lad, but they were too far for me to register specific characteristics on their faces. I cannot tell you if they had any birth marks, or scars, on their faces, but the girl caught my fancy. Don't ask me why."

Vlad thanked her for talking to him, handed her two rubles, and took off for the kafenio, hoping to find someone who could help him trail the mysterious woman. Upon entering the coffee-making establishment, he instantly received suspicious looks from the owner and the customers. No one saw him there before. Several groups of men were seated around small tables, drinking coffee or ouzo, playing poker, and arguing about the political establishment back home. Vlad approached the owner behind his counter, sat at one of the empty stools, and asked him for coffee.

"Heavy-sweet, sweet, or just black?" the coffee maker asked.

"Just sweet," Vlad said to get out of the peculiarity of a hardcore Greek specifying the sweetness of his coffee. While the coffee maker was brewing the coffee, Vlad reconnoitered his surroundings and found no women among the customers. A short, blond, overweight lady, behind the counter, did not raise her head to look at Vlad. She was preoccupied with her work. She had her hands in a sink filled with soapy water, washing cups and glasses. She did not fit the description of Georgia that Vlad got from the woman in the public restroom.

A burly man, who appeared to be a local Slav, a bit arrogant with his conduct, walked in and sat on the stool next to Vlad.

"I haven't seen you around here before," he said to Vlad. "You are a Russian, I can tell." He shook hands and gave his name. "Alex Bookas."

"Vladimir Moraska," Vlad responded. "Everyone calls me Vlad. You are correct in guessing my nationality. Russian, 100 percent, fresh from Stalingrad."

The coffee-maker returned with Vlad's coffee and said to Alex, "The same for you, I assume."

"Yes," Alex responded and turned his attention to Vlad. "What brings you here to Macedonia, Bolshevik?"

"The climate here is more agreeable with my poor health." Vlad sized up the strength of the burly man next to him. He didn't like Alex's arrogant behavior or his offensive comment, calling him a Bolshevik.

"I often stop here, looking for my ex-wife. She walked out of my life over a trivial disagreement with my parents," Alex said, suddenly. "It's almost a year and a half since she disappeared, but I still love her, more than ever." Throwing his first shot of ouzo in his mouth, he refilled the glass and readied himself to repeat his ouzo-drinking step.

"Go easy with that stuff, young man! Drinking like that will kill you," Vlad advised. "You are still young, and there are more young women walking the surface of this earth."

"Not like my Georgia," Alex declared, and threw his second drink in his mouth.

The thinking wheels clicked faster in Vlad's mind upon hearing the name Georgia. He mastered all the diplomacy of a former KGB agent and said in a sympathetic voice, "She must be a girl worth dying for."

"Here," Alex said, and retrieved his wallet from the inside pocket of his leather jacket. He unfolded it to show Vlad the picture of his missing wife, but at the same time, someone called Alex over to his table. Alex left his wallet unattended next to the glass with his ouzo and walked to another table in response to the call. His ID card was behind a clear cover on one side, inside his wallet, and the picture of a lovely young woman was behind another cover. Vlad, using his dexterity he had with his miniature camera, snapped several shots of the wallet and, unnoticed, hid his camera back in his pocket. Seconds later, Alex returned to his seat, downed a third glass of ouzo, removed Georgia's picture from where he kept it, and handed it to Vlad.

"Have you ever seen a woman that stunning? I wish I could have her back."

Vlad, fearing misconduct from the drunken Alex, returned the lady's picture to its owner, quietly sneaked out of the kafenio and returned to his hotel. The next day, he stopped at the local photography studio with his camera and made several prints of Georgia's picture and Alex's ID card. The photographer, a rather immature young man, took a second look at Georgia's picture and exclaimed, "Yeah, I know this hard-headed Greek. She abandoned her husband and went away with a nobody, a homeless bum. I photographed her wedding with the richest young man in town, Alex Bookas."

"Do you happen to have the picture of the guy that took her away from Alex? A friend of mine is looking for him."

"Nope," the photographer responded. "I don't even know his name, but he was one of those Greeks who wandered around town, a Paithomazoma remnant, you know!"

Vlad couldn't extract any more information from the photographer, so he thanked him for the information about Georgia and her mystery friend and returned to his hotel. He did not want to return to the kafenio, fearing that he might run into an intoxicated Alex.

Reading the evening newspaper, Vlad located the place where the Aria group was scheduled to appear tonight. He was performing in a town close to Bulgaria, two hundred miles east from there. He decided to take an evening train, meet Arian after the show, give him the pictures, and verify whether the woman in the picture was indeed his sister. He boarded the train late at night, and as soon as he arrived at the city where Arian's band was performing, he learned that the band had boarded another train to Sofia, the capital of Bulgaria. The band gained popularity and grew to a full-size traveling orchestra, thanks to Arian's musical talents. It consisted of twenty-five musicians and supporting technicians. Vlad commandeered a taxi and before the train was there, he was at the train station, waiting for him.

"Good morning, Arian."

"Good morning, Vlad." Arian was half-asleep. "What urgent thing brings you to Sofia at this hour?" Instantly, he froze in his tracks, just like a hunting dog, when it locates a rabbit hiding in the cover.

"Any news of my sister?"

"I have three pictures of three different women. I want you to look at them and tell me if you recognize anyone of them." He took the pictures out of his leather jacket and attempted to show them to Arian. He realized that the lighting was not enough for Arian to look at them and quickly said. "Let's move under that streetlight, over there. We need more light." The two men stepped under a post with a bright lamp, and Vlad handed the three pictures to Arian. He, in turn, gently arranged them in the palm of his hand, took several glances at them and turning to the detective, he returned two of them. He pointed at the picture he kept with his finger and exclaimed.

"My God, Vlad! This is my sister Georgia! Where did you find it?"

Before Vlad had time to answer, Arian fired two more questions at him with the rapidity of a well-lubricated, automatic pistol.

"Is she alive? Where is she?"

"As recently as six months ago, she was alive and well, in the company of a boyfriend. I have no reason to suspect that something bad happened to her, since then. Let's find a quiet place to sit down, and I'll tell you everything I know about her. I don't know where she is at this moment, but, by golly, I'm sure she is alive and well. I'll find her!"

"My hotel room is the best place. I will have my fiancé sleep alone tonight. She is one of our other vocalists in the band, and we are serious about getting married. We spend most of our free time together. She will be there now."

"Arian, what I have to tell you is general information about your sister. In no way will you be offended or feel uncomfortable listening to my presentation while your girlfriend is with us. Unless you feel otherwise, your girl can stay and hear my story."

In the back of Vlad's mind was the thought that Arian might go on a premature drinking spree to rejoice at the discovery of his sister. Premature, indeed, for he had no proof that Georgia was still alive, living somewhere, above grass and under the sun. He just wanted to give Arian the facts, retire to a hotel room, clean up, and get a badly needed rest.

Entering Arian's suite, Vlad found himself face-to-face with a half-nude young woman. She came out of her shower with only a Turkish towel covering her. She quickly disappeared into the next room to make herself presentable. Vlad pretended he hadn't noticed her semi-nudity and fixed his attention elsewhere. In the meantime, Arian went to a cabinet, retrieved a bottle of vodka, and filled three glasses with the colorless liquid.

"Who is the distinguished visitor?" Vlad heard a feminine voice behind him. He rose to his feet, turned around, and saw the same woman, now wrapped in an oversized bath robe and with a towel coiled around her head. He took her hand and bowed.

"Vladimir Moraska, my lady, private investigator."

"Ah, you are the man who is looking for Georgia, aren't you?" she responded with a pleasant voice.

"Yes, dear," Arian interjected. "He is the man who is here to bring us some very important news about my sister." He handed out the drinks.

"Sit down, friend, and tell us everything you know about Georgia." Arian and his girlfriend sat down on a couch opposite Vlad's chair. "Please sit down and tell us what you know about her. We are dying to hear where Georgia is and her health condition."

"Just recently, she was seen at a kafenio, close to where the camp was located. She was married once, but her marriage did not flourish. Recently, she was with another man at the same place. This time, she was well dressed and looked prosperous. Here I lost her tracks, but my instincts tell me that she went back to Greece with her new man. My intuition tells me that she is still alive and well, somewhere in Greece. Give me more time and I'll find her. I know people in Greece who can find a needle in a haystack.

"Tell me, Arian, your true name and, most of all, any members of your family and the places they reside. Human nature dictates that a desperate person, especially a woman, will look for friends and relatives for help and support. Just Imagine her returning home, finding the house ransacked, and no other place to go. Logic tells me that she will reach out for relatives, regardless how distant they might be. The Greeks say that 'the blood does not change to water.'"

"Let's start at the beginning," Arian said. "My true name is Fotis Liakos, the twin brother of Georgia. My parents were 100 percent Greeks. My father, a teacher, came to Vivitsi from the Peloponnese and met my mother. Mother came to Greece with her parents from the northern part of Turkey during the population exchange between the two countries. To the best of my recollection, my maternal grandparents never said anything about a family they left in their birthplace, and my father never told us anything about his family back home. He probably talked about it, but I do not remember anything about any of his relatives back home.

"Things were normal with us until my parents were picked up and executed by the rebels," he continued and drew a deep breath. "Georgia and I became the victims of Paithomazoma, years later," Arian continued and wiped tears from his face. "I want to keep the rest of my life private for it is the gory part. Besides, the events will not help you with your investigation. It is the segment that I will keep to myself until I will face my creator."

"Your assumption is not necessarily correct, Mr. Liakos, but as an investigator, I will honor your wish. I am leaving for Greece tomorrow morning and I will not stop looking for your sister until I find her, dead or alive. Expect to hear from me in about two to three months from now. In the meantime, count on me. I will find her, trust me, I will."

"Vlad, for all you know, my name is Arian, the Gypsy guitarist. No person should know that Arian is Fotis Liakos," and escorted the investigator to the door. He handed him some more money and wished him a safe trip to Greece. Vlad walked out of Arian's hotel, flagged down a taxi and went to the nearest motel. Arian returned to Voula's company.

It was still early for an ex-KGB agent to go to sleep. He phoned an old friend in Sofia and invited her over for a nightcap. The two ex-comrades had a couple of drinks and relived old times working together. Vlad's comrade gave him the name of a secret agent in the Greek National Police force and told him that this man was able to help him with his investigation. "Go and see him. He is a bit arrogant in his manners, but he is smart. He will be helpful." Two hours later, the meeting between Vlad and the other agent ended with just a friendly handshake and a wish for good luck. "Agents are not allowed to develop any personal relations with one another," the KGB code of conduct specifies.

Vlad bought several maps of Greece the next morning and spent most of the day getting familiar with the southern part of the Peloponnese. He was convinced that Georgia must have contacted her father's family when she returned to Greece from Slavic Macedonia with her boyfriend. He spent the next day in leisure, all by himself, and the next day after that, he boarded a train to Salonica, Greece. He arrived there in the early afternoon and devoted the rest of the daylight hours visiting historic and other cosmopolitan sites of the city. At 9:30 p.m., he walked into an outdoor restaurant by the seashore and had his dinner. Ouzo and fried octopus were his appetizers. His main course was a large, Mediterranean brown snapper, cooked over a wood fire and smothered with plenty of olive and a splash of fresh, lemon juice. Aromatic oregano was brushed on the perfectly cooked, succulent fish. For dessert, he chose a big slice of galaktoboureko over the baklava that his waiter recommended.

A dinner by the shore is not complete without music for the fun-loving people of Salonica. Before Vlad finished his dessert, dancing performers poured on stage and the humming voice of a vocalist, supported by several stringed and wind instruments, filled the air. As time went on, the vocalist changed his singing from Turkish to Greek and the air was filled with applause. A belly-dancer, wiggling her slender body like an eel, entered the stage. That's when the whistling of the exuberant crowd, the beat of a drum set, and the shrilling of the string and wind instruments climbed above Vlad's tolerance level. He got up, paid his bill, and went directly to his hotel room. "Wow. Now I know why we call the Macedonians, 'the crazy descendants of Alexander the Great.' They are the best in war, and they know how to have fun," he murmured in the elevator to his room.

The next morning, Vlad only had coffee and yogurt for breakfast at an outdoor restaurant. He took a short walk around the

White Tower, the symbol of freedom for the proud Macedonians, and visited several boutiques in the area, looking for a book to read while traveling. After a while wasting his time going from store to store, the proverbial expression of "do not leave for tomorrow, what you can do today," popped into his mind. The office building where his contact had his office was within walking distance. He decided to walk there and pay him an unannounced visit. He entered the impressive edifice, approached the receptionist, and stated that his name was Vladimir Moraska.

"Yes, sir. We are expecting you. Please take the elevator to the fourth floor and find room 410. It is an impressive office. You cannot miss it." Vlad thanked her, entered the elevator, and a minute later he was in front of a large door with a fancy brass name tag. He pressed the lit button and heard a command from the interior.

"Come in, the door is open!"

Vlad entered, closed the door behind him, announced the secret code that only his listener understood, received a coded response that only Vlad recognized, and approached the desk where the other man sat.

"They called yesterday and told me that you were on your way here," the man behind the desk said drily. "What can I do for you?" he added without even raising his eyes to look at his visitor.

"Captain, I'm looking for a lady who is twenty-three years old, from Vivitsi. She goes by the name of Georgia Liakos," Vlad responded.

"Liakos, eh! Let's see what this thing hides in its pages," he mumbled and opened a manila folder in front of him. He glanced through several pages and stayed silent for a few seconds. Then he raised his eyes from his desk and said, "Sorry, pal! Please sit down. Would you like to have a cup of coffee?"

"Just sweet," Vlad responded and took a mental photograph of the captain's general appearance. The man was dressed in a freshly pressed uniform. He was about forty years old with an olive complexion and healthy, wavy, black hair that was smartly combed away from his forehead. A powerful square chin was under his broad mouth and an unusual pair of pitch-black eyes pierced through Vlad when he looked at the old KGB agent. Then he returned his attention to his manila folder. While he was thumbing through the file, he pressed the button on the monitor in front of him.

"Just sweet, dear," and before receiving a response, he cut off the person who was on the other end of the monitor.

"Liakos, Liakos, Liakos," the captain kept saying, while looking at his folder. "There are several of them, all staunch supporters of the king. All from an isolated region of Mani in the Peloponnese, probably related to one another. Aha! Here is a Liakos who was active as a guerrilla fighter during the civil war. There is another one who is listed as a candy specialist on the island of Siros. If I was you, I'd start my digging with the Liakos who lives in Mani. I'll give you the name of the police sergeant who has jurisdiction over that area. He will be the one who can help you." He picked up the intercom and said.

"Is the guy back from Colombia with the coffee for my guest?" he demanded sarcastically to emphasize his expectation that his orders have to be carried out in a punctual manner.

Seconds later, a woman holding a tray with a cup of steaming coffee and a glass of sparkling water appeared in the office. She placed the tray in front of Vlad, smiled broadly at him, glanced at the captain, and left without saying a word to either one of them.

"Sergeant Furkas is a good guy. I know him. He is one of us. He will be expecting you." He handed Vlad a hand-written note with the word "Telos" on it. "Telos is the name of the village where you can find the sergeant and the Liakos families. Here is a brief story about the village. Back in the time when the rest of Greece was under the authority of the Turks, this part of my country (Mani) refused to be under their authority. Local, freedom-lovers, took advantage of the mountainous terrain and kept the invaders out of their villages. You should know that Telos means the 'end' in Greek, and legend has it that the local folks erected signs by the road leading to their village to warn Turkish military expeditions to stay out of there. It was the end of the road, so to speak," he concluded with a chuckle.

Vlad finished his coffee, thanked the captain for his help, shook his hand, and left the office. He returned to his room, closed the door, spread the maps on the table, and focused his attention on the area the captain indicated as being the best place to search for the missing Liakos girl. Working through one map at a time, he found a little black dot marked with the word "Telos" printed next to it. He drew a circle around the word and went to another map that emphasized roads traversing through the mountain peaks in the general area. The altitude where Telos was located was only a fraction of the heights he had climbed when he was trained as a KGB recruit. He highlighted the railroad lines and all the roads that traversed through the general area where Telos was. At the end, he packed his backpack with a few things for his expedition, placed it under his bed, and took an unhurried walk through town to reconsider the things he was planning to do during the next month. Although he learned nothing new about Georgia Liakos, he felt that he will find her. The premonition that he was on the tracks of his hunt kept coming back to fortify his gut feeling. He just knew that it was a matter of time.

The comment the captain made that some Liakos was a guerrilla fighter kept coming back to Vlad's mind. He wondered what unspoken secrets Arian the Gypsy (Fotis Liakos) kept under the shrouds of his silence. Were there some shameful things he did not want to talk about, or were there events that might jeopardize his future, even his life? Was he a heinous criminal? "Well, the question of who Fotis really is has to wait until we finish the search for his sister," Vlad said to himself, and dismissed the nagging thought that Fotis had a dark page in the book of his past. He stopped at a little kiosk, bought a gyros sandwich and a beer, and sat at a bench under an acacia tree. He slowly ate his sandwich, washed it down with the beer, and belched several times with satisfaction. He felt refreshed after a while. The details of his investigative work were out of his mind and he decided to take a week off and live like the rest of the people around town. For the week that followed he slept late, skipped breakfast, had a cup of yogurt with honey and coffee for lunch, took walks all by himself, and ate fresh fish with boiled greens for dinner. Toward the end of living like a local, he was rejuvenated. He felt young again, and the urge to have a woman in his private hours triggered memories of his youth in France. Eleni, a vivacious street girl, took him out of his quandary until he resumed his snooping for Georgia Liakos.

It took Vlad three days, traveling on trains and hiking through villages, to get to the general area of Telos. Folks he met on his way were friendly, yet suspicious of a stranger claiming he was just going through the area. He slept under the stars at night and only bought things he needed to survive. Friendly village people gave him bread, cheese, and olives, for they felt sorry for him. The man had not shaved for a while, his shirt and slacks were stained with mud and perspiration, and his boots looked worn out. Several people avoided meeting him face-to-face, for they thought he was an escapee from some mental institution. The mayor and several elders from a village became overly concerned about a ragged hobo roaming their village and summoned the authorities of Telos. Sergeant Furkas sent his deputy to investigate the nature of the stranger. He found Vlad taking a snooze under a fig tree loaded with ripe fruit.

"Stranger," the deputy commanded with authority, "you are under arrest for trespassing on private property and taking figs that are not yours. Get up and let's go and see Sergeant Furkas at the station." Vlad's plan to find Sergeant Furkas worked to perfection. He got up and followed the deputy to the station. Moments later, they entered the office of the sergeant.

"Man, state your full name for the sergeant," the deputy ordered Vlad.

"That's enough, deputy," Furkas interrupted. "You can go now. I'll handle the rest."

"Am I correct to assume that you are Vladimir Moraska, the famous investigator of the Russian KGB?" and getting off his chair, Sergeant Furkas reached over, took the hand of the other guy in his, and continued without waiting for an answer.

"It's my pleasure meeting you, sir."

"The pleasure is mine, sergeant," Vlad responded with the composure of a former KGB agent and a seasoned investigator.

"Before we ask the question of why you are here, we should make you comfortable. You need to take a shower, shave, put on fresh clothes, and eat something. The best place to clean up is our lock-up area. Get in there, put yourself together, and join me for lunch." Vlad took his backpack off his back and with it in his hands, entered a room with only four walls and two narrow windows toward its ceiling. He closed the door, undressed, and walked under the shower. A half hour later, he came out looking like a different person. He was shaved and in clean clothes. His hair was smartly combed and his boots looked new again.

"Throw your dirty clothes in this basket," the sergeant suggested. "I'll have someone clean them, courtesy of the station." Vlad obeyed orders and after he placed his dusty, old jeans, and smelly socks, shirts and underwear in the basket, he made himself comfortable on a woven chair on the other side of the roomy desk that Furkas occupied.

"While waiting for our lunch, tell me what brings you to Telos."

"I'm trying to locate a young lady by the name of Georgia Liakos. I have reason to believe that she was recently around here visiting relatives."

"Hum … Liakos, eh? We have three families living here in Telos by that name and they are related, genealogically speaking. If your lady visited one of them, all three of them will be aware of her visit. I'll bring the elder of the Liakos here and we will ask him. He is a God-fearing fellow and he doesn't lie. What's so interesting about this woman? Can you tell me?"

"There is a fellow who claims that she is his lost sister, and he hired me to find her," Vlad stated coldly. He figured that it was not the other man's business to know the details of his investigation. The deputy appeared at the door with a plate of cold cuts in one hand and a liter of wine with two empty glasses in the other. He approached the desk, placed the plate, glasses, and wine on the table, picked up the basket with the items to be washed, and walked out of the office. On his way out, he heard the voice of his superior calling his name and stopped.

"Deputy! Go and bring the senior Liakos here. Tell him I want to talk to him. Tell him it's important," he reiterated and lifting the flask with the wine in his hands, decanted some of its content in the empty glasses. The deputy left and the sergeant picked up his glass.

"To your health, investigator. Spartan as it may be, the spread on the plate is enough for now. Dig in."

Vlad stuffed some cheese and bread in his mouth, took a sip of wine, and when his mouth was free to say something exclaimed.

"Plenty! Plenty of everything, Sergeant."

A half an hour later, the plate was empty and the wine flask was void of its contents. The two men made themselves comfortable on their chairs and an aimless conversation about the political systems in Greece and Russia consumed their time until late in the afternoon. Vlad pretended that he was interested in knowing things about the Greek king, and the sergeant kept asking questions about the famous Joseph Stalin. Neither was critical about the other guy's leader or about their political system. They only kept up an affable conversation to be polite to each other.

"Hello, Mr. Liakos," the sergeant said when the senior Liakos entered his office. "Please come in and sit down. It will not take long. Just a simple question from your vigilant captain."

Liakos Sr. sat on an empty chair next to Vlad, stroked his long, white mustache several times, and said, "Okay, captain. Lay it on me! What is it?"

"Sometime in the recent past, one of your nieces came here from up north. Can you tell me anything about her and the nature of her visit?"

"Oh, she is George's daughter, my brother's kid! George was a teacher in some God-forsaken place, close to Yugoslavia. The kid was here with her husband, Demos, looking to mend family ties and get help to fix George's old house up north."

"Curious. Where is she now?"

"My other brother hired her husband in his candy business on the island of Siros. As I understand it, he is doing well in the Liakos Candy Co. Her name is Georgia, and as I was told, she became a mother, recently."

Sergeant Furkas sent a quick glance at Vlad and receiving no answer, he said, "That will be all, Mr. Liakos. You can go."

The old man unfolded himself off his chair and balancing on his walking cane, walked toward the door. At the door, he momentarily stopped.

"She is not in any trouble with the law, is she?"

"No. Not at all, Mr. Liakos. It's my job to know what's going on in my jurisdiction, that's all!"

As soon as Mr. Liakos was out of the door, Furkas turned around and said to Vlad.

"Are you ready for a little excursion to our lovely island of Siros? They tell me that this island is the crown jewel of the Aegean. If your luck is good, this trip will mark the end of your search for Georgia Liakos."

"I look forward to consummating this saga," Vlad responded. "I want to return to my hiding place, back in Serbia, rest for a while, collect my thoughts, and write my memoirs. I have so much to tell the world, and I ran out of time, I'm afraid. I had an interesting life as a KGB agent and along the way, I made a few friends and several enemies. I stepped on the toes of mighty folks and one of my most powerful adversaries is after me." The sergeant was listening with his mouth wide open. He wanted to ask questions but, respecting the other man's privacy and professional dignity, he kept his lips tight.

"Telos is not the last place in Mani to disappear to Mr. Moraska. You can adopt a monastic life in a monastery, for example, change your name to father somebody, dress in a black robe, and live as a monk for the rest of your life." Vlad made no comment on the other man's suggestion. Instead, he asked.

"How can I get back to Athens from here?"

"Coming tomorrow morning, we will take you to the train that goes directly to Athens. From the seaport of Piraeus several ferryboats depart for Siros, daily. By the way, let's be sure that your clothes are clean, before we go to bed tonight. You must be at the train station early, unless you want to hang around Telos another day or two."

"Thank you, sergeant, for the offer, but I would like to be on my way to Athens tomorrow morning. One of the most famous persons in the world once said, 'do not leave for tomorrow, what you can do today.'" In reality, he did not want to stay in Telos, face additional questions about his KGB life, and jeopardize his true identity.

"As you wish, friend." Later that afternoon, Furkas called his deputy and inquired about Vlad's laundry.

"Everything will be sparkling clean, mended in places, pressed, and ready to go, before bedtime," the deputy responded.

Right after dinner, Vlad withdrew to the lock-up room of the police station, re-packed his backpack, threw himself on a cot, and went to sleep early. The next morning, he put on his clean attire, shook hands with Furkas at the train station and boarded the train to Athens. While resting comfortably in his seat during his train ride, he thought a lot about the idea Furkas had. "Adopt an ascetic life and become a monk to save yourself," Furkas said. "Nah," Vlad said to his other self. "Walking away from danger is not characteristic of a KGB man. I'll stick with my original plan. After I'm through with the Liakos hunting, I'm going back to Slavic Macedonia, period."

The train spent all day traversing the 290 miles from Telos to Athens, for it made numerous stops on its way. Vlad made several trips to the rest room, just to exercise his numbed legs and to stretch his sore back. The man next to him was a real bore. He was either chewing his gum looking out of the window, starring motionless like a marble statue, or dozing in his seat. When the train arrived in Athens, Vlad picked up his backpack and walked away from the buzzing noise of the passengers. He walked to an inconspicuous hotel and took a room under a fictitious name. At six o'clock, he ordered the evening paper and a light dinner and retired early. He was tired. The strange fellow next to him at the train occupied his mind constantly. There was something odd about the behavior of the stranger, something that Vlad could not explain.

The next morning, he went to the seaport of Piraeus and bought a ticket for Siros. He returned to his hotel, paid his bill and with his backpack strapped securely over his shoulders, returned to the port and boarded the ferry on time. Two hours later, he walked out of the ferry in the small seaport town of Siros, all alone, not knowing a soul in town. He readjusted the load on his back and took the main street toward the section of the city with tall buildings. He was hoping that he could spot a hotel along the way. Meandering along looking at the displays of the store windows, he came upon a door with a hand-written sign tapped on its glass panel. The sign said that the place was a hotel and had vacancies for the evening. Vlad took another look at the sign and read it one more time. He couldn't make up his mind whether to knock at the door or keep going. It was getting dark and he only needed a bed under a roof to rest his aching back for the night. He did not care for luxuries or night activities. He just wanted a quiet place to get his rest and collect his thoughts. Finally, he rang the door with his bare knuckles, several times.

"Is this a hotel?" Vlad asked the man who appeared behind the screen door. "I need a place to stay for a couple of days."

"Read the sign," the man snapped. He thought that Vlad was another drifting hobo, asking for alms, but when he saw Vlad's face, he realized that he spoke prematurely and tried to mend things up. "Sir, of course this place is a hotel. Please come in. We get strange people from the port around here, and we have unpleasant experiences with them. Sorry for my unfit conduct. Please come in and make yourself comfortable." Vlad walked in the place, introduced himself as a tourist from Serbia, and told the owner that he would be around town for only two to three days. The other man escorted Vlad to an empty room and started to talk about a little box of candies that was resting on the night table.

"Liakos, the owner of the company that made our town thriving, came here after the Germans left. He converted a 'mama-papa' shop into a loukoumi-making company. He supplies this small box of four loukoumi, free of charge, to all the hotels in town," he added, and pointed at the small box of candies on a night table next to a single bed.

"He had a clever idea making something that the public wanted, and I bet he has expert help to do it," Vlad said. He was fishing for information about Demos who, according to senior Liakos back in Telos, was the husband of Georgia and foreman at the candy factory.

"My daughter works in the office and has the best words to say about Mr. Liakos. The husband of Mr. Liakos' niece, a guy by the name of Demos, is a roaring tiger at the place. He runs the show. On the other extreme is Georgia, his sweetheart wife! She will never miss the opportunity of opening the door to say hello to me and my wife, every time she passes by to go to the butcher shop or the fish market. Lovely people, all around. And that lovely baby they, recently brought into the world is something else. He is cute like a China doll. Before I forget, let me tell you that breakfast and dinner are available here for a few drachmas a day. My wife does the cooking and the baking. She is a good cook and an expert baker. Try her culinary creations. You will not be disappointed."

"I'll take you up on your offer," Vlad responded. The talkative owner of the hotel went back to his duties and Vlad sat at his bed and recorded the information he had gathered about Georgia and Demos. The next day and the following two days, Vlad walked around town, savored the assorted flavors of loukoumi, and learned more things about Georgia and her husband. For example, he discovered the last name of Demos and their home address. The last day in town, Vlad walked through the neighborhood where Demos and Georgia had their new home. Casually, he walked down the street in front of a new house and saw a woman teaching her one-years old baby to make his first steps. She was stooping over the baby holding the hands of the infant encouraging him to walk. As Vlad went by, the lady turned her face toward the oncoming stranger. Vlad confirmed her identity from the picture he had in his pocket. He also noticed a shining pendant dangling from her neck. This pendant was identical to the one Arian retrieved from his chest when he was describing Georgia to him in his hotel room. He also heard the woman calling her baby "George," an additional piece of information confirming that the baby was named after his late grandfather.

Returning to his hotel room, Vlad made his final notes in his diary and made up his mind to leave the lovely island. There was nothing else to learn about Georgia and Demos and certainly he did not want to blow his cover. He preferred to be unnoticed. He took a walk to the port and bought a ticket for Piraeus for early the next morning. When he returned to his hotel, he had a delicious supper and informed the owner that he was leaving early the next morning. He cleared all his bills, packed his backpack, and curled in his bed for an early rest. Early the next morning, the private detective embarked on another ferry, and sailed for the Greek mainland. At the seaport of Piraeus, he bought the evening editions of three major newspapers and located the place where Arian's band was performing for the next two weeks. Without any undue haste, he purchased a train ticket to the town where Arian was scheduled to appear.

CHAPTER SEVEN

I t was a year earlier when Georgia and Demos arrived at her parents' house in Vivitsi. Fotis had left the place just a day before them with Mr. Angelis to join the International Red Cross. The door was ajar and the old sleeping blanket the neighbor gave him was still there, folded neatly on a broken table next to the fireplace.

"Someone lives in here," Demos said to Georgia with suspicion and pointed at the bedding resting on the table. "Let's get out of here before we get in trouble with some mentally disturbed, derelict person."

"Before we leave the place that belongs to me, let's try to find out who was or who is sleeping here at night. While you are checking the rest of the place, I'll go next door and introduce myself to whoever lives there. The person who is next door might have seen the trespasser." Georgia walked over to the next house and knocked at the door.

"I'm sorry to disturb your peace, my lady," Georgia said to the woman who answered the call. "The house next door belongs to my late parents. Do you know who lives there now?"

"There was a nice young man who showed up here one day out of nowhere. He was penniless, and I felt sorry seeing him sleeping on the bare floor without a cover. I gave him an old blanket I had to cover himself during the chilly nights. Yesterday, he mysteriously disappeared, just the way he showed up in the neighborhood a month earlier. He was a nice young man. I could tell from his manners. Are you planning to stay or are you just passing by?"

"It all depends on finding work to make a living. My dream is to fix the house up, find jobs for me and my husband, and establish ourselves right here in the house of my parents."

"I'm glad to hear that someone will live permanently in this house. I'm tired of seeing folks go in and help themselves to whatever they need. Welcome to our neighborhood! Remember that I am here, willing to extend my hand to you."

"Can you spare another blanket? I'll pay for it."

"Here is another one," the neighbor said, and reaching for the pile of her bed covers, she handed Georgia a lighter blanket. "This is a house-warming gift to you, dear," she proudly declared. "Use your money for something else."

"Thank you, madam. My name is Georgia! Can you tell me yours?"

"Of course, dear. My name is Olga."

The neighbors exchanged friendly hugs and Georgia returned to Demos with a cuddly blanket around her shoulders.

Things did not work out for either Demos or Georgia for the next eight months. He was not able to find a job in town and the little money she had stashed away in her backpack was not enough to make the house livable. It was barely enough to buy food and other bare necessities. They replaced the entrance to the house, bought eating utensils, and a second-hand bed. From their neighbor they bought a large, home-made bar of soap to clean their underwear and take a sponge-bath using a dishrag they found in the old kitchen. Demos was thinking that it would be best if he returned to his smuggling trade. Georgia felt *forgotten,* once again. In the midst of their financial squeeze, Georgia discovered that she was pregnant.

"Demos, come and sit down next to me. I have something very, very important to tell you," she said one evening when he came home disappointed after looking all day for a job. He gave her a surprised look and assumed that she was planning to tell him that their relations did not work the way she was expecting. He sat next to her, ready to receive the bad news. He was prepared to hear that she was through with him. Instead, she threw her arms around his neck and kissed him.

"Demos, I'm going to have a baby!"

"Are you sure of what you are telling me? My God, this is great news!"

"Yes. I feel the baby moving in my belly! There is no doubt in my mind that I am going to be a mother. My God, you will be a father! We will become parents, Demos. We will have a third mouth to feed and no money to buy things for all of us," she concluded and broke down, weeping and sobbing. Demos' heart shattered. He reached over, took her in his embrace, and he, too, lamented with her about their poverty.

"I wish my parents were here!" Demos said in tears. "I know my father would offer us a helping hand. Unfortunately, he sold the few things he had and went to Australia with the rest of the family. I'm sure he assumed that I was dead.

"Do you know where your father was born? We may be able to track down the place of his birth! He may have relatives there, who may be willing to help us face our present crises. There must be someone, somewhere to give us a hand, sweetheart!"

"Phooey! I don't even know the name of the place where he was born," she lamented.

"You say no, without hearing me. Please, pay attention to my reasoning love! He was a teacher at the school, right? To teach, he should have a teacher's certificate that would show the place of his birth. A copy of this document should be in the archives of the school. Better yet, a copy of his birth certificate must be on file. Bingo! Let us go there tomorrow and find out."

"Your idea will work only if there is such a document at the school. A shot in the dark, isn't it!"

"We will not have answers to your if, unless we go there and find out," he responded with a hint of optimism. His idea took shape and form, as their conversation on the lineage of Georgia's father went on for the next hour. At last, the excitement of learning that they would become parents and the trickle of hope in solving their financial dilemma wore them out. They spread one blanket on their bed, covered themselves with the other blanket, and went to sleep.

Early the next morning, Demos and Georgia went to the school where George Liakos was a teacher. The principal of the school received them in his office and heard that they were there to find the name of the village Georgia's father was born in. The cooperative, friendly principal went to the back room, retrieved several folders from that era, piled them on his desk, and took time to go through them. In the middle of a disjoined conversation with his guests, the principal stopped talking and exclaimed.

"Aha, here we are," and produced a piece of paper with the picture of a young man pasted on its upper-left corner.

"George Liakos was born in Telos, Laconia," he declared. Handing the document to Georgia, he asked, "Do you recognize him? He is, supposedly, your father!"

"Hard to say," she responded, and focused her attention reading the writing. Seconds later, she handed the document back to the principal. "I was just eight years old, the last time I saw my dad and mom. My husband and I plan go to Telos. I'm dying to meet my relatives."

"In that case, I will try to alert one of the Liakos family in that village that you are going to be there in the near future," he added, and returned the document back to its folder.

Returning home, Demos and Georgia stopped at the train station and inquired about the cost of traveling from Vivitsi to Telos, Laconia. They also stopped at the local general store and bought a few things for their evening meal. At home, Georgia reached into her old knapsack and dug out the last money she had tucked away in one of its inside pockets. She counted it to the last drachma and asked Demos to do the same. They had more than enough money for two people to travel on a local train, from Vivitsi to a town closest to Telos. "I hope the station is not very far from the town! But whatever the distance is, we will manage to get there," Demos declared.

When the sun rose the next morning, it found the daring young couple standing at the train station with a backpack containing a set of clean undergarments for the woman, two pairs of worn-out socks (one for her and one for him), and an extra sweater and a warm dress for Georgia. It also contained a pair of worn-out jeans and a home-made sweater for Demos. As soon as the train stopped at the station, the two new passengers climbed aboard and started a new adventure. The train traveled day and all night through picturesque mountains and valleys. It stopped at several places to either pick up travelers or allow someone to get off. Finally, in the late morning of the second day, it made a brief stop at a station in a valley close to Telos.

"You paid up to this point," the conductor announced and opened the door for Demos and Georgia to get out. The couple exited the train and found themselves strangers and alone in a place they had never been before. The arrow on a metal sign ahead read: TELOS 4km. Demos took Georgia's hand in his and like two little children going to grandma's house for supper, started to walk in the direction the arrow pointed. It was noontime and the sun was hot and uncomfortable for the plodding and struggling travelers to reach the summit where Telos was located. Out of nowhere, the rumbling engine of a car disturbed the tranquility of the day. A young man, escorted by an attractive woman, stopped his old Citroën next to Demos and said politely, "Are you going to Telos? Hop in. I'm going there."

Demos and Georgia welcomed the opportunity for a free ride. They sat in the back seat of the vehicle and thanked the driver for giving them a lift to town.

"I'm the vet in the area and I have an emergency call in Telos. I'll drop you at the center of the village, for I have no time to look for your exact destination," he added and concentrated his attention on his driving. Georgia and Demos kept quiet for the rest of the ride until the car made a complete stop.

"Thanks for the ride," Georgia managed to say before the vehicle sped away. Demos looked around and saw a sign that read KAFENIO several doors down the street. "Let's get there," he said to Georgia. "There should be someone in the place who knows your folks."

Georgia retrieved her charm from her bosom, kissed it with reverence, and said, "Virgin Mary, mother of God, please help me one more time!"

There were only two people, in addition to the keeper, in the kafenio. When the strangers entered, they stopped talking to one another and fixed their glances at the newcomers.

"We are looking for Liakos," Demos said.

"Which Liakos are you looking for?" the keeper responded.

"Who are you, anyway?" another man added and all three of them fixed their gazes on the strangers who wanted to see one of their village's residents.

"My wife, here, is the daughter of the late George Liakos, the teacher. We are here to visit her family. Can you call one of the Liakos and tell him that his niece is here?" Demos said. "They are expecting us."

"Niko," the keeper hollered. "Go and tell Liakos to come here. Tell him that I have something important to tell him." A teen-age boy appeared from behind the kafenio and answered the man's call.

"I'm on the way, Dad," he responded and disappeared up the street.

"Come in and sit down. You look tired, kids! What can I offer you?"

"Thanks for the offer, I'm okay," Demos responded.

"Just a glass of water will do it for me," Georgia said.

While they were waiting for the boy to return, the keeper of the kafenio asked Georgia some pointed and direct questions about her father.

"I don't remember much of my parents," she responded with sadness. I was only four years old when they took them away. I hardly remember their faces," she remarked and swallowed several times to suppress the pain she felt in her heart. The keeper felt uncomfortable hearing Georgia's response and changed the line of his talking. He turned his attention to his other two customers and started conversing about the upcoming, presidential election. As soon as the boy and an impressive senior citizen appeared at the door, the storekeeper interrupted his conversation with the other two men and turned his face toward the newcomer.

"Come in, Mr. Liakos. Come and meet one of your family members! Did you know that she even exists?"

"My dear child," the senior Liakos said. Extending his huge arms toward Georgia, he embraced her just like her father used to do, when she was a little girl. "They called me and told me that you were on your way, but I did not expect to see you here so soon." He then released her from his embrace, took a better look at her face, and that's when Demos interrupted the scene. Up to this instant, he stood there motionless, waiting for the initial outpouring of emotions between Georgia and her uncle to subside. This was the instant that he felt was appropriate to make himself known. He reached over, took the hand of Mr. Liakos in his, and humbly announced, "Mr. Liakos, I'm Demos Prasinos. I'm the husband of your niece, Georgia."

"Welcome to the Liakos family, young man! You are welcome!"

A few seconds later, Mr. Liakos walked out of the kafenio, holding close to him Georgia on one side and Demos on the other. They walked to his home in a cheerful state of mind, met Mrs. Liakos at the door, and the outpouring of love was repeated, anew. A neighbor went out to the rest of the Liakos in town and informed them that Georgia and her husband were in town. Within the next hour, the house of Mr. Liakos was filled with loving relatives and family friends. The havoc of introducing each other continued for a while, until the old man asked everyone for their attention.

"My dear family and beloved friends. Tonight is the happiest evening for the Liakos family. Tonight we welcome home our Georgia and her husband, Demos. Unfortunately, we were not prepared for this happy occasion. Tomorrow at three o'clock I expect all of you back here. We will have a family fiesta to officially welcome them and hear their life story. Please go home now, and I'll see you tomorrow, yeah?"

When the house was empty of guests, Georgia and Demos had a late supper with their hosts and then went to sleep. Mr. and Mrs. Liakos were exhausted from the excitement of the evening, and they, too, went to bed as soon as they kissed their newfound niece and her husband goodnight.

The next day started early. Some members of the family cooked food for everyone in copper cauldrons and others made fresh bread in the wood-burning oven. At three o'clock, everyone sat on a long picnic table and gorged themselves on mutton stew with fresh bread and home-brewed wine. After dinner, Georgia told everyone the story of her life from the point where her parents were taken away to the present moment. She purposely omitted the part about being Alex Bookas' wife. Demos narrated his life experience of being the victim of Paithomazoma and his struggle to survive after the camps were broken apart. At the end, a voluntary, monetary donation followed the fiesta, and the evening ended in cheers and sincere wishes for a successful new beginning for Demos and Georgia. The senior Liakos, the hero of the Greek-Bulgarian and Greek-Italian wars, the survivor of two civil wars and the father of five grown-up children, sat proudly at the head of the long table, savoring the pleasure of seeing his family together.

Demos and Georgia spent a whole week in Telos, visiting friends, relatives and getting acquainted with neighbors of the Liakos clan. Finally, the day for them to pursue their destiny came. They traveled to the island of Siros and met another Liakos, the loukoumi maker and the youngest brother of Liakos Sr. A brief get-together at the house of the rich uncle culminated in the permanent employment of Demos at the candy factory. Additionally, the wealthy uncle provided temporary housing for the couple.

Things went well for Demos at the factory. He started making and saving money, and Georgia gave birth to their first child. That was the time when Vlad came to the island, snooping around for Georgia.

*

The notorious ex-KGB investigator, arrived in Salonica from Athens two days after he left the island of Siros. He bought a local map of the city where Arian was to perform and boarded a non-stop train that was going there. He made himself comfortable on one of the seats, spread the map on his lap, took out a pen from his pocket, and began to circle several spots where Arian was to appear soon. His training as a KGB agent made him aware that a suspicious character was eavesdropping on him as he was reading the map. Vlad decided to move to another car of the train. Minutes later, the suspicious character walked by, took an inconspicuous look at Vlad and at his marking on the map, and sat directly opposite to him, pretending that he did not even notice him. This event made Vlad fear for his life and he decided to escape any impending danger. As soon as the conductor announced the approach to the next station, Vlad went to the men's room and when the train came to a complete stop, he squeezed through the open window and disappeared in the darkness. Purposely, he left the map and his backpack on his seat to give the impression that he was planning to return.

Almost a year went by and Arian did not hear a word from Vlad. The idea of hiring another sleuth to find his sister crossed his mind, but his involvement with the band was taking priority over his life. Additionally, he was working hard to cement his relations with Voula. He was convinced that Georgia was well somewhere, and he was planning to resume his search for her as soon as possible. Georgia had given up hoping to find her brother. She believed that he was one of the victims of the civil war, and she concentrated her energies on being a good mother and a model wife.

Ten months went by and Vlad came out from his hiding place. He sailed to the island of Siros, verified that Demos and Georgia were still there and returned to Salonica disguised as another common, European tourist. The next day, he bought the local newspaper and located the place where Arian was performing that week. With extreme caution and utmost care not to be noticed by anyone, he sneaked into the parking garage next to the club where Arian was to appear for the night. In the confines of that public place, Vlad hid between parked cars, and waited for Arian to show up. Two hours later, a limousine arrived, and Arian came out. Vlad rushed to him, hurryingly gave him his final report of his investigation and told Arian that all the information about Georgia was in his report. "She is fine," he whispered and turned around to go away. Arian was elated upon receiving the news that his lost sister was still alive and well. He reached in his pocket, took out a fat wad of money, and handed it over to Vlad. He thanked him warmly and said with genuine sincerity. "I want to stay in touch with you, Vlad! I want to see you again."

"I don't think so, friend. You will never know me. You will only know of me," Vlad responded, and without another word, he vanished between the rows of the parked cars around them.

"Wait! Who are you?" Arian called. But Vladimir Moraska from Stalingrad was gone forever.

Arian read Vlad's brief and concise report several times and handed it over to Voula who stood next to him.

"I remember her as a teen-ager with an angelic face and a slender body," Arian said to his wife. "She is twenty-five years old now, and according to Vlad's report, she is the mother of a child and the wife of my childhood friend. If she is the girl I remember, she must be a real beauty to behold and a model mother and wife to be proud off. Demos is a lucky fellow," Fotis said, and threw himself in the arms of Voula.

"Compose yourself, dear," she responded and added. "Let's make plans to go and see them. I'm dying to meet her, too. The band will survive for a few days without us."

Arian's voice on stage and the feelings he delivered with his guitar were more cheerful and more melodious than before he received the good news about his sister. He was a happy man and everyone who knew him could tell that something extraordinary had happened to him. People close to him knew the real reason, but most of his admirers wondered if the man was going soft. The band leader noticed the changes in Arian's conduct and suggested that the couple should take a little vacation.

"Take a few days off and go to see a friend," Mazurkas suggested. "It will do you good to get away, after all this time! Take your wife and go, man! I might give a few days off to the rest of the group, until you guys return. We all worked hard and need a break. I'm dying to see Santorini myself and soak up the sun on its seashores."

A week later, Arian and Voula packed their suitcases, boarded a passenger train to Athens, and checked into a hotel in Piraeus. Before they had their dinner, Arian walked to a travel agency, purchased two tickets for Siros, and returned before Voula was through with her shower.

"We will spend the evening and early morning here," he informed his wife. "The ferry leaves at eleven o'clock tomorrow."

"I'll be ready for the big day," she responded and continued getting ready for a quiet dinner by the ocean front. An hour later, dressed in designer blue jeans and identical yellow cashmere sweaters, the two celebrated musicians entered a small restaurant by the seashore. Unnoticed by everyone around them, they had a flavorful and quiet dinner, away from loud hand-clapping and noisy notoriety. They wanted to be alone and away from friends and admiring listeners. They were fully aware that the tomorrow would be an unforgettable day. They were to meet Georgia, Demos, and the baby of the Prasinos family.

It was early when they returned to their hotel after dinner. Arian stopped at the corner kiosk by the public square and purchased the evening edition of the national newspaper. It was his habit thumbing through the paper before bedtime. In their room, Voula made herself comfortable in her bed attire, turned the radio on, and spread herself on their bed to rest and digest her dinner. Arian kicked his shoes off his feet, pulled a chair close to the bed and under the light of their night lamp, opened the paper, and aimlessly began to turn its pages.

"Oh, no! My God! No!" he exclaimed and with the paper still in his hands, he jumped off his chair. His wife, alarmed by her husband's sudden reaction to something he read in the paper, jumped off the bed and grabbed his hands.

"Look! Vlad is dead!" Fotis pointed at a short article in the newspaper with the title: VLADIMIR MORASKA, DEAD. Voula snatched the paper off her husband's hands and read the short article. "...The authorities suspect that the famous ex-KGB investigator was strangled to death. The man was known as Vlad Moraska from Stalingrad, but his true name was Vangelis Moraites from the island of Ithaka," the announcement said.

"You live by the sword you die by the sword," she declared. "Besides, what do we know about him and his true history. He might have been a mole for the Greek Secret Service, or even a guerilla leader disguised as a Russian agent."

"Voula, he was a good man, and he was still young. He did not have to die so early in his life and in that barbaric fashion!"

"Same as your parents," she said. "When your time comes, it comes, dear! Just forget Vlad. He was another man who reached the end of his life. Let's get some rest, for tomorrow is a big day for both of us. We will meet your lost sister and her husband after ten years, and we will hold the new Prasinos in our arms." Arian had difficulties falling asleep. He tossed in their bed for a while and kept Voula up. Finally, he calmed down in her arms and went to sleep, too.

The next day, Fotis and Voula Liakos boarded a passenger ferry and two hours later were at Ermoupoli, the seaport of the island of Siros. Until this moment, neither Demos nor Georgia knew that Fotis was still alive. Not a soul in the world knew that he and his wife were on their way to pay them a surprise visit.

Georgia fed the baby lunch and kissed Demos goodbye. He was walking out of their house to return to his work, when a taxi with a man and a woman inside it, pulled in front of their house and blocked the driveway.

"Hey pal, move it. You block my driveway! I'm getting out to go back to work," Demos hollered at the taxi driver. At that instant, the doors of the taxi opened and a face they had not seen for five years came out, accompanied by an attractive young lady. They both rushed toward Georgia with her baby in her arms and with Demos standing next to her. No language of any man has descriptive enough words to express the outburst of human emotion at that moment, and no person possesses the skill needed to tell the passionate drama that followed thereafter!

EPILOGUE

T he heroes in this story are the products of the author's fantasy. Only the events and the settings are drawn from episodes that took place during the civil war of the 1940s in Greece.

My nostalgia to tell the story of *Forgotten* powered my fingers to press the keyboard of my computer enough times to form the words you just read. Still, the labor I spent to put my story together is only a grain of sand in the Sahara Desert compared to the yearning and sacrifices my heroes made to survive the perils of Paithomazoma and return home. The rest of the children, estimated to be anything between 45,000 and as many as 100,000, are still unaccounted for. It is safe to assume that most perished during their struggle to stay alive in countries behind the Iron Curtain. The others obeyed the Darwinian law of survival, through adaptation. The dead and the survivors of this human travesty are the innocent victims of the uproar of a nation trying to shape the system of its government. Against their choice, these innocent human beings were thrown into the streets of other European nations. They became dispersed into a new society, and those who managed to survive were forced to spend their lives away from their motherland with its rich cultural heritage. These pathetic souls are the *Forgotten* of the story you just read.

www.ingramcontent.com/pod-product-compliance
Lightning Source LLC
LaVergne TN
LVHW090026090225
803301LV00006B/44

* 9 7 8 1 4 9 0 7 9 8 4 7 9 *